# THEIR WILL BE DONE

A DARK NEW ADULT REVERSE HAREM ROMANCE
(THE SINNERS OF SAINT AMOS BOOK 2)

LOGAN FOX

# WARNING

This dark romance is a work of fiction. The aim of this book is to entertain, not educate. While it includes elements of BDSM, it in no way depicts a healthy relationship (kinky or otherwise). That being said, you can expect some pretty dark content such as non-con, dub-con, public humiliation and degradation, violence, knife play, breath play, choking, murder, mention of suicide and abuse. Please tread carefully if you have triggers.

# JOIN THE FOX DEN

Can I send you my secret dark romance novella that's never been published…?
Join my VIP newsletter and you'll receive your own exclusive copy of My Darling, and I'll keep you up to date with my new releases and promos!
https://authorloganfox.com/my-darling-signup

# PLAYLIST

**Theme Song**
*Scorpio* — POUR VOUS

**Playlist**
*Oh My God* — HELLYEAH
*Heathens* — CORVYX
*Something in the Way* — AT SEA
*How Far Does the Dark Go?* — ANYA MARINA
*Kvrt in Space* — FRANHOFER DIFFRACTION
*King Night* — SALEM
*A Conversation with God* — KING 810
*Amen* — ΔAIMON

To view this playlist, please visit my website at https://
authorloganfox.com/playlists.

# 1

## ZACH

I flick on my indicator and make the turn into Redwater's main street. My decade-old SUV rattles every time I strike a rut in the road. I'd have to buy a new one soon—this battered car was part of my persona as Zachary Rutherford, a kid from a low-income home who dragged himself up by his bootstraps, worked two jobs while he got his Bachelors, and couldn't be happier with the menial wage Saint Amos pays first-year teachers.

If I were to cash in all my assets, I could probably *buy* Saint Amos. And in a few weeks, my wealth is set to triple.

Another clank. This time it's internal and it comes as I hit another rut. Probably the shock absorbers. The roads around here chew through them.

It's risky, heading out today. When I left my brothers, the atmosphere was taut as a bowstring. If I'm gone too long, they might fall on Trinity like a pack of wolves. I'd have stayed, but I always go to town on Saturday. It would seem strange for me to stay at the school, especially this close to break.

I snort at the thought.

This is the first time I've even *considered* going off-script.

All because of one girl. A girl I can't get out of my mind since the day she showed up at my class. Even more so after our time in the shower. After we had her trapped and helpless in our nest. She thinks we're humoring her. Letting her decide which side of the battle line she wants to stand.

My lips twitch, but I smooth them before they can twist into a grimace.

With Trinity in the picture, everything's changed. Now I'm no longer just driving into town to buy Apollo a new camera, a few cartons of cigarettes, and to empty out my post box.

We'd originally planned to kidnap Gabriel. Apollo found an abandoned wood cutter's hut in the woods—a place straight out of the sixteenth century. We were going to do whatever the fuck it took to retrieve the names of each and every Ghost Gabriel handled, and find out who it was that he reported to. Because we know the Guardian had a superior.

And then we'd kill him.

We'd have done it over summer break, while Saint Amos was closed for repairs. No one would have missed him, and by the time the police were notified, we'd already be away on our killing spree.

The timing was perfect.

*Everything* had been perfect...until Trinity arrived and put a wrench in the works. That's what I'd thought, anyway. Now it turns out this unexpected development might work in our favor.

There'd always been a chance Gabriel wouldn't have handed us the information or that, under torture, he'd give us any bullshit just to make the pain stop.

But since Trinity's so fucking adamant Gabriel is a true man of God, we'll make her *prove* it. And in doing so, she'll inadvertently get us everything we need.

I park outside a photography store, ducking to look through the window. Then I take a piece of paper out of my pocket and glance at Apollo's horrific handwriting. I can't even remember how many cameras I've bought him over the years. He's as clumsy as he is introverted. Today's shopping run is going to be pricey, but it'll be worth it. Because one thing is for sure. Once we have the information we need, Gabriel becomes expendable.

My brothers and I agree fully that inflicting even a fraction of the pain and suffering he orchestrated over the years is the least he deserves.

That we deserve.

And Trinity?

I'll let my brothers decide what they want to do with their new toy—keep her, or discard her.

## 2

## TRINITY

A rough shake, accompanied by an even rougher, "Hey!" drives me out of a deliciously tangled dream. I knock away Jasper's hand and scramble into a sit, clutching my blanket to my chest like he was trying to cop a feel.

But that had been Cassius. And a dream.

"What?" I squint up at him with scratchy eyes. "What is it?"

"Where were you last night?" He's still standing, forcing me to crane back my head to look up at him.

I turn my back to him. "None of your fucking business," I mutter.

He grabs my shoulder again. "You can't do shit like this."

"Shit like what, Jasper?" I yell, twisting around to face him. I kick off my blankets, glaring at him so hard he actually takes a step back and drops onto the edge of his bed. "What do you think I did that's so fucking wrong?"

He fidgets, smoothing his hair with a palm. "If the hallway monitor catches you outside your room at night, you get lashes. And I'll get them too."

I briefly consider telling him that I'd been with the hallway monitor. But then I remember Zachary's moss-green eyes, and the way he'd stared at me in the shower like I was an ice cream sundae and he was a self-destructive diabetic with a craving for cherries.

"Yeah?" I cock my head to the side. "Do they hurt, those imaginary lashes you keep getting on my behalf?"

I shouldn't be baiting him like this, but dear Lord I was enjoying that dream, and the blissful sleep that came with it.

Apollo and Cassius snuck me back here just before dawn. I made sure not to wake Jasper, watching him like a hawk as I'd changed into my pajamas and slipped into bed. And unless he'd woken up just after I'd gone to shower, how else would he know I was gone?

"Do they hurt—?" He cuts off with an angry sound and stabs a finger toward me. "You know what? Fuck you. Do whatever you want. But I swear, if I get punished again when you fuck up, then—"

I sneer at him. "When did you ever get…?"

Jasper stands, turns to the side, and tugs down his boxers. Mustard-colored bruises mar his skin.

My stomach turns over before logic can take hold. "You're lying," I tell him, standing to get my clothes so I have an excuse to get the hell out of our room. "Those look old, anyway."

"I got them the first day you arrived because you went to class without your school uniform."

"I didn't have one!" I whirl around to face him, thrusting out one of the dresses that miraculously appeared in my closet the day after Ruth took my measurements.

While Apollo watched.

My cheeks catch flame. I hope Jasper takes it as anger and not…something else.

"Think that matters?" he mutters.

"You want to know what I think? I think *you* did

something," I say, walking closer until he's leaning back to get away from me. "Something bad enough to get you stuck with a roommate. And now you're trying to blame me for it."

This shuts him up, but from the sulk on his mouth, it won't be for long.

I huff and pause a moment to rub at my temples. There's still a faint headache lurking from all the weed and alcohol I consumed. "Where do I get painkillers from?"

He smirks at me. "Go fuck yourself."

"Asshole." I storm out, heading for the restroom. I hear him calling after me, but I ignore it. Probably just trying to blame more shit on me. The fucking nerve.

I find the closest restroom and change in the stall. After washing my face in the basin, I spend a few minutes trying to sort out my hair.

No luck—it will need another wash before people stop confusing me for a clown. My gaze tracks to the small window on the side of the restroom.

What time is it?

I bundle my pajamas against my stomach. The only laundry hamper I know of is the one in the showers, but I'm sure as hell not going there. I'm sure it's full of naked boys. And the only naked boys I want to see are a select few who I'm pretty sure wouldn't be caught dead in that place again.

I'm still blushing at that thought when I let myself back into my room and shove my dirty clothes under my bed.

"Idiot," Jasper mutters from his bed. He's lying on his back, a dog-eared copy of *Metamorphosis* propped on his stomach.

"Jerk," I snap back. I tug at the hem of my school dress and flounce out of the room.

My stomach keeps alternating between a hungry pit and a maelstrom of bile and stomach acid. Apollo had murmured something about coffee to me when they'd been sneaking me back inside, wrapped in a blanket with nothing but underwear beneath. If it hadn't been for them, I'd have peed myself at the thought of having to get back to my room without someone seeing me.

So coffee. Possibly breakfast.

Oh Lord. Do I have more gruel to look forward to?

I pause in the hallway, a hand on my stomach. I have to stop thinking about that or I'll fucking puke.

I'm used to the hallways being empty around here. It seems the only time there're lots of activities is in the morning when all the boys rush to go shower before pray—

Wait. Did I miss prayer?

I peek down the hallway and spot a boy heading toward me, hair wet and a towel dangling from his shoulders.

"Sorry?" I call out, stepping into the hallway.

He takes me in with a frown. "Yeah?"

"Were there prayers this morning?"

"It's Saturday," he says, frown deepening as he moves past me.

I throw up my hands at his retreating back.

I risk a peek outside. There's not a cloud in the sky and, judging from the position of the sun, it's early. I should have checked my schedule. Were the weekend activities even on there?

Opening the door wider, I step outside to catch some sun on my face before heading for the dining hall.

I'm not the last to arrive—there are a handful of trays still left on the table. Including mine—bright pink post-it still intact.

. . .

# TRINITY MALONE

I grimace before I notice there's a little heart above each of the I's in my name and then a butterfly starts fluttering around in my stomach. I grab my tray and turn to look for an empty spot.

On cue, the snickers begin. I spot a few gaps, but every time I get near, they miraculously close up.

*Not all miracles are divine.*

Assholes.

There's something different about the boys today, but I'm too busy trying to ignore their awful giggles to figure out what it is.

Movement draws my eye. Apollo's waving at me through the kitchen door's window.

A second butterfly joins the first.

Zach said he'd send for me to discuss what they wanted me to do next. Is that why Apollo's calling me? I hadn't thought it would be so soon. I'd hoped to get my head straight by then.

I swallow and walk across the dining hall.

I haven't had a chance to process the past twenty-four hours. I've never felt this conflicted in my life. I want to hate those guys —hell, *of course* I hate them—but after hearing their stories…is it any wonder they're so fucked up?

But what about Father Gabriel? The stuff they told me about him? I can't even begin to process that.

Zach told me Father Gabriel would be back tomorrow.

Apollo pushes open the door when I get close, and beckons me inside with a charming, lopsided smile.

"Hi," I say, fumbling with my tray as I push a stray curl behind my ear.

He cocks his head and leads me to a steel door. Daylight streams in when he opens it. I step into a courtyard that smells of damp bricks. There's a concrete table and four stools in the center.

There's a sickly pot plant in one corner, and another steel doorway opposite. Someone left their boots next to that door.

"Where does that go?" I ask, digging the edge of the tray into my stomach and trying not to look like a complete idiot.

"You don't have to wear your uniform on weekends," Apollo says, his back to me as he pulls out a packet of cigarettes and lights one. I look down at myself, close my eyes, and curse inwardly.

That's what was different about the boys. They were wearing normal clothes, not their usual drab brown.

Is that what Jasper was trying to tell me?

I *am* an idiot.

"Still have to get used to things around here," I murmur, heading for the table so I can put my tray down.

"Why bother? Not like you're going to be here much longer."

My tray clatters onto the table. I turn to Apollo, mouth gaping. "What do you mean?"

He points to one of the stools. "Sit. Eat."

"No." I cross my arms over my chest. "Tell me what that's supposed to mean."

Instead, he smokes his cigarette and stares at me through a gap in his blond hair. Did he wash it? I bet *he* has his own bathroom. "Sit."

I sink down, wincing when the icy concrete touches the back of my thighs.

"Eat."

Glaring at him doesn't work, so I let out a huge sigh and tear the plastic wrap from my tray.

Someone cut my toast into the shape of a heart. I look up at Apollo, deadpan.

He grins with one side of his mouth, blowing cigarette smoke my way as he drags his hair out of his face. "For the shit food I made you yesterday," he says.

I grab a piece of toast and start nibbling on it. "Please tell me what you meant." Maybe good manners will help me get through to this guy because being rude sure as hell didn't.

He puts his foot on the stool opposite mine, the table now between us. Taking another drag of his smoke, he leans his elbows on his raised knee, studying me for a few seconds before speaking.

He holds up two fingers. "We got two scenarios here."

I frown at him.

"First...we're right, you're wrong." He shrugs. "When it all comes to light, shit's going to go down. Big time. This place—" he flicks his fingers up, taking in Saint Amos towering above us on all sides "—will probably get shut down. Feds would ransack it. Everyone gets arrested. Etcetera, etcetera."

A chill shivers down my spine. I'm so convinced they're wrong about Father Gabriel I never even considered what would happen if, by some slight chance, they turned out to be right. I couldn't stay here. I'd be back in foster care until...when? I'm finished school? Then what?

Lord, but it's difficult to keep eye contact with Apollo. Paired against Zach and Reuben and Cassius, he seemed almost forgettable. But with his hair out of his face, his high, sharp cheekbones are more distinct. And his mouth? It's impossible not to watch him every time he takes a drag of his cigarette.

Eyes, Trinity. Eyes!

My gaze snaps back to his eyes. The crinkle in the corner of each tells me he knows exactly what I'm thinking.

My cheeks grow warm.

"And what if I'm right?" I blurt out before biting off another mouthful of toast.

Apollo tilts his head, and his hair slides back into his face. "Even if it's not Gabriel, Gabriel knows who it is." He shrugs, drags at his cigarette, and walks around the table to me. "And you'd probably go running your mouth if you think we'd hurt him, so...we'd have to make sure you didn't do anything like that."

I'm so shocked at what he's insinuating. I don't move when he brushes his fingertips down my jaw. "I wouldn't do that," I whisper.

"We're not exactly trusting of strangers. Nothing personal, pretty thing."

We.

All those years they spent together in that basement. I can't even imagine the bond that created between them. I'm guessing it goes far beyond hatching a plan of revenge. They're not just buddies—they're brothers.

"Please, you *have* to believe me." I widen my eyes as I turn to face him.

There's uncertainty in his eyes. But there's something else there too. I can't be sure, but I'm hoping against all hope that he wants to believe me.

"It's not me you have to convince," he says, his lips curling into a smile as he takes another drag of his cigarette.

His fingers trail down my throat. He traces the outline of my collarbone, sending a flurry of shivers through me. Toying with the top button of my dress, his smile hitches up. "Lunchtime, a day like this?" He tilts back his head and looks up at the patch of sky. "Everyone's gonna picnic in the field." He stands and goes to kill his cigarette in the pot plant. "No one will miss you until tonight." He walks over to the kitchen door, pausing with his hand flat on the steel.

"We'll fetch you in an hour. Wear something pretty," he says around a smirk.

"Wait!" I call out before he can disappear inside.

He steps back, waiting.

I scrounge up every ounce of courage to ask, "Do you guys have a private bathroom?"

## 3

## TRINITY

If anyone ever wanted to conduct a study on the effects of blushing, I'd be the perfect candidate. In the past half an hour I don't think I've stopped blushing even once.

I'm in a room in the east wing. It's nothing like the one I have to share with Jasper. It's three times the size, and it has its own en-suite bathroom where I'm currently standing buck naked and terrified that someone's going to walk in on me.

Reuben, to be precise. Since it's his room, he accompanied me up here. I think he's in the small study-cum-dining area of his apartment, but his carpets are too thick for me to hear if he did move about.

Steam fills up the shower cubicle, turning the frosted glass white. I slip inside that heavenly cloud, and the water draws a deep sigh from me as it cascades down my body.

There was no way I was going to have lunch with Zac's boys while I still had traces of sticky alcohol over my breasts and crazy person hair. So I brought my clothes up here and slipped into Reuben's room while Cassius watched the hallway to make sure no one spotted me.

Apparently, I could get into a lot of trouble being on this floor. More so if I'm discovered inside someone's room.

Lathering rosemary-scented shampoo into my hair I try and squeeze every last drop of indulgence from the most blissful moment I've had in the past month.

For a few minutes, there's nothing but me, the warm water, and that delicious scent. It should smell like Reuben, but on me it smells different.

I'm glad it's his bathroom I get to use. I'd have refused if it was Cass's, and it would have felt really weird to use Apollo's. Strangely, despite how big and scary he is, Reuben feels...safe.

It must be amazing having someone like that in your life. Someone who can knock the teeth out of anyone who dares look at you funny. I'd never be scared again. Not wrapped in his strong arms.

My hand slides down my hip, and I hesitate, biting down on my bottom lip for a second. I peek behind me, but I can't see the bathroom door through the glass and steam.

Skimming lower, my fingers brush against my clit. A thrill flutters through me as my eyes slide closed. It should have been Reuben's black eyes that appear, but instead all I can see is Zachary. His solemn expression, that almost permanent crease between his brows.

I took it for severity, but now I know it's some kind of anger. Anger hardened into a diamond over time. But diamonds aren't pretty when they first come out of the ground. They're rough and murky looking. To sparkle, they have to be polished.

I doubt Zachary will ever let anyone close enough for that to happen. He or any of his brothers.

Sinful bliss flashes through me. I haven't done this in ages, and the guilty pleasure of it makes me bite down even harder on my lip. What do they do in that lair of theirs? Drinking and smoking like they own the place. Do any of them ever slip behind that curtain to do what I'm doing?

Alone.

Together?

*Fuck.*

A tiny moan escapes my lips. I'm so close I can almost—

There's a knock on the bathroom door.

"Trinity?"

I gasp and flinch away from my throbbing clit. Reuben's deep voice sends a tremble through me that congregates deep in my belly.

"I'm done!" I call out in a cracked voice. "Be out in a sec."

He says nothing, but I can imagine him frowning at the door, perhaps considering coming in to make sure I'm okay.

It wouldn't be the worst thing in the world. I've never considered what type of guy I would like—honestly, I've never met enough for that to ever have been a consideration, but out of all Zach's brothers, Reuben strikes me as the sanest. Sure, he's a bit hot and heavy with his bible, but on him that kind of zealous fervor seems pure and right.

Maybe because that's the only kind of crazy I understand.

I rinse, turn off the faucet, and dart out of the shower to grab a towel and wrap it around me.

After I've dried off and draped Reuben's rosary around my neck, I slip into one of my own dresses. Mom would have thrown this one out a long time ago, but I'd kept it because it was the prettiest thing she'd ever bought me.

Father wasn't always a priest. They married young, and tried for years to have a child. Father eventually turned to religion, expecting answers from God for why Mom kept having miscarriages. I guess they ultimately found their answer, because a year or two after my father joined the clergy, Mom became pregnant with me and carried to full term.

She bought this for my sixteenth birthday, but I never got to wear it. The moment my father saw it on me, he sent me back to my room to change.

They had a huge fight that night, and Father left without bothering to stay around for cake.

The cream-colored dress has lace at the bosom and on the hem, and because she always bought everything at least a size too big, I'd grown into it since I last wore it. I'd put it on when they were sleeping and twirl around in front of the mirror, pretending I was just like all the other girls I saw in church, or walking down the street. Girls whose parents let them wear makeup and jewelry and high heels.

I don't have heels, but this dress doesn't need them. It comes mid-thigh and clings to me like a second skin. I saunter out of the bathroom all casual like, pretending to focus on untangling my hair as if I wear stuff like this every day, even when my heart feels like it's going to pound out of my chest.

Reuben is busy texting on his phone. He glances up at me as I walk across the room. My stomach somersaults at his double take.

"Ready?" he asks. I nod, keeping my eyes away from him in an attempt to cool down my cheeks.

It doesn't help, of course, but I have no right to complain. I know this dress is trouble—that's why I chose it.

While I'd been rifling around in my closet wondering what clothing best suited a date with the devil—or four of them, in this case—I'd realized something.

They've been controlling me like a puppet. They wanted me gone so they bullied me. And if I'd had a choice, I'd have left. They want to turn me against Father Gabriel, and expect *me* to prove that he's not a pedophile.

I guess alcohol does put hair on your chest, because I'm done being their marionette doll.

I'm wearing this dress because that means Zach's brothers—and hopefully Zachary himself—will be so distracted that, for once, I'll have the upper hand.

It's not the best plan, but it's *a* plan.

What could possibly go wrong?

# 4

## TRINITY

When the Brotherhood had invited me over, I'd expected to meet them somewhere inside the dorms. I get that they can't be seen together or it would blow their cover, but I didn't realize we'd be going back to their man cave.

I'm sitting in Zachary's wooden chair. It's hard and too high—my feet dangle unless I point and touch my toes to the carpet. The guys are sitting on the big sofa staring at me like they can't decide whether to kill me or fuck me.

Apollo just makes Reuben look even brawnier by comparison, especially since Reuben's biceps are almost bulging out of his t-shirt.

"Where's Cass?" I ask, shifting in my seat.

"He'll be here soon."

"And Zachary?"

"Gone to town," Reuben says. Apollo immediately elbows him in the side. "Shut it!"

"What?"

"She doesn't need to know that."

"Why not?"

Apollo frowns at him in reply before they turn their gazes back to me. I lick my lips and shift uncomfortably.

"Do you want a drink?" Reuben asks, standing before I have a chance to reply. He pours one for each of us and hands them out before sitting down again.

My nose wrinkles when I catch a whiff of the eye-watering booze in my glass. "What is this?" I ask, swirling it around.

"Whiskey," Apollo answers. "Not the greatest, but this far away from civilization it's this or moonshine."

"What's moonshine?"

Reuben chuckles wryly. Apollo snickers. Then both their faces go blank. "Fuck, you're serious," Apollo murmurs. He shakes his head as he lifts his glass to his lips. "God help us."

I frown at him, about to ask just what the hell that was supposed to mean when there's a snap of fabric behind me. I twist in my seat, facing Cass as he storms into the lair.

"We've got company," he says, and then his eyes fall on me. A smug smile replaces his frown. "Welcome back, my little slut." His eyes rove over me like a physical touch. "Damn. You look good enough to eat."

I drop my eyes and try to hide behind my glass as he strides deeper into the sitting area. I'm starting to regret wearing the dress.

"Guess who's back?" he says, stabbing a thumb over his shoulder.

"Not Zachary," Reuben says. "Not unless he left early."

"No, not Zachary," Cass says, deepening his voice as if trying to imitate Reuben. "Those other two fucks."

"Again?" Apollo sits forward in a rush, dragging his hair out of his face. "Christ, you'd think they'd have better things to do."

"You going to stop them?" Reuben asks, putting his empty glass on the ground.

"They're already headed down here." Cass grabs his hips, twisting to face me. "We should gag her."

Reuben's already on his feet. I throw up my hands, miraculously still holding onto my tumbler. "No. No gagging. I'll be quiet."

"Can't take a chance," Cass says, shaking his head as he goes over to the bookshelf and rifles through a pile of clothing. He whips out a bandanna and twists it into a thick rope like he's done this a thousand times before.

I'm on my feet a second later, my glass tumbling out of my hand and landing silently on the carpet. "No, please, Cass."

"Grab her," he says through his teeth.

I make a dash for the exit, but a thick arm slings around my throat and drags me back. "They won't be long," Reuben says, almost kindly, as he turns me around for Cass. "But they can't hear you."

"I wasn't going to—"

Cass shoves the bandanna between my lips and ties it off behind my head. Then he pats my cheek and draws me out of Reuben's grip.

I'd been willing to hear them out.

But this?

It's obvious they'll never trust me, so what's the point in trying to change our fucked up dynamic? I've gotten myself enmeshed in their plans, and the only way out is along the path they've chosen for me. I hate them for not letting me choose. But why did I expect any different of the big bad world my parents kept warning me about?

"Put her in there." Cass points to the bedroom. Apollo grabs my wrists and starts dragging me across the room.

I shake my head and dig in my heels.

"Relax, Trin," Cass says.

I'm one-hundred percent focused on Apollo, but I can

practically hear Cassius rolling his eyes at me. "Your virginity is
safe." He lets out a dark chuckle. "For now."

My enraged shriek comes out as a manic moan.

"Shh," Apollo says, hauling me the rest of the way. Reuben
holds the curtain back as Apollo pulls and Cass pushes. I end up
tripping the last yard and falling on hands and knees inside their
soft, dark sleeping pit. I scramble up in a rush, my fingers
tugging at the gag.

Reuben's hand closes over mine. He's just a shape in the dark,
if a *massive* shape, but his presence calms me. He doesn't try and
shush me, or drag me, or do anything. He just gently guides my
hands away from the knot at the back of my head until they're in
my lap.

Two more shadows slip inside and merge with the darkness.

Despite the blood singing in my veins, I can hear them
breathing.

And then the muted sound of fabric rustling. I sit up
straighter, and Reuben's hands tighten around mine. It should
have calmed me, but now I can feel his pulse, and it's racing.

Who the hell is coming?

"Here?"
        "Further back."
"But this is where we—"
"Want someone to find us again like last time?"

I sit up straight, my lips going slack around the gag. What
the hell are Jasper and Perry doing down here? Did they follow
Reuben and me when we slipped into the crypt? Do they suspect
something?

It's only when Reuben starts stroking my knuckle with the

pad of his thumb that I realize I'm gripping him hard as I can. I try to ease up, but my fingers refuse.

If they discover me down here, it will put an end to everything. Is that why Cass gagged me? He can't honestly think I'd make a noise and attract their attention—I could have done that any time in the past few hours I've been alone in the dorm. But since I'm past the point of complaining about their treatment, I sit and bear it.

At least until this fucking gag is loose. Then they'll get a mouthful.

A thump rattles a bookshelf a few yards away, back in the sitting area. Crap, what was that? Are they fighting? Fabric rustles, this time not nearly as muted as before.

If my eyes were to go any wider, I swear they'd pop out of my head.

They can't be doing what I think they're doing.

Can they?

Reuben peels open my fist and laces his fingers through mine. Something brushes my leg, and I turn my stricken gaze on Apollo who managed to move right up beside me without making a noise. Then again, I hadn't been focusing on them, had I? Apollo takes my other hand, mimicking Reuben.

Do they think I'll try scratching my way out of here or something? I shift on the layers of blankets and mattress beneath me, and squint in the darkness, looking for Cassius.

Maybe he thinks Apollo and Reuben have me taken care of, because I can't spot him in the shadows even though my eyes have adjusted to the dark.

Outside, Jasper and Perry start kissing. From those desperate sounds, it seems this tryst of theirs is long overdue.

More rustling.

A stifled moan.

Mother of God, I can't stand this. My brain seems very eager to fill in the blanks of what's happening. In my mind, those two boys are doing some very, very naughty things to each other.

I shift again, and then freeze.

No, this can't be happening.

Are those sounds turning me on? It can't be. It's more likely the fact that Zach's brothers have my hands clasped like kids on a first date.

The weirdest first date imaginable.

But there's definitely something happening between my legs. I'm starting to feel slick and tingly. Even my underwear's becoming damp.

There's another thump, a harsh indrawn breath, and then a deep moan.

Guess Jasper and Perry couldn't care less about keeping quiet —they think they're all alone in the abandoned library.

Oh my God! Jasper and I went through a whole lesson with him knowing he'd done this very thing just a few yards away? The pervert! Is that why he couldn't concentrate?

I flinch when a hand slides around the front of my throat.

Damn it. When did Cass move behind me?

Outside the lair, Jasper and Perry break into a furious, grunting rhythm. I can't make out if they're in pain or ecstasy. Probably a little of both.

Cass's other hand glances over my knee and up the inside of my thigh. I twist my shoulders, trying to get away from him. Reuben and Apollo tighten their grip on my hands.

I freeze.

No.

Bastards!

They weren't holding my hands because they were damn well sweet on me. They're keeping me still for Cass.

I grunt at them through the gag. Definitely not loud enough for Jasper and Perry to hear—although I doubt they'd notice a bomb going off—but I still end up with Cass's fingertips digging into my throat.

His hand starts moving again, inching toward my center.

Outside, books rattle on the shelf as the boys' pounding grows slower, but harder. I hear a muffled, "Fuck!" but I have no idea who said it because right now I have problems of my own.

Cass's fingertips slide under my dress and skate over my hipbone. He hooks a finger over the elastic of my underwear and tugs it down an inch. The hand around my throat travels up until he's cupping my jaw. He tilts back my head until I'm staring up at the silhouette of his head and shoulders.

"Lift your cute little ass so I can take these off," Cass murmurs into my ear.

What the fuck?

I start struggling, but that somehow translates into me agreeing that he can yank off my undies and leave them tangled around my knees. I buck, and that's when Reuben and Apollo grab my hips and shove me back onto the floor.

Panting into my gag, I toss hair out of my eyes and try to think of my next move while ignoring the fact that my body thinks this is all above board.

Lips brush my cheek as Cassius rains soft little kisses over my face and neck. There's a tug at my underwear before he groans into my ear. "You're fighting pretty damn hard for someone who's already wet," he says.

Heat washes over my face and sinks into my cheeks. I don't think I've ever been this humiliated in my life.

Outside, there's one last thump, and a groan to rival the one Cassius just let loose in my ear.

Another drawn-out, "Fuuuck," and I'm sure it's coming from Perry.

Frantic motion, skin on skin.

A deep sigh.

My mind is going haywire. The more I try and keep it blank, the more it fills with graphic images of what they're doing out there.

"Yes. *Fuck*," Jasper grunts.

Goosebumps break out over my skin, and I have no idea if it was that outburst, or Cass's teeth grazing the back of my neck.

Another thump.

Then a breathless, "We have to go," from Jasper.

"Not yet," Perry says, and my chest tightens how frantic he sounds. "Please, Jay. Just five more minutes."

They start kissing again. Cass's hand is less than an inch from the hot, throbbing mess between my legs.

"I'll fuck you first," Cass whispers in my ear. "Then Apollo, then Rube. Hopefully you'll be stretched out enough for him by then."

My body shudders, and Cass chuckles low and deep in his throat.

"Damn right you should be scared. I don't think you can handle him, my pretty little slut. Not that you have a choice, of course. Not if he ends up splitting you right down the fucking middle."

There's a soft, angry growl from Reuben.

"Wait!" Perry's voice makes me stiffen in surprise. "Did you hear that?"

"Let's go!" Jasper whispers furiously. Metal clinks against metal and fabric rustles. "Quick, before—"

A whistle pierces the air.

I gasp behind my gag. Zach's brothers fall back, releasing me.

Zachary's voice cuts through the air like a whip. "You two!"

"Shit!" Jasper hisses right over Perry's panicked, "Oh, *fuck!*"

"What on God's green earth are you doing?" Zachary bellows.

Again, we're all holding our breath. Waiting for the other shoe to drop.

Jasper yelps.

"Come here!" Zachary yells.

Off to one side, further away than he had been before, Perry starts crying. "Please, Brother, we were—"

"I know *exactly* what you two were doing."

My blood runs cold at the sound of Zachary's voice. Before I can stop myself, I'm hugging my arms over my chest. I don't ever want to hear him speaking to me with such frigid anger.

"Sister? It's Zachary. I'm sending Jasper and Perry to you." His voice moves away. "Twenty each. No, I'm afraid I have other matters to attend to. And no dinner for either of them."

I almost swallow my tongue when I hear the sound of the curtain hiding the lair's entrance being whisked away. Reuben and Apollo are on their feet a second later. Orange light blooms around the edges of the curtain shielding this side of the room, and then cuts a slice through the darkness when Zachary throws it back.

"What the fuck?" he demands in a deep growl that makes my hackles rise.

"I can explain—" Cass begins.

Zachary points back to the living area. Cass cuts off and steps into the living area without so much as a backward look.

Then he points to Reuben and Apollo. They follow Cass.

Zachary stares down at me, his face unreadable.

Without taking his eyes off of me, he tilts his head to the side and calls out, "Go get my things."

## 5
## ZACH

When I move forward, Trinity leans back like I'm gripping a blood-stained ax. I hold out one hand, then the other, showing her I'm in fact unarmed.

Fucking savages.

I knew this would happen. Which makes me a bigger idiot than they are. Luckily, those two queers were so busy fucking they probably wouldn't have noticed if Armageddon came and went. It's sad that I have to perpetuate the school's canon on homosexuality, but just like the fucked up car I'm forced to drive, some things are an intrinsic part of my persona. I can't break out of character yet.

Except here, in our nest.

I'd decided to cut my trip short after all. It's a blessing in disguise that Jasper and Perry agreed to sodomize each other down here—Miriam will be so caught up in giving them lashes that I'm sure she won't notice I'm back an hour early.

They gagged her again. I'm not surprised. In fact, I'd honestly expected her to be hogtied and deflowered already.

As soon as the gag is off, she scowls at me. "What's so fucking funny?"

I briefly close my eyes and let out the chuckle I'd been suppressing. "You should be thanking me," I tell her.

I try to help her up, but she shakes off my hand with a muttered curse. She stands, and then hurriedly tugs at something around her knees.

Her panties?

Jesus H. Christ.

I hold out my hand. "Give."

She looks like she might disobey, but then her shoulders sag and she hands over her underwear. I scan her as I untangle the fabric. For once, she's wearing something that fits, but that pale, clingy dress is like a red flag to a bull.

"Nice dress."

She doesn't look at me as she slips past to go out. "What, this old thing?" she mutters.

Underwear finally untangled, I go to fold it and stop.

It's soaked.

I turn a little, frowning after her as she disappears into the living area.

Why, I believe our little Trinity has a crush on us.

She's sitting stiff as a board in my chair, hands placed just so on her lap and her eyes down. But I can see her watching me through her lashes as I go to put her underwear in one of my tins. I had no intention of keeping it, but it will drive her mad knowing she'd left evidence of her presence down here.

Cass is gone. Probably hoping I'd cool off before he comes back with the things I bought in town.

"Twenty?" Apollo says. "That's a bit harsh, isn't it?"

"Second offense," Reuben says before I can open my mouth. "Should have gotten thirty."

"No one can stand thirty," Apollo says, sounding aghast. He flicks his head, tossing his hair from his face as he looks my way. "That Miriam's got a good arm."

"What is she doing here?" I ask them.

Trinity replies. "I'm here to talk."

I turn, my eyebrows quirking up before I can school them. "You came down here after I expressly told you not—?"

"We fetched her," Apollo says, sounding bored. I'm sure, without his camera, he's about to die. "Made sure no one saw. Right, Rube?"

"Right." Reuben stands. "Drink?"

"Double." My eyes are still on Trinity. "And for her too."

"I don't want—"

She cuts off when I shake my head, and drops her gaze back into her lap.

Such a pretty thing. Is that why Gabriel brought her here? I'd been thinking about it all of last night. Relocating Trinity to Saint Amos was a risky move for the Guardian. So risky, I'm still trying to figure out why he'd do it at all.

If he was in fact such a close family friend, then there's a strong possibility she might have seen him interacting with a Ghost from their church.

We're not a hundred percent sure how he chooses the Ghosts he works with. We assume they're all clergy members, but from a different diocese, or all from the same? I'd expect there would be nothing tying them together except Gabriel, and that he'd keep his distance.

Bringing a remnant from his previous life here, to Saint Amos, is not keeping his distance. Maybe he thinks he's safe now, after all these years. But he's never been reckless.

Until now.

Until Trinity.

But why risk everything…for *her*?

Unless his plans for her are short-term.

Because the only reason I can think Gabriel would bring Trinity here is because he knew she wouldn't be staying. So where is the poor orphan girl headed?

My thoughts go to the worst possible conclusion.

Trinity isn't here to finish out her senior year. She's here to meet someone very special. Perhaps a *few* somebodies.

My gut tells me Gabriel is planning on introducing her to her very own Ghosts.

# 6
## ZACH

I sit in Apollo's armchair, and he sits beside Reuben. Trinity's barely touched her drink, but every time I make a point of looking in her direction, she does at least take another sip.

Gabriel's back tomorrow. There's nothing we can do—short of breaking down his door—to speed up this process. And if that had been a possibility, we'd have done it by now.

There's time to kill. I should be grateful for the diversion Trinity affords us.

Cass arrives with my things and sets down the bags alongside the back wall of the library. "Two cameras?" he asks a moment later.

"Couldn't make out your handwriting," I say, directing my voice at Cass, but staring at Apollo.

But he's so busy scrambling off the sofa, I don't think he even notices. I drop my eyes and let out a soft chuckle as I drain my whiskey.

It's taken us years, but we're finally starting to find joy in the little things.

"This is the one," he says, snatching the offending box from

Cass's hands. "But I'll keep this as a spare." He tucks both boxes under his arms and looks about to leave.

"Sit down," I tell him, holding my glass out for Reuben.

He comes and takes it, but instead of going to refill, he stops beside Trinity's chair, his back to me. "Finish," he says quietly, tapping a fingernail against her glass.

She cranes to look up at him, and slowly swallows down the rest of her glass.

Well, that's one mystery solved then. I shouldn't be surprised it's him that she fancies most. When Reuben looks at you, it's like you're the only person in the world.

I think that's what his Ghost liked most about him. It's one thing controlling a little kid who can't fight back, but controlling someone like Reuben? He'd always been stronger and bigger than the rest of us. Our rock.

That's the funny thing about erosion, though. It weathers mountains. Reuben's Ghost ground him to dust over the years. If we hadn't escaped when we had, there'd have been nothing left of him, just an empty shell.

But what will Trinity do when Reuben realizes he doesn't need to save her anymore? Because that's around about the time he loses interest in people.

"This all you could get?" Cass asks.

I don't have to look to know what he's talking about. My trips to town are like Christmas around here because I always come back bearing gifts. Cass's comes in a few dime bags that cost a fuck load more than a dime these days.

He opens the seal on one and takes a deep sniff. "Jaysus," he mutters, grimacing. "You tell him he has to cure his stuff longer than a fucking day?"

"I'm not getting into a debate with your dealer, Cass."

Trinity glances from Cass to me to Reuben to Apollo, her eyes flickering around like a nervous dragonfly.

"Did you know Jasper was gay?" I ask her.

I smile when she flinches at the sound of my voice and turns her wide, amber eyes on me. Rube brings me my drink and then hers. This time, she takes it without looking at him.

"No." She lifts a shoulder, sipping absently at her glass. "But some things make sense now."

"Like what?"

She takes a tiny sip of her drink. "Perry told me Jasper hated girls."

Cass snorts as he moves over to the sofa. He sinks down, nudging Apollo aside with his elbow. Apollo's so busy starting up his new video camera and going through the settings, he doesn't even seem to notice.

I tap a fresh cigarette from my pack and light it, standing to a crouch to hand it over to Reuben. All while Trinity tracks me with that dragonfly gaze.

The lacy bodice of her dress keeps catching my eye. Not because of the perky tits they barely cover, but because I keep wondering why she wore it. For someone who doesn't seem comfortable in her own skin, exposing so much of it must have taken courage. Courage I didn't think she had.

Does she think we'll start salivating over her to the point where we let slip something important?

I look away when Reuben hands back my cigarette.

My paranoia knows no bounds. And although I'm fully aware of how fucked up my mind is, I can't stop these intrusive thoughts any more than I can stop breathing.

Something else I was considering last night as I lay sleepless in bed. What if Gabriel brought her here because he knew his time was short? What if he suspects—or *knows*—who we really are? What if, this entire time, he's been tracking us as carefully as we've tracked him?

There's nothing in this nest of ours that would give away our true identities, but the mere fact that we know each other, that we've kept in contact…

*Paranoia.*

We barely resemble the kids we once were. There's a box of hair dye in one of the bags. Colored contacts in another. Cass's Ghosts loved his long hair, so it was the first thing he did when we escaped—shaving his head. We're no longer grimy, malnourished, basement-pale boys full of bruises and sores.

Still, from the day I arrived here and shook Gabriel's hand, I couldn't get rid of the feeling that he'd stared at me just a second too long.

Like he'd recognized me.

She could be telling the truth.

Or she could be a spy. He could have brought her here to infiltrate us, spread dissent, find out how much we know.

My fucked up mind is dead set on the latter.

# 7

# TRINITY

Alcohol seems pretty good at calming my nerves. I'd been shaking when Zachary arrived, but not anymore. I guess it's also because I only have Zachary and Reuben's attention on me at the moment. Cassius is rolling more weed, and Apollo hasn't looked up from his camera yet.

Zachary doesn't speak again until Cass is done and the weed has passed around a few times. I don't bother refusing. I've never smoked before—weed or cigarettes—but I can understand why people do it. Once my lungs grow used to the hot smoke, the sensation is utterly delicious.

"This tastes different," I say, and instantly wish I'd kept my mouth shut.

*You're not here to make friends, Trinity. You're here to figure out how the hell you're going to get yourself out of this mess.*

"That's because it's absolute shit," Cass says. He quickly lifts a hand, palm out to Zachary. "Not that I'm complaining. I'd take ditch weed over no weed any day."

"Damn right you will," Zachary mutters, sounding more playful than serious.

His armchair is at an angle to mine, so I have to turn my head to look at him. I risk a quick peek now, trying to see his expression.

He's staring at me.

I quickly face forward, blushing.

"Give me my seat back," he says through a sigh. I bolt up off his seat, standing idle in the middle of their ill assortment of chairs and sofas like I'm showing off a new fashion line, before my brain starts working again. I sink into the armchair he'd been sitting in, squirming on the warm leather. Zachary takes my chair and spins it around on one leg, straddling it and laying his arms across the back before resting his chin on them.

It's the most relaxed I've ever seen him, but he still looks ready to pounce.

"You'd make a shitty poker player," Cass says.

"No I wouldn't," I snap back, hurriedly looking away from Zachary.

"Yeah, you would." Cass sits forward, ducking his head as if he's trying to imprint his statement on me. "Your face is an open book. Large print edition."

This makes Apollo and Reuben laugh, and puts a scowl on my face. Which I quickly smooth away.

Shit. I guess subterfuge isn't on the menu until I'm sober again.

Idiot.

I shouldn't have smoked or let Reuben bully me into downing my drink. Why do I feel like I have something to prove to these guys?

Everyone's attention is on me again. So I try and move it away. "You never told me your story," I say to Zachary.

Just his eyes move. "My *story*?"

"You and Reuben." I wave a limp hand. "The basement? How'd you end up there?"

Everyone stops moving. Even Apollo, who I'd thought wasn't listening.

Cass sits back and crosses his arms over his chest as he lets out a low whistle. "Presumptuous little slut, aren't you?"

My cheeks heat up again, but I force myself not to look at him. I keep my eyes on Zachary as he stares deadpan back at me. He takes a deep breath, and lets it out as a soft sigh before pushing away and straightening in his seat. "Our story," he repeats quietly, looking down as he smooths his jeans over his legs. "Our *story* is none of your fucking business, little girl."

My chest closes up, squeezing my heart like a fist.

"I just—"

"Gabriel will be back tomorrow," he cuts in. "How about you start focusing on that instead of sticking that pretty nose where it doesn't belong?" He stands without waiting for my reply.

I drop my head, willing myself to disappear into the armchair. I hadn't meant to be nosy. I just want to understand what I'm dealing with. I get that it's probably a horrible subject for them, but Apollo and Cass had told me theirs without biting my head off.

Maybe that's why *they* spoke up yesterday, and not Reuben and Zachary.

Holy shit…what did Zachary and Reuben go through?

I hug myself and risk peeking at Reuben through my lashes. He has a hand flat on his chest, his eyes boring into me. I hurriedly look away and on instinct reach for the rosary around my neck.

Then I freeze and look back at him.

His rosary. I've had it this whole time. Should I—?

"Keep it. I bought him another one," Zachary says.

I jump at the sound of his voice.

Dear Lord. Whatever nerves I had, they're shot again.

Keeping cool around these guys is impossible. It's like trying to keep an eye on four moving targets. I'll just have to get used to the fact that they'll always have an advantage over me.

Strength in numbers, I guess.

I drop the rosary I'd been about to pull over my head.

Zachary hands a slim case to Reuben, and he stares at it for a few seconds before opening it. He lifts out a dull black rosary and slips it over his head. Then he tucks it away under his t-shirt.

They're all in casual clothes today.

Zachary is wearing a button-up shirt, pale blue, and jeans that look like he bought them at a thrift store. In fact, all the guys look like they got their clothes from the Salvation Army.

I'm assuming it's on purpose, seeing as Zachary just bought a brand-new laptop. Then there're the two video cameras…

Either he's rich, or he has a ton of credit card debt. I guess if you're planning on offing someone, you wouldn't really care about your finances.

"Do that later. I need you to set this up." Zachary leans across and hands Apollo the laptop.

Apollo flicks his hair out his eyes as he looks up at Zachary, and then gives a grim nod.

Zachary takes out a much smaller box and goes back to his seat. He toys with it as he watches Apollo remove the laptop's packaging and start it up.

I tip my glass against my lips and look down in surprise. It's empty. I hurriedly wrap my fingers around it, trying to hide the fact, but I'm too slow.

Reuben gets to his feet.

"In a bit," Zachary says as if he's reading Reuben's mind. "We need her to focus."

My throat moves as I swallow. With Zachary handing things out to the guys, there'd been an almost festive air inside this strange lair. For a moment, I'd forgotten where I was. Who I was with.

*These are not normal people, Trinity. Your life is the furthest thing from ordinary right now.*

I drop my head and snort quietly to myself. Like I'd ever had a claim to being normal.

"Gabriel has a laptop," Reuben says.

I start fidgeting with my glass. "Okay."

"It's hidden somewhere in his room."

I nod and glance at the other boys. Cass is smoking what's left of the weed, leaning an elbow on the armchair and slouching like he's waiting for his photoshoot to begin. He's wearing a white t-shirt made of flimsy fabric that drapes his body like silk. If it weren't for the hole in it, I'd have thought it was an expensive designer piece. But the hole is big and ugly—it definitely didn't ship like that.

Apollo's still busy with the laptop. His long fingers fly over the keyboard, his shoulders hunched and his hair hiding his face.

Zachary toys with the box while his eyes search me.

"So you want me to steal it?" I ask, when it seems Reuben's done talking.

"Of course not," Zachary says through an impatient sigh. "We need you to clone the hard drive."

I frown at him. "I don't know how—"

"It's easy," Apollo says without looking up. "Zach will give you the drive. You just plug it into a USB slot and it'll do the rest."

I nod, my eyes going to the box Zachary has. I'm not going to ask what a USB drive is—I'm hoping it will be one of those self-explanatory types of things.

"How am I supposed to sneak that into his room?" But then I hold up a hand, briefly closing my eyes. "How am I even supposed to *get* into his room?"

Zachary gives me half a smile. "You're a bright girl," he says, his smile turning sarcastic. "I'm sure you'll figure something out."

I clench my jaw as I tap a finger against my glass. "Why do you need me? Couldn't one of you just—?"

"You're so convinced he's a saint," Zachary says. "Time to prove it." He tosses the box to me.

I fumble it before opening it up and taking out a thin device barely longer than my thumb. "So I just plug this in," I mumble, turning it over in my hands. "After I sneak into his room and track down his hidden laptop."

"You have until Wednesday."

I look up at Zachary. "Why Wednesday?"

His smile is anything but merry. "Because by then, I would have lost my patience with you."

# 8

# ZACH

Trinity gets up to leave. I scan her body as she does, and she folds in on herself like an origami swan. "Where do you think you're going?" I ask lightly, shaking out another cigarette.

"I have the thing," she says, holding up the thumb drive. "I know what do to. Surely I can…" She trails off before glancing at the exit.

"Leave?" I finish for her, getting slowly to my feet as I drag at the cigarette. "Now why would we let you do that?"

Her mouth opens, but she says nothing. Instead she grabs the blood-red crucifix around her neck.

Reuben would have preferred to have his rosary back but he needs to learn to let go of things. The crucifix is a start. A *good* start. I could never get him to abandon it. But all it took was a desperate soul and he handed it over like it was nothing.

Although I suppose he expected to get it back.

We all have to learn some hard lessons if we're to piece together the remnants of ourselves. Reuben has to understand that his past isn't encompassed in that cheap trinket.

*We're* his past.

Trinity flinches when I grab her wrist.

I drag my eyes down her body again. She looks up and meets my eyes, but there's uneasiness in those amber irises. "I think you should dance for us," I tell her.

"W-what?" she splutters out, her mouth lifting into an incredulous smile. "No."

"Fucking *fantastic* idea," Cass says.

"I can't dance," she says through a laugh. "And even if I could…" Her eyes dart around before she puts her hands on her hips and tries to look casual. "There's no music."

"You don't need music," I say, drawing her closer.

She steps back hurriedly, pulling her wrist free and letting out a huff. "I'm not dancing." Her eyes flicker over my brothers. Then they flash back to me and narrow. "Not unless I get something in return."

Cass whistles through his teeth. Apollo even stops messing around with the laptop long enough to look up at her with wide eyes and a slack mouth. Reuben snorts and rubs his jaw like he's trying to hide his faint smile.

I tilt my head at her. "Do you really think you're in a position to bargain with us?"

"Hang on," Cassius says through a chuckle. "Let's hear her out. What's your offer, Trin?"

She replies without taking her eyes off me. "I want to know how you factor into all of this," she says. An absent wave of her hand takes in my brothers, then the packages against the wall. "You're older than them. And a teacher, which means you've studied at college, right?" She steps close, until the rose-scented wood of her rosary beads tickles my nose. "And you're rich. So how did you wind up in that basement? How did you become a part of this?"

My eyes narrow. She gasps when I grab her jaw and squeeze dimples into her soft flesh. That sound ripples through me like a stone tossed into a pond. My cock starts paying attention for the first time today. I want to force her to her knees and make her swallow every rock-hard inch of me until she passes out from lack of oxygen.

I resort to fisting her hair instead, keeping her head in place. Fear turns her amber eyes a sullen bronze.

"For a dance from someone who can't even dance?" I sneer at her. "I don't think so."

There's utter silence from my brothers. Are they holding their breaths like she is?

I force a smile. "How about you dance, and I'll consider *not* giving you five lashes for being such a presumptuous little slut?"

Cass snickers at the fact that I'm using his words, but I ignore him. Trinity is all I'm interested in right now.

She would be pissing herself if she knew how deadly it was to attract my full attention.

Her face pales. "Lashes? Just for asking—?"

"Six."

Her lips begin to tremble.

I shrug, tilting her head back another inch as I close the distance between us. "We could demand worse things from you," I murmur. My hard-on presses into her stomach, and her eyes flare wide. She tries to arch away from me, but I release her jaw and press my hand into the small of her back. "Dirty, *sick* things." I grind into her even harder.

She shudders against me.

"Fine," she says through her teeth. "One dance."

My eyes fall to her lips. When she licks them, I almost kiss her just to taste her mouth.

Instead, I push her away and drag at my cigarette as I sink back into my seat. Then I click my fingers at her and again at the spot between us.

"Get to it then."

She moves to the center of the room, and hesitates before looking over at Reuben. "Can I have another drink?"

Reuben doesn't bother confirming with me first. Now that our business is done, I'm not anyone's boss anymore.

We agreed a long time ago that we couldn't all lead the charge and drew straws to determine our hierarchy.

Just because I drew the short straw doesn't mean I dominate them twenty-four-seven. By now I know when to step back and let them have their fun.

Our blessed Keepers knew that too.

It was their responsibility to feed us, shelter us, keep us hidden. And, most importantly, to make sure we didn't escape.

Keeping us tied up all the time damaged our young bodies.

Bruises became welts.

Welts turned into sores.

I still have kinks in both my ankles where the constant ligature of a too-tight rope altered my bone structure.

They were also instructed to keep our spirits up. Most of our Ghosts liked it when we fought back. But you stop fighting when you lose hope and our Keepers eventually figured that out.

So they made sure there was always a sliver of hope. Just enough to cling onto until our Ghosts' next visit.

Once a day while we ate, they'd let us out of our bonds. In that hour we'd search every inch of our cage, just in case a Ghost had dropped something, or we'd missed something the thousand previous times we'd searched.

Apollo found a rosary one day. Reuben recognized it as the one his Ghost would wear. We drew straws to see who would keep it.

Rube lost.

Trinity folds her hands in front of her as she waits, making an obvious effort not to look at any of us. Which is probably a good thing, because even Apollo's put away his toys to watch.

And if she can't feel Cass's hungry gaze already peeling off that flimsy layer of fabric...

She takes the tumbler from Reuben and downs it in a rush. Her face scrunches up as she fights not to cough. She nods at him and hands back the glass.

"No music," she says softly, as if to herself.

"You're boring us," I tell her, my chair creaking as I shift my weight.

She throws me a panicked look and quickly starts swaying her hips.

"Slower, little girl."

I love the way her eyes flare when I call her that. But as if she picks up on the fact, she smooths her expression and instead closes her eyes.

A minute later, I bark out, "Enough."

She stops, her eyes fluttering open as she whirls to face me. "What?"

"You're terrible," I tell her, shaking my head. "Cass, give me your belt."

Her eyes go wide. She holds up her arms, one palm facing me and the other to Cass as he stands and starts taking off his belt. "No. No! I can do better. I just have to—"

"Here, I'll show you," Reuben says.

My lips quirk up. God, he certainly took long enough. He's a clever fucker, but he's so damn cautious you'd think he was simple.

I light another cigarette. Cass lights a joint. We pass them to each other as Rube gets up. Trinity takes a hurried step back when he looms over her, but then he grabs the back of her neck and hauls her back.

He slides his hand down her shoulder, her arm, and over to her hip. Then he takes her waist in both hands and swivels her hips in a figure eight.

"Loosen up," he grumbles in his deep voice.

"I'm trying," she mutters back, staring up at him like she's wondering when he plans on snapping her neck.

"Close your eyes, if it helps," he suggests calmly. "Pretend I'm one of those boy band idiots you girls are always crushing on."

I'm smiling full out now, and it has nothing to do with the whiskey-and-weed concoction wreaking havoc on my brain.

Reuben and Cass were the only two of us that had something resembling a normal childhood after we escaped the Ghost House. I'd fought to keep us together, but we were all from different states. Rube and Cass went to foster homes in West Virginia and Georgia, Apollo back to North Carolina, and I stayed behind in Virginia.

It took years for me to find them again.

Reuben ended up in a foster home with three other girls, which we'll never let him live down, especially seeing as he never fucked any of them. Although I doubt it ever crossed his mind. He became their big brother, and that's the persona he stuck with. And he did such a good job, that foster family almost ended up adopting him.

It was practically a done deal until something triggered an episode of psychosis. He destroyed that family's home and badly injured two of his foster sisters before the police arrived to restrain him. He landed in juvie for a year before being spat back into the foster system. Months went by before I could track him down. A lot of money exchanged hands before I finally got him relocated to Saint Amos.

Times like that, I honestly wished I'd had parents I could turn to. Having legal guardians to sign off on legit paperwork would have been so much easier than all the palm-greasing I did. But my parents were long dead, and after we escaped from the Ghost House, I no longer trusted *anyone* except my brothers.

Luckily, money can buy just about anything.

"Good," Reuben says. "Now your shoulders. You have to dance with your whole body."

"It's really hard without music."

"You don't need music," Rube says.

On cue, I tap my thumb against the back of the seat.

*Thud.*

*Thud.*

*Thud.*

Rube glances up at me, and gives me a ghostly smile. "All you need is a rhythm."

Cass and Apollo pick up the beat, Apollo with one of his rings against his glass, Cass tapping the back of the tin he keeps his weed in.

And Trinity starts to dance.

Her hips sway, and her shoulders undulate to the slow, steady beat we create.

"That's it," Rube murmurs. His head hangs low, his lips brushing the top of her head. "Do you feel it?"

I expect Cass to make a snide comment—he's got a fifth-grader's sense of humor—but when I look over at them all I see is a most familiar hunger.

*That's how our Ghosts would look at us,* a sinister voice hisses.

My jaw clenches.

No. This isn't the same. That was a sick, contaminated lust. This is pure and natural.

*That's what* he *said about us. That's what* we *were.*

Pure. Innocent. We were the cure for our Ghost's perversions. Our lot in life was to ease their suffering—a sacrificial offering to appease their depraved hedonism.

And they accepted us time and time again.

I falter on the beat, but Cass and Apollo don't even notice. Taking my cigarette with me, I stalk into the bedroom.

There the darkness swallows me, shields me, comforts me.

But my respite is brief and bittersweet.

*That's what she is. Pure. Innocent. Is she our cure?*

I try to block the voice, but clapping my hands over my ears does nothing.

*You know what you have to do, don't you? To her, to* them.

I go to the back of the room and lift up the corner of a mattress.

*Killing Gabriel won't make the pain go away, Mason.*

*Not for you, not for them, not for* her.

When I don't find what I'm looking for, I clamp my lips over the filter of my cigarette and shove both hands into that cool dark as smoke burns my eyes.

"Looking for something?" Cass asks, sinuous as a fucking serpent.

I rock back on my heels and snatch my cigarette from between dry lips. "Where is it?" I grate out.

"If I can't have my smack, then you can't have your—"

I spin around and grab him by the throat, pressing him into the solid wall. He chokes, and then chuckles into my face. "That shit's unhygienic as fuck," he says hoarsely.

"Where. Is. It?"

"You don't scare me, Boss. Never have, never will."

I can barely see anything in the dark, but there's a glimmer of light where his eyes are.

I bring my cigarette up, instantly mesmerized by the red glow on his wet corneas. He blinks, but he doesn't close his eyes.

"She's messing with all of our heads," Cass whispers. "Let's get her out of here. We don't need her."

"*You* need her," I counter, bringing that glowing ember closer to his eye. His cheek lights up faintly but he doesn't even bat a fucking eyelid.

"Do we?" He shrugs and lays his hand casually over the stiff arm pinning him against the wall. "I thought we didn't need anyone."

"Just tell me where it is," I say through my teeth. I hate how my voice shakes, but I'm past the point of being able to control it.

"That shit's like slapping a fucking Hello Kitty band-aid on a gunshot wound," he says. His voice drops low. "Come on, Zach."

He's right, and that makes me feel even more pathetic for allowing myself to be caught between shame and guilt and utter desperation. "I just need—"

"I *know* what you need," Cass cuts in quietly. "And I told you before, all you gotta do is ask."

His hand slips off my arm. Fabric rustles. Then he grabs hold of the hand holding my glowing cigarette. "Just not the face, bro. That's my moneymaker."

I clamp down on a near-hysterical bark of a laugh as I let him guide my hand down.

"We should try for a smiley face. Nirvana style. What do you say?" His voice is tight, light, steady.

I don't know how the fuck he so easily accepts my breakdowns.

"Fuck," I grate, squeezing my eyes shut so I can't see that tempting glowing ash. "Cass, no."

"Come on, you pussy. I've had worse."

"Fuck off."

"Jesus, the tension's killing me," he says through a grin I can hear but not see.

So fucking easy for him. For them. I should never have drawn the short straw. Rube would have made a better leader than me any day. Any of them would have. But it was me. So I had to man-up and fucking lead them.

"You know it's the worst part, right? The waiting? You fucking know it, Zach. So just do it, you cunt."

He guides my hand lower and closer, until my knuckles graze his bare skin where he's hiking up his shirt. I trail his skin with the pad of my thumb. My chest is so tight I can barely breathe, and what little air does come in feels like I'm sucking it from a fucking chimney.

Hot. Full of ash.

"Fuck," I say again, trying to ignore the erection straining against my jeans. Pain and pleasure—I've never had one without the other.

"Cass—"

"Just fucking do it," he grates.

My thumb skims over a puckered burn mark. Then another. Another.

"There." He sounds as breathless as I feel. "Right there."

"Christ."

My lungs fill with powdered brimstone as I press the tip of the cigarette into his flesh.

He stiffens, letting out a short, soft gasp. Then he shoves me so hard I fall back and land on my ass. I'm anticipating the boot heading for my stomach, but that just makes the impact ten times worse.

My breath rushes out in a pained grunt I can't possibly keep quiet. I roll onto my side, curling up as he kicks me again. Then he's gone, orange light blooming against the back of my eyelids before the room goes dark again.

I open my fingers and let the crumpled cigarette fall out. Then I bring my hand close and lick off the streak of ash smeared over my palm.

The almost constant ache in my wrists and ankles fades away as I lie there listening to Apollo tapping out a beat for Trinity as she dances for Reuben.

Tap. Tap. Tap.

*Sounds like the leaking pipe in the back of the basement, doesn't it, Mason?*

The pain makes it easier to push away the voice.

And that's always been the case, even back then.

*Tap.*

*Tap.*

*Tap.*

## 9
## TRINITY

I t has to be the weed. Or the booze. *Something's* doing weird, weird shit to my brain. That bit in a Disney movie where a magical light zooms around the heroine and lifts her up? That's me right now. It feels like I'm suspended inches from the floor, a glittering aura whirling around me.

In my wildest dreams I would never have imagined anything could feel this good. This…right.

Reuben's got one hand around the back of my neck, the other at the small of my back. Using his hands and body, he guides me.

Moments later, faint noises in the background clamor for my attention but they sound wrong and violent so I push them out of my mind.

This…this is the complete opposite.

"See?" Reuben murmurs into my ear. "And you thought you couldn't do it."

I wasn't about to tell him I'd danced before. A *lot*. My mirror had been my only audience, and my worst critic. For all I know,

I probably looked a right idiot back then as I swayed to my own quiet humming.

I'd really hoped to use my feminine wiles to strike a deal with these men, but I guess I still have a lot to learn about the art of seduction.

Also, dancing for an actual audience is much harder than watching yourself in a mirror. So much so, I hadn't even known where to start.

Reuben saved me.

This whole time I'd had my hands at my side, limply moving along with my arms. But as soon as Reuben's breath brushes my skin, I suck in a breath and force myself to reach out and touch him.

My fingers trace the outlines of his perfectly sculpted muscles. I tilt my head back and open my eyes. They flutter and then go wide in surprise.

Reuben's glaring at me.

He stops moving, and snatches my wrists together in one meaty hand. "What are you doing?" he demands in a low voice.

"I was just…I thought we were…"

Movement draws my gaze away.

Cass storms out of the curtained area of the room, a hand on his stomach like he's sick. The snarl on his face sends a chill through me, but as soon as he looks up and sees me, it disappears.

My mouth opens to ask him what's wrong, but by then everything's moving too fast.

"Enough of this bullshit foreplay," he grates out, whipping his hand away from his stomach. He points straight at me and advances so fast that I wheel back from him with a stifled yell.

He grabs my arm before I have a chance to get away, and throws me into the armchair I'd been sitting in.

I gasp—more in shock at how fucking strong he is than in actual pain. Then he's on top of me, straddling my waist and yanking my dress up my legs.

Cool air caresses my upper thighs as he hikes my skirt up my hips. Since my panties are still in Zachary's tin box, there's nothing to shield me from the dark lust gleaming in his eyes.

"Stop!" I yell. I start bashing at him with my fists, but he knocks my arms away with a flick of his hand, the other going to his belt.

"Keep singing that pretty song, little blackbird."

The hair on my arms stands up straight. His voice is low, rough, and has an English accent, like he's mimicking someone.

What. The. *Fuck*?

The button on his jeans pops open with a twist of his hand.

I scream, my fists turning into claws. He grimaces, now straining to keep back my attack while working his fly. I buck my hips to try and shake him off, but that just makes him laugh.

*Why is no one stopping him?*

*Mother of God—are they just going to watch?*

I obviously put up too much of a fight. Cass grabs my hair, wrenches back my head, and slaps me.

A shock wave coruscates through my skull. My vision swims with tears. My face goes numb. I blink hard, sending those tears down my cheeks.

I watch in dumbstruck silence as Reuben rips Cass off my lap and throws him against the wall like he weighs nothing. Zachary appears by the curtain, but his head hangs low, and there's a strange set to his mouth.

My Disney movie has just turned into a horror show.

Reuben's got Cass against the wall, his arm pressed to his throat. Cass's face reddens, but he doesn't fight back.

He's fucking *grinning* at Reuben.

Reuben's muscles bulge beneath his shirt as he uses his arm to shove Cass a couple of inches up the wall.

But there aren't any blows exchanged. He's just restraining him. Zachary lumbers over and tries to pull Reuben off. Reuben doesn't even shift.

A cool hand slips around my wrist and tugs. My neck feels stiff as I turn to look at Apollo. I'm dimly aware that I'm exposed, but my hand's shaking too much for me to successfully pull down the hem of my dress.

"Let's go someplace else, yeah?" Apollo says, smiling so calmly you'd swear he hasn't noticed someone was about to get murdered. "Come on. I wanna show you something."

When I don't move, he dips his head a bit and then presses a quick peck to my slap-stained cheek. "There. All better now."

Again he tugs at my wrist.

Somehow I stand.

He leads me out of the lair just as I hear the thump of flesh on flesh and hear Cass groan in pain.

*What. The. Fuck?*

**B**right sunlight bathes my face when we leave the crypt. Apollo hangs back at the doorway, his hair shifting as he checks left and right.

There's no one in sight, but he still seems hesitant to leave the shadows and step into the light.

*Vampire.*

I laugh at the ridiculous thought, and Apollo throws a concerned look at me over his shoulder as he starts toward the dormitory.

"Okay there, pretty thing?"

I giggle at him.

"Sorry…it got a bit rough in there," he says. We're walking at a brisk pace, his fingers handcuffed around my wrist. "They'll calm down. A few punches and they always do. Like Fight Club, right? And shit, how was that cinematography? Did you know Cronenweth deliberately underexposed the actors' faces to force the audience to pay more attention in each shot?"

I say nothing, instead willing the world to stop bobbing up and down so hectically. I couldn't have had more to drink than yesterday, but yesterday I'd had a good long nap before I'd attempted to walk anywhere.

Now I feel like everything I've consumed today has only just kicked in. I feel like I'm walking on a trampoline an inch off the ground. And every time I shift my eyes even a little, the world blurs.

"I'm drunk," I announce.

"That's the spirit," Apollo replies without slowing. "Nice day for it, too."

I finally find it in me to pull back. "No. I mean…*really* drunk." I sway as soon as we come to a halt, and he steps forward to steady me by slinging an arm around my waist.

"Easy there," he says and then starts walking again. "There's nothing to it, see? You just keep your eyes on something that's not moving. Like the bell tower. Can you see it?"

My head tilts back.

Fuck, that's a big building.

"Yeah."

"Good. Just keep looking at that. I'll make sure you don't step on any snakes."

"Snakes?" My head bobs forward, and I stumble as the world takes a slow somersault. "Fuck."

"Sorry, bad joke. No snakes. *Holes*. That's what I'll keep an eye out for. Just holes."

"Holes," I agree, tilting my head back again. "Who rings the bell?"

"Not a hunchback, that's for sure."

I giggle like a fucking idiot at that. Cool shadows replace the sun, and I sag in relief. "Made it."

"Not yet, pretty thing. Should I carry you?"

I snort. "You can't carry me."

"Bitchy much?"

The world spins around me. I'm looking up Apollo's face, his victorious grin partially hidden behind a few locks of hair.

"You jus' call me a bitch?" I demand.

"Keep your voice down," he says. "And yes. Because you're being one."

I snort again. "You're a...you're an asshole. You all are."

"Quiet," he warns in a low voice, his hair shifting as he glances left and right. My teeth click together as he starts up the staircase. "Or I'll take you back to your room."

I hesitate, my head bobbing against the crook of Apollo's arm as he hurries up the stairs with me. My room? Jasper might be there? I grimace. I'm too drunk to deal with him. Or not drunk enough.

"Here," Apollo says. He sets me down and props me against the wall like a broom as he fishes in his pockets. He takes out a bunch of keys. The keychain used to be a furry cat face. Now it's grubby as fuck. While he looks for the right key, I start to slide down the wall. He props me back up with an absent tug on the shoulder of my dress and then herds me inside the room.

"Hey! I've been here before!" I head for the closest chair.

"Sure have."

When I sit down, I see he's leaving. "Hey, where are you going?"

He pauses at the door, turning to me. But then he closes the door without answering.

And locks it.

I sit up a little straighter and stay conscious, remember that I'm too drunk to give a shit, and pass out on the couch.

# 10
## ZACH

**M**y jaw pulses, the heat emanating from within a stark contrast to the ice pack pressed against my bruised flesh.

"Shit, man. We can't let anyone see you like this," Apollo says.

"No fucking shit," I snap, squinting over at him. I click my fingers at the tumbler he's supposed to be filling for me, and he hesitates only a second before filling it with whiskey.

"Is this going to mess with the plan?"

"I don't know, Apollo," I tell him through gritted teeth. "How about you ask Cass the next time you see him?"

"Man, you can't blame him for this."

I slam my fist into the arm of my wooden chair. "The fuck I can't."

"Here." Apollo hurries over with my glass. I drain it and hand it back.

"Just give me the fucking bottle."

"Yeah, right," he laughs, skipping back and snatching the bottle away like he honestly thought I was in any state to tackle him for it.

Besides the two solid kicks Cass got in earlier, he punched me in the jaw, the groin, and my fucking kidneys. *Twice*. Because by that time, Reuben had hurried off to check if Trinity was okay, not giving a fuck who survived the fight.

Cass has always been like a fucking rat in a corner. You wouldn't think he was even capable of throwing a punch, and then you're lying on your back wondering why the stars had come out in the middle of the fucking day.

All because I'd held back.

Because I'd thought Trinity was still in the room.

Watching. *Judging*.

I thump the wood again, wishing the arm would break and growling when it doesn't.

"She's done." I shake my head and point at Apollo as I breathe through a wave of pain. "Too much fucking trouble. Tomorrow, you take my car, you throw her in the trunk, and you fucking—"

"What, Zach?" Apollo cuts in with a snort, shaking his head at me. "We tell Gabriel his girl child wandered into the woods and got *et* by bears?" His lips twitch and he smooths his fingers over his mouth as if he could wash away his words.

A dark smile slowly spreads over my face. "I knew you weren't just a pretty face."

## 11

## TRINITY

I wake up to the sound of muffled voices and intense nausea. Pushing up to my elbows, I scan my dark surroundings to try and figure out where I am. This can't be my room. There are too few lumps in the mattress. The sheets are too soft. And it smells like Reuben, not mothballs.

*Reuben.*

Shit, I'm in his room. His *bed*room.

And I need to puke.

I slide off the bed onto wobbly legs. The room is so dark that I hit my knee against the side of the bed as I head for the glowing outline of the door.

It opens before I can reach it. Reuben's silhouette blocks out almost all the light.

"Bathroom," I say in a tight voice.

He grabs my shoulder and herds me out of the room. Everything's a blur until I reach the bathroom, where all I can focus on is the toilet.

Thank God he opens the lid for me, because I barely bend over before I puke.

Fingers brush my temples, drawing my hair away from my face. A large, cool hand caresses the back of my neck as I puke out my guts, stomach lining, and a lung.

I finally rock back on my heels. Reuben's holding out a washcloth for me.

Deliciously warm.

I wipe my face with it and stand on shaky legs. He points to the basin. There's a bottle of mouthwash there, the sink already filling with more warm water.

"We'll be outside," he says, turning to the doorway.

Apollo moves aside as Reuben approaches.

I clean myself and the bathroom as well as I can and try to ignore the fact that I still feel tipsy. When I step into the living area of Reuben's room, the smell of coffee hits my nose.

I still can't believe seniors get an accommodation like this if their grades are good enough. I guess Father Gabriel really wants me to work my way up from the bottom.

Apollo brings me a cup. "Cream and two sugars."

I can't help but smile. It's sweet that he still remembers how I take it, although the day he saw me putting in sugar I'd given myself a double dose.

Hell, I probably *still* need the energy. Maybe this will become my regular serving from now on.

"What time is it?" I ask, glancing around. The lights are on and the curtains are drawn, but it doesn't feel like it's night time yet.

"Five," Reuben says. He's sitting on one of the two couches that make up his living area. "Come sit."

His quiet command makes my hackles rise. I glance at Apollo with raised brows, but he just gives me his usual lopsided smile. "We need to talk," he says. Then he goes and fetches another two cups of coffee, handing one to Reuben before sitting down beside him.

Thank God. I'm not sure if I would dare to sit beside any of them after what happened in the library. My chest goes tight just thinking about what Cass had tried to do.

Suddenly the coffee doesn't taste as nice.

I sit on the fabric couch and hurriedly tug down my dress when it inches up my leg.

"Cold?" Reuben asks, already standing before I can answer. He disappears into his room and comes back with a wool blanket that he hands to me without a word.

I throw it over my lap and give him a grateful nod.

"Zach wants to get rid of you," Apollo says.

My sip of coffee goes down the wrong way. I cough and almost tip the entire cup over me. Thankfully it only spills on the blanket, else it would have burned me through my dress. I quickly put the mug down on the coffee table. "Excuse me?"

"You're causing disruption," Reuben says.

"Disruption?" Great, now I've turned into a parrot.

Apollo waves a hand. "Don't worry, we talked him out of it. But shit's still a bit tense right now."

Really? I thought Cass trying to fuck me on the armchair was a normal day for these guys.

I pick up my coffee again. It's instant, but it's warm and sweet and I need all of that right now.

"You should keep out of his way until you've cloned that hard drive," Apollo says before taking a noisy slurp from his cup.

"Zachary's my Psych teacher," I say dryly. "I have a class with him."

"Then get it done tomorrow."

I sit forward, frowning hard at Apollo. "How the hell—?"

"It's for your own safety, Trinity," Reuben says. "If Zachary says you have to disappear then—"

"Then the three of you will do what he says like the good little soldiers you are, right?" Of course I regret the words the moment they leave my lips, but I blame the headache and the lingering taste of bile in my mouth.

Oh, and don't forget the scratch marks Cass left on my inner thighs. I don't have to peek under my skirt to know they're there. I can feel them throbbing in time to my headache.

Reuben drops his head and lets out a heavy sigh. A humorless laugh huffs from Apollo, disturbing the surface of his coffee as he brings it up for another sip.

"How will you do it, huh? Mince me up into burger meat? Hit me over the head and bury me in a shallow grave there in the cemetery?"

Apollo purses his lips. "Hadn't thought of that." He shakes a finger at me. "That's a good one."

I glare at him. "You *can't* get rid of me. Gabriel will find out, and he'll start looking around. He'll find you—all of you—and then…"

I don't know what happens then, but I know they've been trying to avoid it for years so it's as good a threat as any.

Apollo stands and heads for the kitchenette. There're a microwave and a kettle and a few odds and ends on the counter. He brings back the device Zachary had been toying with earlier and holds it out to me.

"Do it tomorrow, soon as Gabriel's back."

"Yeah, I'll just invite myself to his room, ask him where his super-secret computer is, and copy everything while he pours me a drink or something," I mutter sourly as I snatch the box from Apollo. "Great plan, guys."

"It'll take like five minutes to copy. This shit's high tech," Apollo says as he sinks back into the seat beside Reuben. "And we'll help you."

"How?" I sip at my coffee as he and Reuben share a look.

"We'll create a diversion," Apollo says. "You get yourself into Gabriel's room, we'll do the rest."

I open the box and take out the device before weighing it on my palm. "How am I supposed to sneak this in?"

Reuben lets out a long-suffering sigh and gets up, putting down his mug as he passes the coffee table en route to me. "Give," he says, holding out his hand.

I pass over the device.

"Sit forward."

I do as he says, but with a frown for Apollo. He just shrugs, quirking an eyebrow at me as if he has no idea what Reuben's doing.

Reuben crouches in front of me, one of his knees clicking. He pulls down the bodice of my dress and slips the device between my breasts. Then he uses his thumb to smooth the fabric over my breastbone.

I look down. And then up at him.

"If he's the saintly priest you say he is, then he won't be staring hard enough at your tits to notice it," Reuben says.

"I can't wear this dress around Father Gabriel." Just the thought makes my cheeks heat up. Which is weird, because Reuben's touch hadn't.

"He's not going to find it." Reuben stands, putting his crotch directly at eye level. I hurriedly sit back and bury my face in my mug as I take a sip.

"Why are you helping me?" I ask quietly, glancing between them. "Why not just get rid of me like Zachary wants?"

At this, they share another look. Apollo drops his head, avoiding eye contact. Reuben doesn't say anything.

"Why?" I ask. "Tell me."

"Because we're all coming undone," Reuben says.

"And as much as Zachary likes to think getting rid of you will help, it won't," Apollo adds.

"Only one thing will," Reuben says.

"What?"

"Finding our Ghosts," they chorus, faces deadpan.

A pollo leaves first to check if there's anyone in the hallway. As I wait for Apollo to come back, I peek at Reuben standing in the doorway. He's resting his shoulder against the jamb, arm barring my way as if he's worried I'll bolt out before the coast is clear.

"Thank you for helping me," I say.

He glances at me and then does a double take. I stiffen when he reaches for me, but it's only to slip the blanket off my shoulders. "They'd ask questions," he says with an apologetic shrug. "Else I'd let you keep it."

I don't know what comes over me. Maybe it's the alcohol that's still flowing through my veins or surviving Cass's attack with my virginity intact.

More likely it's the simple fact that Reuben's always been kind to me. Taking into account how his friends treat me, I'm starting to think it's something I shouldn't take for granted.

I step forward, go onto my tippy toes, and immediately realize my mistake when I pucker my lips a good two inches from his jaw.

I forgot how tall he was. Other than kissing the side of his neck, there's no other way to express my gratitude.

My cheeks catch fire. I sink back to my heels, dropping my gaze as I pray for the earth to swallow me.

A hand slips around my waist. Before I have a chance to protest, Reuben presses me to the wall beside the door.

I lift my legs and wrap them around his waist, if only so I won't hit the floor if he decides to let me go.

But he doesn't drop me.

He pins me to the wall with his body and uses his hands to smooth my curls out of my eyes.

"I wish you weren't part of this. You're too innocent to be mixed up in this shit. But then I wouldn't have met you," he murmurs.

My heart twists as he comes close enough for me to feel his breath on my lips. "And I can't imagine not having met you."

His lips crush mine.

I have time for a gasp, but then I'm swept under. His commanding lips fight mine, urging me to open and let him in, but I'm so terrified that I'm doing this wrong, that I taste gross, that he'll stop...

He makes a sound deep in his throat. Somehow, my body takes it as a signal. Resistance flees. My lips part to let him in and it's like stepping into the middle of a raging river. In an instant, I'm swept under.

Electricity courses over my lips as our kiss slows.

Seconds—*centuries*—later he pulls away, grabs my ass in both hands, and slowly lowers me to the floor.

I swoon like some corseted lady from the eighteenth century about to succumb to a fainting spell, and lean against the wall before my legs can buckle.

"You two done? Because we gotta go." Apollo's standing about a yard away, a deep frown creasing his brow.

Did he see everything?

I press the back of my hands against my hot cheeks. "Sorry," I murmur, yanking the hem of my dress down my legs and dropping my head as I hurry out of the door.

Behind me, Reuben lets out a throaty chuckle that does sinful things to my insides.

I breathe a sigh of relief when Apollo and I arrive on my floor and I see the hall is empty. The last thing I need is another run-in with Cass.

"Thank you for walking with me," I say.

"You gonna kiss me too?" Apollo asks dryly.

I stop to frown at him, but he just keeps walking. Is he jealous because I was nice to the only person who's treated me like a human being?

I push back my shoulders and hurry after him, catching his shirt sleeve. "You make it sound like I go around kissing boys at random."

"You don't?"

"Reuben's been super nice—"

"Super *nice?*" He glances at me, his face expressionless. "I can be super nice too, you know."

I stop walking again, my mouth working as I try to find words. "Jealous much?" I call out after him.

He spins around, eyes darting this way and that before narrowing and settling on me. "Would you keep it down?" he says, shaking his head. "We're trying t' be circumspect."

I lick my lips. "Sorry."

"Yeah, fuck, me too." He waves at my closed door and then frowns hard at me as he walks past me again, heading back the way he came. "Dinner's in an hour." Disapproving eyes scan me. "I'd suggest you wear something less conspicuous."

At the sound of the dinner bell, I swallow down a surprised yelp. I'm in the restroom washing my face after changing into jeans and a sweater. Not because of what Apollo had said, but because every time that dress moved against my skin I would either think about Cass or Reuben. And that would either make my skin crawl, or give me goosebumps. And not always in a logical order.

I must have had a meltdown of epic proportions if I can't keep straight what's supposed to feel good, and what definitely should feel bad.

I emerge from the restroom and immediately hang back as students stream into the hall from their rooms.

When the bulk of them have disappeared down the stairs, I merge with the remaining few headed for the dining hall, doing my best to ignore how they keep looking back at me like I'm some creature everyone thought went extinct with the dodo.

Extinction's starting to look really good.

For the first time since I arrived at Saint Amos, there's a queue to get into the dining hall. I crane to see past the boys instead of falling in line.

My mistake.

"Follow me."

I flinch at Apollo's voice. He's headed in the opposite direction of the dining room. With a casual glance back in my direction, he beckons me to follow with a cock of his head.

My choice is to follow him or to go stand in a long line while everyone stares at me.

Apollo leads me outside the building and then around the back. We end up at the back door of the laundry. He takes out a set of keys and unlocks the door, ushering me inside with a hand on the small of my back.

Then he unlocks a metal door set in the side of the room beside one of the massive steel basins and leads me into the small courtyard I was in earlier today.

Seems like a century ago.

He closes the door behind us. "See, I can be nice too," he says right by my ear.

A cluster of candles illuminates the concrete table and the two silver domes on top of it. A jug and two glasses stand to one side of the serving dishes, beads of water condensing on the side.

"Couldn't risk bringing any wine," he continues, snagging my wrist as he walks past, tugging me after him. Then he slips something out from behind his belt. "But I got something to keep us warm."

He flashes me a silver flask, takes a sip, and then hands it over.

I wave it away. "You did this for me?"

"The candles give it away?" he says through a playful smirk.

I smile, but then immediately school my expression into disinterest. I bet he expects a kiss for going to all this effort.

Well...it's kind of romantic, what with the candles and everything. I push away the thought, ignoring the heat creeping onto my cheeks.

I really *am* a blasphemous little slut.

"Well? What d'ya think?"

"It's lovely, thank you."

There's a mischievous sparkle in his eyes. Is he planning something, or is it just the candlelight?

Apollo offers me the canteen again. This time I don't say no.

Despite having invited me out here for what I assume is some kind of date, Apollo doesn't say another word until our plates are empty. Dinner is accompanied by crickets chirping in the dark corners of the courtyard while cutlery scrapes against crockery.

Apollo grins at me as he collects our empty dishes, and tosses his hair from his eyes with a flick of his head. "I'll be right back," he says before disappearing into the kitchen.

I tip the flask against my lips, clearing my throat after the fiery liquid scorches its way into my stomach as I consider my next move. I could use this time alone with Apollo to my advantage. He must know how Zachary and Reuben ended up in the basement. Can I persuade him to tell me?

Apollo comes back with two bowls and sets one down beside me. I snag his jeans before he can move away. He wears them baggy, but thankfully they're not falling halfway down his ass like some of the boys I've seen in the mall.

"Why don't you come sit here?" I pat the stone stool closest to me. He hesitates, and then sets his bowl next to mine before taking his seat.

He studies me with a small frown.

I have zero experience in seduction, but I guess there's a first time for everything. I dig my spoon into my chocolate mousse and raise it to his lips.

He just keeps staring at me.

My cheeks grow warmer the longer he leaves me hanging. By the time he moves, I feel like I'm melting. But thankfully he eventually ducks forward and cleans my spoon.

"Rube's not a nice guy," he says as he leans back and brushes his hair from his face.

"I didn't say anything about—"

"People assume a lot." He points at me. "People like you." He points at the bowl of mousse and opens his mouth for another serving.

I resist the urge to jam the spoon down his throat. "I'm sorry I'm so transparent. And you're right. I *do* think Reuben is a good guy."

He chuckles at me. "That's because he's been practicing being nice for years now."

"Well he's definitely got the hang of it," I say, another heaped spoon accompanying the statement. My heart thumps a little harder. "How did he end up there anyway? Was he kidnapped too?"

"He didn't exactly wander in off the street, now did he?"

I frown, but I don't get a chance to speak.

"Listen, pretty thing. There's something you have to understand about us. We're not just a 'bunch of friends.'" His air quotes are rife with condescension. "Something happened to us in that basement." He quickly lifts a hand, as if expecting me to interrupt him. "Over and above a bunch of pedophiles repeatedly sticking their dicks in us."

My skin grows cold at his callous words.

"They broke us, Trin." His voice becomes thick and rough. "Broke us into a million fucking pieces. But we picked ourselves —each *other*—up."

His sorrow cuts the nerves to my hand and my spoon tinkles when it hits the side of the bowl. Apollo takes the spoon without missing a beat.

"I reckon we got some of those pieces mixed up when we picked them up." He scoops out a spoonful of mousse. I half-expect him to eat it, but instead he brings it to my lips.

We stay like that for a beat, him staring into my eyes as I get sucked right back into his.

Eyes as deep, dark, and dismal as the bottom of a well.

I eat the mousse. He keeps talking.

"So when we put the pieces together, we got a bit of each other too." He frowns hard as the mousse starts to melt in my mouth. "Does that make sense?"

I nod, because it does.

It makes so much fucking sense it scares me.

It explains why they're so close. The horrors they experienced, they *shared*, wove them together like a rug. Those strands, strong in their own right, became even stronger.

He scoops out more mousse and brings it close, but not close enough.

I lean in a little.

"We're not friends. We're brothers. A brother*hood*. And the only way you're weaseling your way in is if we let you." Apollo smears mousse over my mouth with a flick of his hand.

His eyes drop to my lips.

I reach up instinctively to wipe it away but he snatches my

wrist and draws it into his lap. Then he ducks forward and sucks the mousse from my lips.

Heat floods my body.

I try to lean into what I think is a kiss, but he drops his mouth to my chin, then the side of my jaw, then my ear.

"There's something else you should know, pretty thing."

I freeze at the sinister tone in his voice. He moves my hand deeper into his lap, until I brush against something long and hard.

He nips my ear. "We'll never be jealous of each other, because we *always* share our toys."

# 13

# TRINITY

I'm staring up at the ceiling later that night, toying with my curls as I try to make sense of the day, when Jasper slips into our room.

I've spent a lot of time over the past few weeks awake while everyone else was sleeping with thoughts swirling around my head like water going down a drain.

It never gets any less frustrating, especially when I know sleep could whisk me away to peaceful oblivion for a few hours.

"Hey," I greet him, going onto my elbows.

Jasper walks stiffly over to his bed, kneels on the mattress, and lowers himself down with his back to me.

"Everything okay?" I ask. Pretending not to know what happened to him is as difficult as straight-up lying.

"Fucking peaches," he mutters back.

I wince in sympathy, and then I'm glad it's dark and he's not facing me because I'd probably have given myself away.

My ointment is still in my top drawer. Should I leave it out and hope he notices it, or did Miriam give him his own bottle?

*Twenty lashes.*

*Should have been thirty.*

*No one can survive thirty.*

Fuck.

"I know you got lashes," Jasper says.

I sit up straight. "What—why would you think that?"

"For the drawing," he says without turning to face me.

My heart is suddenly beating too fast. "What drawing?"

Jasper maneuvers around until he's facing me. If it wasn't for the moonlight streaming through our tiny window, I wouldn't have seen him rolling his eyes at me.

"The one of Rutherford banging you."

I say nothing as my cheeks start to warm up.

I'd forgotten about Cass's prank. "Yeah. So what?"

"He likes it, you know."

"What, the drawing?"

"Beating people," Jasper says through a world-weary sigh. "He gets off on it."

He…*what?* I've heard some strange things before, but that? It doesn't make any sense. And Zachary might be cold and calculating, but…a sadist?

"I don't think he—"

"He loves beating people as much as he hates gays." The whites of Jasper's eyes shine in the moon's silver glow. "If you don't believe me, try telling him you're a lesbian. You won't be sitting for a week."

Jasper turns around again.

Even if I could speak, what the fuck am I supposed to say to that?

I need air.

I'm already in my pajamas—yoga pants and a tank top—so I grab my threadbare dressing gown from the foot of the bed where it keeps my feet warm in this ice-box of a room, shove my feet into the fur-lined boots I use as slippers, and shuffle out of the door.

For a while after dinner there was quite a lot of traffic in the hallway. Boys coming and going, laughing and roughhousing. But now all the doors are closed, and the passage is quiet.

Cass came by about half an hour after I'd gotten into bed. It was the first time I'd heard him call 'lights out' since I've arrived. I'd almost peed myself at the thought that he would slip into my room, but I guess he wouldn't risk it in case Jasper was there.

I use the restroom before heading back to my room.

I feel sorry for Jasper. It sucks that he and Perry ended up in a place like this, where their relationship is considered a cardinal sin. I wish I could tell him Zachary doesn't feel that way.

Maybe Jasper and Perry can be open about who they are when they leave Saint Amos. I've never had an issue with other people's sexuality. If you love someone, *truly* love someone, then things like gender shouldn't matter.

That's the one thing I'd admired about my parents. You could tell they were wholly devoted to each other. They weren't passionate lovers or anything like that—I've only heard them making love once, and it only lasted a few minutes. But they spent every moment they could together. I guess my mother's miscarriages brought them closer together. They happened way before I was born, but I'm sure they played havoc on the marriage. Luckily they tried one last time before she had a hysterectomy, else I wouldn't be here.

To hear them tell it, God was the one who saw them through those dark times.

I think it was love. A love so strong, it could survive anything. I guess I shouldn't be surprised that they chose each other—and God—over me the night of the accident. I was never included in that love triangle, because I was never as devoted to their faith as they were.

Not for lack of trying. But no matter what I did, it never felt right.

Father Gabriel would often try to rope me into conversations about God when he came to visit. He was subtle about it, and I give him credit for that. But even he could never convince me.

I still went to church, of course. I still prayed when everyone else did.

Gabriel's coming back tomorrow.

The thought makes my pulse beat a little faster.

What do I do if I find out everything the Brotherhood's been telling me is bullshit? Would Gabriel still take me under his wing after I doubted him? Or would he act like he did all those times I came right out and told him I didn't believe?

I can't handle seeing that disappointment in his eyes again.

Not now. Not after everything.

I walk past my room door without pausing.

I don't know if I can risk hurting my only friend. I need to make up my mind about Zachary and his brothers *before* Gabriel gets back.

There's only one way I can think to do that.

I push back my shoulders, take a deep breath, and start down the stairs.

# 14

## ZACH

I lost control today.

It's the girl.

Trinity has a talent for tearing down the walls I've meticulously built up around my dark heart. When she's around, I can't forget how fucked up I am.

Because of her, I lost control. Now the darkness doesn't soothe me like it should, nor does the joint I just smoked envelop me in its usual mind-numbing fog.

I feel sick, but not in a physical way. Times like this, it's as if the disease in my mind is actual cancer, slowly spreading through my neurons.

Infecting. Weakening. Killing.

What will happen when my sanity is gone? When there's nothing left to hold onto? When I can't slow down the clock?

The things I did today were supposed to give me more time. But instead of resetting that fateful countdown clock chiming out the minutes till my next breakdown, everything I did today sped it up.

Hurting Cassius.

Our fistfight.

Punishing Jasper.

That last one I'm particularly pissed about. It should have been Miriam, that steward of righteous repentance, doling out his punishment. But I thought it would tame the demon clawing its way up from hell through my body, so I did it instead.

I struck him over and over again, punishing him for something I don't consider a crime.

There's a faint noise from outside.

Have one of my brothers returned to our nest? They know better than to disturb me when I've gone dark.

Something could have happened. Something important.

Or maybe they're in as much need of solitude as I am right now. Rube comes here for the quiet sometimes. Just sits on the couch and stares at nothing as he rubs his thumb over his rosary.

Not his anymore.

But does that change anything?

I have to get up and confront whatever—whoever—it is, but I don't trust myself yet.

Maybe I never will.

Orange light from one of the lamps on the other side of the partition spills through.

Something's wrong.

My brothers know the dark soothes me. They might dare to come close, but they wouldn't risk provoking me.

I rally myself, calling back the tendrils of my mind from the far-away places they drift to when I don't keep them contained. It takes effort, and time.

By then, I can hear soft noises as the invader starts hunting. Tins rattle. Clothes rustle.

I push into a sit and hang my head between my knees for a moment. The cool air slides against my bare back as I breathe deep and try to center myself before standing.

I head for the edge of the curtain, the padded floor masking my footsteps, and zone in on the sound of a tin rattling. Sliding a finger behind the curtain, I part it far enough to see a sliver of the room beyond.

My chest tightens painfully.

I'm suddenly too aware of the slow *thump-thump-thump* of my heart.

She shouldn't be here.

I shouldn't go out there.

She's a blast of warm air to the glowing coals of my mind, and everything around us is mere tinder.

But I guess I like the flames, because I slip out of the dark anyway.

I've *always* liked the flames.

# 15
## TRINITY

There's nothing here. I thought they'd have hidden things between their clothes and porno mags and booze and cigarettes.

But there's nothing. Nothing!

Everything here has a purpose. Not a single object is decorative or sentimental.

It's fucking creepy.

I guess it was stupid of me to think they'd leave anything incriminating lying around.

I'm just about to leave when I spot the corner of a book sticking out under a heap of clothes.

My bible.

I pull it out, running my palm over the cover as I trace the embossed letters with my fingers.

I'm about to open it and take out the photo of my father I'm hoping is still inside when the hair on the back of my neck stands up.

"Find anything interesting?" Zachary asks, his voice inches from my ear.

I spin around with a strangled gasp, clutching the thick bible to my chest like a shield. But it falls from nerveless fingers when I see his face.

He catches it absently before it can hit the floor, and sets it down on the shelf behind me.

Dead eyes the color of pond algae regard me for long moments before he leans forward and rests his palms on the shelf. First one hand, then the other, boxing me in.

It's strange seeing him bare-chested in a pair of jeans. It feels wrong. A *sinful* kind of wrong. But when I try to look away, my gaze darts to the tattoo on his pec before I can force myself to look up at him. The combination of that sinister tattoo and his dead eyes is chilling.

"I was—"

"Lost?" he rasps as he narrows his eyes. "Browsing? *Spy*ing? Tell me if I'm getting warmer."

I'm trembling inside. His proximity, his intensity…it's too much. I can barely breathe. But instead of bowing my head and begging him for forgiveness, I shove my nose into the air and glare up at him.

"I'm taking you on your word about all of this," I say. I lift up a finger. "You couldn't give me a shred of proof. But I'm willing to give you guys a chance, anyway."

"Liar." He lets out a long sigh that shifts strands of hair against my face. He ducks down, leaning in until his nose is almost brushing mine. "If you believed us, you'd be snug in your little bed right now, not wandering around sticking your nose where it doesn't belong."

I have to cleave my tongue from the roof of my mouth before I can speak. "Fuck you! I *do* belong here."

We frown at each other.

"I mean, I have every right to be here. I have every right to ask questions. You can't expect blind faith from me."

He throws back his head and laughs. When he looks at me again, my body goes cold. That crazy laugh didn't add a single degree of warmth to his dead eyes.

"Do you honestly think we live in a world where you have rights?" He arches against me, pressing me into the ridge of the shelf. I wince, but quickly smooth my face.

Don't show a flicker of what you're feeling, Trinity. Cass says they can read me like a book? Well it's time I closed the goddamn cover.

"Of course I have—"

"Wrong," he cuts in, grabbing my jaw. "This is the real world. And in the real world, you're not special, Trinity." His eyes grow hooded. "None of us are."

I grab his wrist. He's too strong for me to pull him away but at least this way I can feel his pulse.

It should be racing, like mine.

But it's dead calm.

Fear worms deep into me and starts squirming around in my intestines like a fat snake.

I didn't expect anyone to be here. I could have sworn they'd said it was risky staying out here. That they all went back to the dorms at night. But I guess he couldn't go back reeking of weed and booze like he does. Or with that purplish bruise on his jaw. He's in no state to be seen outside of these walls.

And I'm not safe down here with him.

"I should leave," I say.

"You should never have come." He ducks lower, his glare pinning me like a butterfly to a corkboard. "Tell me, little girl, why *did* you come?"

He'd see right through me if I lied. And honestly, how much worse could I make this?

"Because I don't trust you. Any of you." I swallow hard and

muster up every bit of courage I have left. "But you can change that. Tell me. Tell me everything."

His lips quirk into a dark smile. "Everything?" he murmurs.

He tucks a curl behind my ear before trailing his fingers down my jaw. It shouldn't, but that touch sends a thrill down my spine.

It could be fear masquerading as something else, but I have a feeling it's not. I'm trapped in the lion's den and instead of looking for a way out, I'm poking the fucking lion.

I *know* Father Gabriel isn't capable of hurting anyone. But that doesn't matter to the Brotherhood, does it? I've been drawn into their war, despite my protests.

I don't have a choice but to fight but I'm going to make sure I'm on the right side of the battle line first.

"You couldn't handle hearing what happened to us in one day, never mind the *years* we spent down there," Zachary says.

"We? It's always *we*." I poke him right between the dripping fangs of his snake tattoo. "I want to know about *you*. I want to know what kind of person *you* are. How else can I trust you?"

He laughs. "You want to know what kind of person I am, Trinity?"

The only warning I have is the darkness shadowing his eyes as he scans my body.

Zachary grabs me, spins me, shoves me.

*Hard.*

I tumble over the arm of the couch, barely stopping myself from bouncing onto the floor. Expecting him to pounce on me —perhaps even try what Cass tried—I scramble into a sit. But he just stands there watching me, his chest heaving like he went three rounds with the world champion.

"I used to think I was a good person, back when I was a kid." His hands curl into fists and then open again as he steps closer.

"Thought I'd become something great. Astronaut, doctor. The usual shit kids fantasize about."

In my fantasies, I was a ballerina. But my parents made it clear that the only career they approved of was me becoming someone's wife and, eventually, someone's mother.

It didn't faze me that much. I was probably too short to be a ballerina anyway.

Zachary moves to the front of the couch. And I stay right where I am, because for the first time since I've been pressing him for information about his past, I'm actually getting what I want.

So instead of bolting, I pull my legs into my chest, hugging myself as he stands in front of me.

Does he like towering over people? My neck's already aching from craning up to look at him.

"So what happened? What changed?"

There'd been a faint smile on his mouth. It fades as his hands slowly unfurl again.

"You really want to know?"

I nod.

He inhales deep and lets out everything as a long sigh through his nose. "There's something I want, too."

His smile returns.

I wish it hadn't.

It makes my stomach coil.

"But you're not going to like it."

# 16

## ZACH

No one's ever shown such interest in my past. My brothers already know everything, and we're not exactly the type to sit around a campfire trading anecdotes. Not any that touch on the basement, anyway.

So what is her ulterior motive? Why is she still here?

"Deal?" It says a lot that I'd give her a chance to back out.

She nods.

It's possible Trinity doesn't fully comprehend what she's agreed to. Not because she's dumb—far from it—but because she's literally that naive.

"Get up."

She stands, her eyes not staying on mine longer than a second before flickering away.

She *should* be nervous.

I move behind the couch and pat the headrest. She visibly steels herself, lifting her chin and pushing out her chest before following.

When she's close enough, I grab her hips and shove her into the back of the couch. My cock stiffens at her surprised gasp. It's still a long way from being hard, but just the thought of what I'm about to do to her sweet, innocent little ass has my body readying itself.

"Hold on."

She hesitates and then spreads her arms, digging her fingers into the headrest's cushion.

"Like thi—?"

I grab her dressing gown and yank it off her shoulders, letting it pool by her feet. When I grab the waistband of her yoga pants she tries to move away, but a shove to the small of her back keeps her in place.

"Do they have to come off?" she asks in a tight voice.

"Obviously." I yank down her pants, baring her panties. My fingers itch to delve inside her underwear, to touch her…but that's not what we agreed.

I could have left her pants around her knees, but instead I draw them down all the way to her feet. I slip off her boots and slide her pants off, tossing them over the back of the couch.

When I touch the elastic of her panties, she stiffens. "Please," she murmurs. "Leave them on."

I should have ripped them off, but I fight back the urge. That thin film of fabric is inconsequential. If I want to admire my handiwork, I can do that when we're done.

"Spread your legs."

When she doesn't obey, I kick them open for her. I run a hand over the curve of her ass and then up her plump cheek, massaging the flesh beneath.

She shifts again. "What are you doing?"

I'm not about to educate this girl on the intricacies of spanking. "Is that your first question?"

She shivers under my hand as she gives her head a violent shake.

My cock stiffens even more.

I take off my belt, willing myself to move slowly so I can warm up her cool flesh and bring enough blood to the surface.

It's surprisingly difficult not to rush this part. The anticipation of hurting her is making me salivate.

I fold my belt in half and then again. I move close to her, my now straining cock brushing the curve of her ass as I reach around and press open her jaw with my fingers.

"Bite."

"Don't I get to ask my question first?"

I slap her ass with the flat of my hand.

She lets out an indignant yelp and glares at me over her shoulder. I hold up my hand, showing her my reddened palm, and her scowl fades a little. She opens her mouth and accepts the belt when I shove it between her pink lips.

"Face forward."

Usually, I wouldn't be bothered if she was making eye contact or not but I can't pretend she's a meek sub if she keeps glaring at me like that.

"This, then your question."

When she doesn't say anything, I smack her ass again.

"I need a yes, little girl."

Her shoulders stiffen, but she doesn't protest the name-calling. Maybe she's finally starting to accept just what a fucked up deal she's struck with me.

Soon, she'll be begging me to stop, and this will all be over. Questions unanswered, I'll send her back to her dorm, a newfound fear embedded inside her.

Deep, *deep* inside her.

# 17

# TRINITY

What the fuck have I gotten myself into? Trading slaps for intel? You'd swear I'd been dropped on my head as a kid. From the third floor.

My ass is already throbbing from the two smacks Zachary delivered. Fuck knows how I'm supposed to survive more.

But that's not what's bothering me the most about this. If I didn't know any better, I'd swear this was turning me on.

Which is ridiculous, of course. What the hell is sexy about having a belt shoved in my mouth? Or the way I'm drooling around the leather? Or the fact that I'm standing here in my underwear, waiting for him to start spanking me?

But if this is what it takes to get the answers I need—

My teeth sink into Zachary's belt as a hard slap thumps onto my ass cheek. I'm so surprised, I don't even cry out.

Whipping my head around, I stare at him with shocked eyes. I reach to take the belt out of my mouth so I can tell him he's hitting me too hard, but I don't get very far.

I catch one glimpse of the dark lust in his hooded eyes before he grabs the back of my neck and pushes me down again.

The next time his hand connects with my ass, I scream.

When I start squirming, he tightens the grip on my neck.

*Slap. Slap. Slap!*

I yell out wordlessly and grab his wrist, trying to pull his hand off my neck so I can straighten.

He steps back, and I stagger to my feet.

I snatch my yoga pants from the back of the couch. He doesn't stop me. My breath hitches as I try to ignore the stings on my backside.

"Fuck!"

"All right there, little girl?"

I grimace at him. "That was five," I tell him breathlessly. Well, technically it was seven, but I have a feeling the first two didn't count.

"So ask your question."

I lick my lips. "How did you end up in the basement?"

A massive erection bulges behind his jeans.

How can anyone enjoy hurting someone else? Even though I said yes, this is just…it's fucked up.

I guess Jasper was right. Zachary *is* a sadist.

He cocks his head a little. "Too vague."

I frown at him as I slide a cool hand behind my underwear. My skin feels hot to the touch, and stings when I touch it. How much will it hurt putting my pants back on? For now, I keep them bundled against my stomach.

"Who took you there, to the basement? How did they catch you?"

"That's two questions."

I grind my teeth. "Who took you to the basement?"

A fond look crosses his face. "My parents."

"W-what?"

"Is that your next question?"

"N-No. But…you have to explain. I mean…your *parents*?"

He surges forward, grabs my hips, and flips me over. I claw at his arms as he tries to pin me but somehow, he gets a hold of my wrists and holds them against the small of my back.

When he kicks open my legs again, my stomach bottoms out.

"No, wait!"

"So many questions, little girl," he says, his voice barely altered from the strain of keeping me in place. "Looks like we're going to be here all night."

There's no belt in my mouth when he slaps me. My teeth clamp down on instinct, and I bite the inside of my bottom lip. A trickle of blood seeps into my mouth.

I let out a Hollywood-style scream that's part rage, part agony.

"Jesus fucking Christ," he mutters, shoving away from me.

I hurriedly spin around, ready to fend him off if he tries to pin me again.

"Get the fuck out of here," he growls as he bends to pick up his belt from the floor. He loops it through his jeans and buckles it up before pointing at the exit, one eyebrow quirking up in a silent command.

My mouth works for a second before I find words. "No, but—"

"You obviously don't have the stomach for this shit," he says, stepping so close that his erection brushes my belly. "Get. The. Fuck. Out."

I keep my ground, but barely. Every molecule in my body wants me to flee, but my mind keeps spiraling in on those two words. I won't be able to sleep until I know more.

His parents.

His *parents?*

I swallow hard and force up my chin. "We had a deal."

He huffs mirthlessly through his nose. "There's a fine line between bravery and stupidity."

"I'm not being brave or stupid," I snap back. Without taking my eyes off of him, and while trying to ignore the fact that my hands are shaking, I grab the front of his belt and start unbuckling it.

He drops his eyes, watching my fingers work. Then he studies me through dark, thick lashes. "The fuck are you doing?"

"We had a deal."

"Not with a belt. You're nowhere near ready for that kind of punishment."

For some unfathomable reason, my insides pulse at the way he says that word.

*Punishment.*

I wasn't sure before, but I am now. This thing he's doing to me? This is turning me on. I don't get it—I don't even think it's *possible*—but nothing else can explain the way I'm tingling down there. When I move, I can feel how wet I'm becoming.

"It's so I won't scream," I say quietly after another hard swallow. "Unless you want to use my underwear again?"

His eyebrows draw together. "Tempting, but no."

Before I can move away, he grabs my bottom lip and tugs it down. "Something to bite down on works better."

I nod as if I already knew this and pull his belt free from its loops. I fold it like he did, and hold it an inch from my lips. "Ready when you are."

He lifts his head as he closes the distance between us, his dick now pressing hard into my soft flesh. I try to ignore it, but it just stokes the fire already building in my core.

His hands slide around my back and down to my ass. I wince when he starts massaging my skin. Then my eyes fall closed.

The soothing pressure eases the sting and sends delicious ripples through my body.

When his breath warms my face, I look up at him. He's watching me.

Hungry.

Angry.

But sad.

*So* sad.

And I need to know why.

I wedge his belt between my teeth and slowly turn around in his arms.

His hands trail down my curves. He hooks a finger behind the elastic of my underwear and tugs it down to the crease where my ass meets my legs. Then he steps back, leaving cool air to circulate over my exposed skin.

I brace myself against the back of the couch and bite down on the belt.

*Slap.*

Air hisses past my teeth as I suck in a pained breath. The sting that follows his slap is immediate and brutal.

*Slap. Slap. Slap. Slap.*

Tears prick at my tightly-closed eyelids, and I scrunch up my face with the effort of not yelling out or letting those tears fall.

Fingers brush my jaw. I reluctantly open my mouth and let Zachary take the belt from between my teeth.

"Your question."

I try to focus on anything but the pain, but it seems impossible to ignore. "Hold on," I murmur, my breathing picking up pace.

"Now, little girl." He caresses my ass, sending fiery licks of pain over my skin. I hiss and try to move away, but there's nowhere to go with me sandwiched between his body and the back of the couch. "Now."

"Your parents," I say through my teeth as my fingers dig into the couch. "Why would they send you to the basement?"

It's the first thing I can think of. The first logical thought of the thousands floating aimlessly through a mind that's coming undone from this exquisite pain.

Zachary's hand pauses. He squeezes me, and I go onto my tippy toes as I gasp at the pain.

I don't understand this. I've had ten lashes, but they were nothing like this. They hurt more, but this...this is a different kind of pain. It has all these layers to it I don't understand. I feel like crying, but not because it hurts, but because...

Because *Zachary* is hurting, and I can feel it.

I can *feel* his pain.

"Good question." Zachary starts massaging my ass again. "And I don't know if I have the right answer for you."

"What? That's not—" I cut off when his fingers stop an inch away from my entrance. Until now he'd been keeping well away from the hot, tingling mess between my legs.

"I'm not sure if it's the right answer, because I can't look inside their heads," he says.

He squeezes me, and I barely hold back a moan of pain.

"I'm not asking you to psychoanalyze them," I say, having to force the words through the pain.

He makes a soft noise in the back of his throat that could have been a stifled chuckle. "Aren't you?"

"You would have asked them. They would have given you some kind of answer. What did they say, when they took you down there? What reason did they give?"

He lets out a laugh that turns my insides into a frozen mush. "It was my punishment," he says. "See, I was a very naughty boy." He shifts behind me and his jeans brush my skin. The rough fabric sends a flurry of hot tingles through me moments before his hard dick presses into my crack, forcing my cheeks apart.

My breath catches.

If he wasn't still wearing his jeans, he'd be inches away from—

*Taking what doesn't belong to him.*

Which he could have done if he'd wanted. Is he holding himself back, or just toying with me?

"What did you do?"

Another laugh. Thankfully, this one isn't as chilling as the one before. "Sure you can handle another question?" He strokes my bare skin with his fingertips. They trace eight lines down my ass, and then converge less than an inch from my sex.

My face heats when he slowly pulls me open. My lips part reluctantly, soaked through from the twisted desire that's been coursing through me the entire time he's had me pinned against this couch.

"I said, are you sure you can handle another question, little girl?"

"Yes," I blurt out, immediately squeezing closed my eyes. "I mean…if you don't hit me as hard. Maybe." Fuck, my heart feels ready to explode from my chest.

He chuckles quietly as he folds over me. "It's sweet that you think I'm capable of mercy." He grabs my wrist, bringing the folded belt up to my mouth. "Open."

And, against all reason, that's exactly what I do.

# 18
## ZACH

I'm barely touching the ground and every breath I take is helium. If Trinity looked around and saw my face, she'd be screaming as she ran out of here.

Which is why I slide my hand over the back of her neck and hold her in place. That way, she can't see the sick lust on my face.

I slip a finger behind the hem of her panties where they're gathered just under the curve of her ass. This time she doesn't plead with me to keep them on. I tug them down to her knees, baring her smooth, shapely legs. I take a few seconds to admire the blurry red handprints on her ass before I start warming up her flesh again.

She shifts as if considering bringing her legs together so I tighten the grip on her neck as I kick them open even wider. This stretches her panties tight between her knees, and that's when I notice the near translucent patch in the fabric.

My cock hardens painfully behind my jeans.

I could unzip my fly and be inside her in seconds, burying myself balls deep inside her tight little pussy.

Except that wasn't the fucking deal.

My fingers dip lower, almost touching her. Her body stiffens, but she keeps still. Keeps her legs open.

I bite the inside of my lip as I give her body one last scan. Then I bring my palm down on her ass with all my strength.

The sound of her shocked yell reverberates deep inside me.

I'm in agony—suspended in ice, drowning in fire. Without conscious thought, I zip down my fly and take out my cock. I stroke myself, keeping my hand on the back of her neck as I inch my dick closer to her wet pussy.

She must feel the warmth coming off my body, because she stiffens again, as if expecting another blow.

*Christ.*

Her heat coats the crown of my dick as I ram my fist down its length. The pain makes me harder. Makes me want to fuck her even more. To spread her open and drench myself in her juices.

She makes a sound behind my belt. It sounds like a plea.

It takes long seconds for me to realize she's shaking. That she's no longer pressing back against my hand, resisting me. She's limp, draping the back of the couch like she doesn't have the strength to hold herself up anymore.

And then I hear her sniffs. The stifled sob.

I shove my cock back into my jeans and move to the side. Her eyes are squeezed shut, her cheeks bright red.

"The fuck is it now?" I ask roughly, ripping my belt out of her mouth. "Finally decided you've had enough?"

As soon as the belt is out, she moves away from me, her hands shaking as she yanks up her underwear. She lets out a string of mangled words.

"Sorry—don't—happening—shouldn't—stop."

I watch her as she tries to put on her yoga pants. When they're halfway up her legs she turns away from me, surreptitiously wiping at the inside of her thigh as another sob wrangles its way out of her mouth.

"Hey." I grab her elbow, but she twists her arm out of my grip. I frown, and this time I grab her waist and drag her up against me. "What's going on?"

"I'm sorry," she says, her lips trembling. "I don't know why that happened."

I stick my hand between her legs, wiping at the slick wetness on her thighs. "This?" I ask roughly. "Are you embarrassed about this?"

She covers her face with her hands, shrinking in on herself like a wilting flower. I make an angry noise in the back of my throat. "You asked for this," I tell her as I yank her yoga pants up the rest of the way. "Don't play coy now."

She rips her hands away and struggles in my arms, but I refuse to let her go. "It was supposed to hurt," she says. "It wasn't supposed to…why did it…*what the fuck's wrong with me?*"

The last is a yell. She glares up at me before her face crumples and her mouth starts quivering again. "What's wrong with me?" she whispers.

"Nothing, my girl." I wipe away her tears with my thumbs as I cradle her face in my hands. "Absolutely nothing."

I stare into amber eyes that demand more from me. But what the fuck am I supposed to say?

She wanted answers, I wanted release. We made a deal. How the fuck were we supposed to know it would turn out like this?

But now, staring into her eyes, I guess I had it wrong all along.

This wasn't about her. It wasn't about me. It was about *us*. All of us. The Brotherhood. The Ghosts. The Guardians.

It was about the basement.

She can't believe what happened to us.

No one can be that cruel.

That perverted.

That sick.

It can't be true.

But it is.

Trinity Malone couldn't accept the truth so she tried catching me in a lie.

A slow, hard ache starts up in my ankles before spreading to my wrists.

I trace the bottom of her lip with my thumb. "I disobeyed them," I tell her quietly.

She blinks, trapping a tear in her lashes. "What?"

"You wanted to know why my parents were punishing me."

Her eyes widen ever so slightly.

"I went somewhere I wasn't supposed to. Saw something I shouldn't have."

My chest closes up. I take a deep breath, but it barely fills my lungs.

She doesn't say anything. Doesn't push me for more. Perhaps she thinks I'll tell her to leave if she does.

Those bright, amber eyes just watch. Not perversely curious, like the policemen who'd taken our statements after we'd finally escaped. Not pitiful, like so many of the parents in the foster homes we'd ended up in.

Just watching.

Waiting.

I manage another breath, this one even shallower than the last. My erection has faded completely, and my skin prickles hot and cold. I move my hands to her shoulders, and she tenses under my hands when I grip her tight.

Her lips move like she's biting the inside of her cheek.

I want to kiss her, which is weirder than fucked up because I *never* want to kiss anyone.

"The basement was in my house."

Her lips move, but no sound comes out.

"My parents were the Keepers." I try to swallow, but I can't. I try to keep quiet, but it's as if she's pulling the words from me. "Gabriel paid them to look after the boys. The Ghosts would arrange times with them. They kept it all a secret, but I started noticing things when I got older. Tracks in the driveway. Strange smells."

Trinity scans my face and presses her hands against my bare chest as if she wants to feel my heart beating.

She won't, though.

"I stole their keys one day. Said I was going to a sleepover. They drove me to my friend's house, but I came back, and I waited until it was dark. Until they were asleep.

"They found me down there in the basement. A silent alarm had gone off. I should have run away, but I couldn't just leave them there." My voice trails away, thickening. I doubt she hears me when I add, "I couldn't leave my brothers there."

Her fingertips dimple my flesh. Still searching for that elusive heartbeat?

No, Trinity. There's nothing for you to feel.

My black heart stopped beating a long, long time ago.

# 19

# TRINITY

I'm already awake when the bell for Sunday service rings, but I lie there for a few seconds before getting up. Tomorrow it will be a week since I arrived in Saint Amos. After almost eighteen years living a life where nothing ever happened, these last few weeks are ridiculous in comparison.

I like to think that I'd have preferred to live a boring life, but then I wouldn't have met the Brotherhood. They're the most interesting people I've ever met but they're also the most fucked up people I've ever met.

I stifle a yawn.

Guess I'll have to take the good with the bad.

Jasper pushes into a sit and presses the heels of his palms into his eye sockets.

When he gets up, I stare up at him in astonishment. "You're going to mass?"

"Why wouldn't I? You're going. Rutherford's going. *Everyone's* going."

*Because your ass probably hurts worse than mine and those pews are fuck hard?*

I frown at him as he grabs his clothes and exits the room. I'm starting to think he's becoming a little obsessed with Zachary. I get being pissed off with him, but this?

Screw it.

My mind's way too fucked up to figure out what Jasper's up to.

I grab one of the two dresses I used to wear to church on Sundays and head to the restroom to wash my face.

Jasper's sitting on the edge of his bed lacing up his shoes when I get back. Guess he didn't bother showering again. I can't blame him—I wouldn't want the other kids seeing my bruised butt either.

I took a quick peek at my ass in the restroom mirror after making sure there wasn't anyone else in one of the stalls. Surprisingly, it isn't as bruised as it feels. Was it because Zachary kept massaging it while—?

Oh no, Trinity. *Hell* no. Your thoughts will remain pure as freshly fallen snow today.

"Want to walk together?" Jasper asks.

"Uh…sure," I manage while battling my shock. Dear Lord, I don't think I can take any more surprises today. I already feel like I'm walking a razor's edge.

Jasper stands, wincing faintly, and then sticks out his hand.

"What?"

He glares at me.

I cringe back when he darts forward and tries to grab my hand. "What are you doing?"

"I'm not going to rape you," he says, rolling his eyes. "Just… give me your fucking hand."

As soon as I give it to him, he hauls me up from the bed.

Halfway down the hall I eventually find my voice. "What's up, Jasper?" I try for casual, but I have no idea if he falls for it.

"Shut up and look like you're in love with me or something."

I barely suppress a snort. Everyone in Saint Amos is on the fucking spectrum. Must be the stuffy air in this place.

Jasper's palm sweats against mine, and he keeps shifting his grip as if he's not sure if he's holding my hand right. We draw more than a few eyes on our way down to the church, and no wonder. He's wearing a thousand-yard-glare that could incinerate anyone who happened to cross his view, and I'm alternating between trying to make myself invisible and keep an eye on Jasper to make sure he's not about to jump out a window—with me in tow.

By the time we get to the chapel, there's a small group of boys tagging along behind us.

You'd think it couldn't get more awkward than this, but then Perry enters the picture.

Jasper stops short. I glance at him and immediately turn to see what he's looking at with a face that suddenly turned to stone.

Not what. *Who.*

Perry's standing under one of the trees dotting the lawn between Saint Amos and the chapel. He *was* heading our way, but as I watch he slows down. A second later he stops, watching us with owlish eyes as Jasper heads for the chapel again.

"Aren't you going to—?"

"Don't be an idiot," he mutters, tugging me after him. I give Perry a timid wave, but he either doesn't see me or decides not to draw any more attention to himself because he doesn't wave back.

I couldn't be happier when we step inside the chapel's cool shadows. I aim for the pew closest to the door but Jasper tightens his grip and hauls me down the aisle like this is our own shotgun wedding.

I guess morning prayers aren't compulsory for staff but Sunday mass is because today the pews are crammed full.

I spot all four members of the Brotherhood as Jasper hauls me down the aisle. Apollo is on the other side of the church in the second row, nestled between a bunch of men I assume all work in the kitchen. Cass and Rube are sitting with the students.

Judging from the way they're staring at me, the fact that my roommate is holding my hand doesn't sit well.

I should probably mention to Jasper that holding my hand isn't going to make anyone believe he's suddenly into girls. What it will do is get him into a ton of shit for dragging me around like he just bought me at a slave auction.

We sit in the second row behind the teachers with Zachary less than a yard to the left. It feels like he's the only one in the entire church who hasn't been watching me since I walked in.

Somehow, that makes me more nervous than if he'd been staring like his brothers.

The bruise on his jaw is barely noticeable now. I'm sure if it was still visible, he wouldn't have dared to show his face this morning.

I wince when my ass hits the pew. Although Zachary's spanking didn't bruise my skin as much as I'd thought it would, it still hurts like hell. Especially on these hard seats.

Jasper must be in agony.

I glance aside at him and then hurriedly look straight ahead. He's glaring so hard at Zachary I'm surprised my Psych teacher's hair hasn't caught on fire.

Although it seems Zachary isn't paying him any mind, I know for a fact he's aware of us.

*Both* of us.

Thanks, Jasper. All I wanted this morning was to remain invisible.

I was exhausted when I got back to my room last night. My ass hurt, my head hurt...my *heart* hurt.

Yes, I'd been digging for answers, but I hadn't expected to unearth a rotting corpse.

A few more kids rush in and hurriedly find seats. A reverential hush fills the chapel's vaulted ceilings. Timing his entrance perfectly, Father Gabriel walks in a mere second after the first bored whisper reaches me from the students seated behind us.

My lungs turn to concrete.

Gabriel looks just like he always does, but now that familiar smile gracing his wide mouth seems fake as margarine. His eyes aren't keen and inquisitive anymore—they're cunning and shifty.

It's like that optical illusion. Once you see the rabbit, you can't see the duck anymore.

As soon as he catches sight of me, Gabriel's gaze strips me bare.

*It's just your imagination.*

There's no reason for him to suspect anything is different about Trinity Malone, daughter of Keith and Monica—devoted parishioners of the Redford Missions of Love church.

I'm starting to sweat.

Gabriel's eyes release me when he takes in the rest of the crowd, and I sag in my seat.

"Good morning, children."

There's still no proof to Brotherhood's claims, but logic doesn't reign in my mind anymore.

*Is it because you want them to fuck you? Is that why you don't need proof anymore, you blasphemous little slut?*

My mouth turns sour.

Father Gabriel starts on a sermon that sounds like so many others I've heard over the years. I find myself studying the side of Zachary's face until I catch Gabriel looking at me.

Adrenaline spikes through me, leaving me tingling and panicked as it recedes. For the rest of the sermon, I keep my eyes locked on Gabriel, but he never once looks in my direction again.

His sermon feels like it lasts for hours. Hours I spend debating my position in this invisible battle raging between the Brotherhood and Father Gabriel.

Finally, we end in the Father's Prayer and begin communion. In Redford, only a handful of people would go up—those that wanted to partake.

I guess they do things differently here. Here, everyone partakes. And as more and more people file out of their pews, I get the feeling it's compulsory.

Gabriel and Zachary make just the right amount of eye contact. Their exchange seems as normal as the one before and after. Gabriel glances up from his paten of bread and locks eyes with me.

He says nothing as he holds out the body of Christ. I lean forward, open my mouth, and let him place the bread on my tongue.

"It's good to see you again, my child."

I stay silent, too scared my voice will shake if I return the greeting.

It could be the play of light on his face, but I swear he frowns at me before smoothing his expression.

The sip of wine he gives me from the chalice tastes like ash.

"You coming?" Jasper asks when I don't take his hand.

"Not yet."

He scowls at me, sends a withering look Zachary's way, and stalks out of the chapel like Satan is nipping at his heels.

I stay in my seat, watching Gabriel through my lashes.

Instead of immediately exiting the stage like he does after morning prayers, he weaves through the loitering students and staff clasping a hand here, patting a shoulder here, murmuring, "Child this, child that."

When it becomes obvious he's ignoring me, I stand up and make my way to the aisle. I'm dimly aware of Zachary from my peripheral view. He's still seated, head bowed over a standard-issue bible as if he's contemplating the word of God before heading off to breakfast.

Gabriel is talking with Sister Miriam when I come up behind him. Miriam sees me and frowns, but I stand my ground. Gabriel turns with a small frown between his thick, dark eyebrows. When he spots me, his face lights up.

Then he turns back to Miriam. "If you'll excuse us, Sister."

Miriam nods, but from the way she adjusts her habit as she leaves, it's clear what she thinks about me interrupting their conversation.

"Are you well?" Gabriel asks, reaching for me.

I sidestep his hand before I can catch myself, and instantly regret it when his smile fades and his frown returns deeper than before.

"Is something wrong, child?"

"Of course not, no," I blurt out. I can't seem to stop wringing my hands. "But, if you're not busy, I'd like to, I mean, could we talk?"

"Certainly." He reaches for my elbow as if to steer me somewhere private, but I step back again.

"Dinner. Um…could we have dinner again?"

His frown deepens. "Are you sure everything is okay?"

I'm itching to get away from his x-ray eyes. I've never been able to lie to him, and I don't think that will ever change. "Tonight?"

"I'm afraid I already have plans with—" He waves away

whatever he'd been going to say. A broad smile replaces his frown, and I hate the fact that it makes me feel warm inside.

"I would love nothing more."

"Thank you, Father."

He watches me with that same enigmatic smile as I strut away on stiff legs.

I don't dare look up until sunlight hits my face. The relief I was expecting doesn't arrive. I could be looking over the side of a cliff.

Why does it feel like I've just set a date with the Devil?

## 20

## ZACH

F abric whisks. Cass slips into the lair, his eyebrows twitching
when he sees me on my chair, smoking a cigarette. I guess
he expected me to be sulking in the dark, fighting my demons.

"Didn't get enough of me yesterday?" he asks, face pinched
tight as he walks past and sticks his head into the bedroom.
Making sure we're alone? "And here I thought we were trying to
be circumspect."

"We set up this place for a reason. No one would think to
look—"

"Might as well install a fucking revolving door at this rate."
He comes back in my direction and snatches the cigarette from
my lips before I can take another drag.

Ash scatters onto his jeans as he collapses on the couch,
draping himself over the cushions like he's desperate to show me
just how few fucks he gives.

I click my fingers, demanding he returns my cigarette. He
whips his head around to study me as he drags hard at it, and
then hands it back.

Just before I take it, he pulls away his hand. "This about the girl?"

I retract my hand, lean back in my seat, and shake loose a fresh cigarette for myself. "You got to make things right."

He turns around to face me and lies back with his head propped up on the arm. "The fuck I do." He hikes up his leg and then crosses an ankle over his knee so he can toy with the hem of his skinny jeans with the same hand holding the cigarette.

I stopped buying them new clothes months ago. But it doesn't matter what Cass puts on, it always looks good. Even old shit like those jeans.

Who knew…maybe when this shit was over, he'd grow out his hair and get a few headshots. He'd easily make it as a model, and preening in front of a camera would be the perfect fodder for his ravenous narcissism.

As long as they never asked him to take off his shirt, of course.

"You scared the shit out of her," I state, deadpan as I tug at my cigarette.

Puffs of smoke spout from Cass's mouth as he laughs. "Thought that was the plan."

I slam my fist into the arm of my chair. "You fucking idiot."

Cass flinches, but recovers in a flash. He considers me for a second before leaning over to flick his cigarette into the cup on the floor by the arm of his couch. "*I'm* the idiot?"

"Who do you think she trusts more? A bunch of strangers on the far side of borderline, or the family friend who's been in her life since she was in diapers?"

Cass's face hardens at this. He despises it when I bring up the fact that the four of us are more than a little broken. He opens his mouth, but I cut him off without waiting to hear what he comes up with this time.

"We're not trying to get her to leave anymore, or have you forgotten? We need her on our side."

"We don't need her," he says. "We don't need any—"

"You're right. We don't."

Cass glares at me suspiciously.

"We don't need her," I repeat as I lean forward and rest my elbows on my knees. "We could go back to the original plan." I flick my wrist and purse my lips. "Wait for this place to clear out. Hope we can grab Gabriel before he gets the fuck out, and then hope we can break him." I spread my hands. "Sure a lot of wishful thinking in that plan, but it's the best we could come up with, remember?"

Spots of anger spring up on Cass's pale face. "She's going to fuck this up."

"She will." I nod.

He shakes his head, laughing through another exhale. "Unless I grovel for her forgiveness, right?"

His bitter words send a rush of heat through me, but I don't call him out for them. It's how I know I'm getting through to him. The harder he fights, the closer he is to giving in.

Like a cornered rat.

It's how he copes. Unlike the three of us, Cass never could switch off his mind. He's too intelligent for that. It would be like trying to dam the Amazon river with a handful of matchsticks.

So he fought.

Tooth and fucking nail.

He fought so hard that his Ghosts would be injured trying to get to him. And that made us happy. We started cheering him on —silently, of course. Even back then we knew we had to keep our Brotherhood a secret. Even as kids we understood that secret would keep us safe.

So Cass fought. Sometimes he'd win, sometimes they'd

overpower him. It went on for weeks, until one of them stuck a syringe filled with heroin into his arm.

"She *will* fuck this up," I say again. "But only if she's not a hundred percent on our side."

"That'll take more than a half-assed apology to—"

"Which is why you're going to make it count."

Cass's scowl pins me. "She won't let me near her, you know that."

"I also know how persuasive you can be."

I'd meant it as a compliment, but for some reason it just makes more angry spots flare up on his cheeks.

We sit for a few seconds smoking our cigarettes, silent, brooding, waiting each other out.

"What's so fucking special about her anyway?" he asks.

Did I hear that right?

I get up and crouch beside him to kill my cigarette in the cup by his couch. When I look up, his iridescent blue eyes glue me to the spot.

I wasn't just blowing hot air up his ass. When he wants something—really, *really* wants something—it's as if the Universe aligns to give it to him.

Even if it's just an answer to a question I'd rather not give.

"I never said she was."

"You didn't have to."

"You're delusional." I start to stand, but Cass grabs my arm, and not gently either. His fingernails bite into my flesh as he tugs me closer.

"What happens when you have to choose between her or us?"

A hard frown creases my brow. "That's never going to happen."

Cass's expression clears. He releases me. "Yeah, let's hope it doesn't," he says as he gets to his feet. I stand too, and he pushes past me to get to the door. "Because it looks like you've already made your choice."

"Cass."

He slips out the curtain.

"Cass!"

I could have gone after him, but then I'd seem desperate. Falling onto the couch, I sit stroking a thumb over the marks his fingernails left in my arm as I let the latent warmth from his body soak into mine.

He's full of shit, but that's nothing new. Of the three of us, his walls are the tallest and the strongest. No one's ever broken through them. He doesn't let his guard down for anyone, not even his brothers. But that wasn't a requirement for joining this war. Every war needs soldiers, and those soldiers need ammunition.

Rage.

Hate.

Vengeance.

In this case, we each had to bring our own. But me and Rube and Apollo? We're weak, flickering candles compared to Cass.

He's the motherfucking sun.

# 21

# TRINITY

After breakfast, I spend a few hours at the tiny desk in our room catching up on my homework. Jasper is there for a while, reading a book, and then he disappears without a word. I decide to close the bedroom door behind him, just in case someone—*Cass*—decides to pop in for an unannounced visit.

I wish more and more every day that I had a damn key.

A few minutes before the lunch bell gongs, I hear a soft sound by the door. I whip my head around to stare at the folded paper someone pushed under the door.

The hair on the back of my neck stands up as I wait, but thankfully the door stays closed.

When my heartbeat goes back to normal, I stand and fetch the note.

SHOWER?

The words all are in capitals, stiff and boxy.

*Reuben.*

He's letting me use his bathroom again. Which is so sweet, especially with tonight's dinner in mind. I guess now would be the perfect time to go—everyone else would be in the dining hall, eating. If I hurried, I might still make lunch once I was done, but I'd happily trade a meal for a private shower.

Plus, I'd get to see Reuben again.

The prospect does strange things to my tummy and I have to push away the thought so I can figure out what I'll be wearing to dinner tonight.

I knock quietly on Reuben's door. Why does no one except Father Gabriel answer their doors in this place? After a third knock I try the handle, eager to get out of the hall before someone spots me.

The handle turns.

The door opens.

I let out a relieved sigh when it opens and quickly slip inside. The apartment isn't massive, but the minimalistic decor makes it seem pretty spacious. How do students get apartments like these? What does Cass's room look like? Zachary's? Apollo's?

"Hello?"

No answer.

I head for the bathroom and then hesitate. Is it weird that Reuben's not here? Maybe he's sleeping. Or studying with headphones on.

"Hello?" I push open his bedroom door and step inside, biting the inside of my lip. I should be in the shower already but damn it I'm too fucking nosy. I know so little about Reuben that I can't bear to pass up a chance to poke around.

After all, it's obvious the Brotherhood doesn't keep *anything* in their lair.

I go through Reuben's closet and find nothing but clothes. Only some books and a lamp on his desk. Notepads inside the drawers, all filled with school work. Something starts nagging at me, but I'm too busy snooping to give it any thought. He could be back at any minute. For all I know, he just stepped outside to make a call or smoke a cigarette.

My eyes move around the room until they settle on the bible on Reuben's nightstand. When it falls open in my hands a hard shiver courses through me.

Phrases in every sentence of every verse on every page have been highlighted.

I flip through, going faster and faster until I can't make out anything but an orange blur, but still the odd phrase leaps out at me.

*Subject to your masters*
*Sells his daughter*
*Lay with him*
*Great plague*
*Fiery lake*
*Seek death*
*Know that I am God*

There's a noise from the living area.

I snap the bible closed and hurriedly put it back on the nightstand, trying to adjust it the way I had found it. Then I grab my clothes, and dart out of Reuben's room, fully expecting him to be standing there.

But thank the Lord, he's not.

I release a noisy sigh, press a hand to my hammering heart, and let myself into the bathroom. After stripping down and folding my dirty clothes in a neat pile, I set Reuben's blood-red rosary on top of everything. I'm not sure how many times wood can get wet before it starts warping or something but I'd rather not risk damaging it. Plus, I'm sure the water will eventually wash away its glorious smell.

The hot water feels *sinfully* good. I start lathering my hair, eyes squeezed shut so I don't get shampoo in them. I'm just about to start rinsing when a hand slithers over my shoulders.

*Reuben.*

I bite the inside of my lip, half-mortified, half-jumping out of my skin with excitement.

I start to turn around, but then his hands sink into my hair and begin rinsing out the shampoo. It hurts when his fingers tangle in my wet hair, but my body still sparks to life—skin tingling, lips quivering, core tightening.

"Mmm, that's nice," I murmur, leaning into his touch.

Once my hair is rinsed, his hands slide down the back of my neck, returning to my shoulders. Strong thumbs sink deep into my flesh, applying pressure right on the precipice between pleasure and pain.

I groan at how magnificent it feels. At how *right* this moment is. It's as if wild electricity sparks between us. If I hadn't been drenched, I'm sure my arm hairs would be standing on end.

"Thank you for letting me use your shower. I really needed…" My words trail away as his hands move lower. He uses the flat of his hands to gently push me forward. On instinct, I put out my hands, bracing myself against the wall.

His knuckles dig into the flesh alongside my spine as he starts working his way down my wet skin.

One hand stays at the small of my back, working the muscles above my hips, the other slides down my ass.

Over the bruises Zachary gave me.

My breath catches at the faint thrum of pain he brings to the surface as he strokes my skin. Did Zachary tell Reuben about our deal last night? Apollo says they tell each other everything.

He squeezes my ass cheek.

I can't help but groan at the deep-seated pleasure that pain forces into my core.

He lets out a strange sound, as if he's holding back a groan of his own.

There's a muted splash as he moves closer. Now both hands are on my ass. My heart stutters as his fingertips sink lower and lower.

"Wait."

He stops.

"I'm not...I don't think I'm ready for...for that." My cheeks heat up at the admission. He must think I'm some kind of cock tease, letting him touch me and then pushing him away when—

His fingers wreath deep into my hair and he uses that grip to tilt my head back. Water streams over my face, some going up my nose. I splutter, starting to struggle, and then his mouth closes over mine.

Suddenly, the fact that I could drown doesn't matter anymore. Eyes closed, heart thumping, I melt against him.

He tastes like toothpaste and something sweet—soda?—and his lips massage mine so expertly that I barely notice when he draws me against him again.

Until I feel his hard-on, of course. I gasp into his mouth, my eyes flickering open. Water pours into them, forcing them shut again.

This is ridiculous. He's going to drown me.

"Let's get out," I whisper through his kisses, blubbering like a fish half the time.

In response, he reaches past me and turns down the faucet. Not all the way—water still patters over my face—but it's more a gentle drizzle than a cloud break now.

His mouth is on mine before I can blink the water out of my eyes.

Lips so warm.

Slippery.

*Demanding.*

Holy hell, how can anything feel this good?

I lose myself to him. My lips open on cue when his tongue slides over them, allowing him deeper inside. He moans against my lips, and my core tightens painfully at that urgent sound.

His hands coast down the front of my body. He squeezes my breasts, and rolls my nipples between his thumbs and index fingers hard enough to make me flinch.

Then he slides his fingers down my tummy. His kiss slows, and with it, his movements.

He presses harder against me, until I start aching deep, deep inside. His hands converge above my pubic bone, resting there for an eternity as he draws every ounce of resistance from me with a hard, languid kiss.

My arms had been dangling at my side. When I reach up to touch him, he grabs one of my wrists and instead urges my hand behind my back, between us, close to his cock.

Then the other hand.

I claw into his thighs. Does he want me to touch him? How do I—?

He grabs my wrist again, slides his hand over the back of mine, and meshes our fingers together. Then he drags my hand up his thigh, over his trunks, and up his stomach.

The fingers of his other hand are still just above my aching center. But when he urges my hand down his stomach and behind his underwear, those fingers sink down too.

I touch his cock the same moment he touches my clit.

I convulse, shuddering uncontrollably as a whiplash of heat and electricity surges through me. I break away from his kiss, my head digging into his shoulder as I arch away from his body.

But he refuses to let me go. He starts massaging my clit— hard and achingly slow—as he curls my fingers around his cock.

He rains kisses against the shell of my ear, using his teeth to toy with my earlobe as he starts pumping his cock with my hand, his fingers wrapped tight around mine.

"Fuck," I whisper, arching again as his fingers press even harder against my clit.

What the hell am I doing? I barely know this guy, and here we are, probably seconds away from fucking? I didn't think my first time would be in a shower. But, God, this feels so fucking right.

He moves my hand up and down his smooth, hard cock, speeding up as his fingers start strumming my clit faster than before.

My mouth falls open, but then I choke on a spray of water. He abandons my clit just long enough to turn off the water, and then dives back between my legs. But this time his hand sinks down lower than before. His fingertips sink between my lips, and he strokes all four fingers over my entrance.

I shudder hard, a broken gasp spilling out of my open mouth.

He groans, low and deep, and then I don't feel his underwear brushing against my hand anywhere.

Shit.

This is happening.

Fuck!

I'm terrified, but ecstatic at the same time. If just this feels so fucking good, I can't imagine—

His lips touch mine, demanding another kiss. I turn my head, and he devours my lips and tongue as if he owned them the second he saw me.

My eyes flicker on the cusp of opening as he applies a hard pressure on my clit and starts rubbing his palm against that nub of nerves.

"Fuck." I moan hard against his mouth, and move his cock down with my hand. I'm still jerking him off, but now his crown can't be more than a few inches from my entrance. I'm too short though. I have no idea how this would even work if I wanted—

"We'd need a stool for that, peaches," he says.

My heart plummets into my stomach when my eyes fly open and I see Cass's face an inch from mine.

I open my mouth for a scream, but he's too fast. In a second, he's flipped me around and pinned me to the tiled wall, one hand over my mouth the other on my throat.

My teeth can't reach him because he keeps his hand cupped. My nails don't seem to leave any marks on his wet, naked skin.

It was a trap.

*That* was what was bugging me earlier. I'd flipped through page after page of Reuben's handwriting, but I'd been too idiotic to connect the dots.

"Would you calm the fuck down?" Cass says, tilting his head and frowning as if I'm working on his last nerve.

So it's easier for him to rape me? I belt out an enraged—if muffled—scream and try to knee him in the groin. He twists away like all of this is second nature. Then he's up against me with the wall of his body, pressing me to the wet tiles.

"What, suddenly my dick isn't good enough for you anymore?" he growls. "And here I thought I'd do something nice for you."

Astonishment turns my bones to jelly.

He studies me for a second, and then slowly peels his fingers from my mouth. "Jesus, I'd have been fucked off with you if you'd gotten me in the nuts," he mutters.

"Nice?" I say, my voice violin-string tight. "*Nice?*"

He slaps his hand over my mouth again. "Keep. It. Down," he growls through his teeth.

I almost try and knee him again, but I have a feeling that would be the worst way to handle this fucked up situation.

He removes his hand again and steps back. I twist my legs

and slap an arm over my breasts in a lame attempt at modesty as I start shaking. Not that it actually matters. His hands were all over me. *Almost* inside me. And I—I was—I'd had his…

His eyes slide down my wet skin. "You cold?"

"Sure. Let's go with that." I circle him warily as I move to the frosted glass doors.

I can't believe I let him touch me. I can't believe I almost let him *fuck* me.

I step onto the mat outside and reach blindly for a towel. Cass shifts as if he wants to get out too, but I lift my chin and widen my eyes at him.

"Don't you dare," I whisper furiously. "Don't you *fucking* dare."

He rakes his fingernails over his buzz cut, eyes narrowing. Then he brings up his hand and licks each of his fingertips, popping them out of his mouth one at a time. "Hate me all you want, your cunt is crushing *hard* on me."

"Get out."

He shrugs and slowly gets out of the shower. Unbidden, my eyes dart over his body as my mouth sets in a furious, trembling line.

Mother*fucker.*

Then I see the burn marks scattered over his muscles. I thought I'd felt something when my fingertips had skimmed his abs but I'd been too lost in his kiss.

Cass grabs the other towel and slings it around his waist. "So you wanna fuck in the bedroom or on the couch?" he asks as a wicked grin slides onto his mouth.

"Get out!" I stab a finger at the door.

He chuckles as he leaves the bathroom, but the sound cuts off as soon as I kick the door closed behind him with a strangled yell.

I should be shocked. Terrified even. But I'm just *fucking* angry.

How dare he?

How fucking *dare* he?

The worst part is, my body hasn't caught up yet. I'm still aching inside, and the more I move about trying to get my wits about me, the worse it gets. I feel like I'm going to implode.

*Fuck.*

I glare up at the ceiling, bite down on my lip, squeeze closed my eyes, and shove a hand between my legs.

But I wrench it away before I touch myself, shame worming through every inch of me.

I deserve this frustration for being such an idiot. Priests remain celibate all the time. Nothing to it.

I dry off and dress, and as I'm about to leave the bathroom, I hear Reuben's apartment door opening.

Thank God. At least I don't have to face him. My hand is on the door handle when I hear voices.

"What are you doing here?" Reuben asks.

I freeze, straining to hear through the door.

"Lady Malone needed a shower. I'm her escort."

"Your hair is wet."

"And?"

"Why is your hair wet?"

"I had a shower too."

My chest clenches so tight, I can barely breathe.

"Alone?"

"That would be wasting water," Cass says through a laugh. "It was her idea."

I bolt out of the bathroom. "He's lying!"

Reuben turns his frown onto me. He's wearing jeans and a tight-fitting sweater. Standing next to each other like that, it's ridiculous to think I'd confused Cass for Reuben. They're close in height, but Reuben's almost twice his size.

*Oh, you knew, you blasphemous little slut.*

The immoral, sinful, hedonistic part of me I always suppress figured it out right away, but the bitch kept silent until it was too late. Until I was so caught up in—

"So you didn't shower together?" Reuben asks, glancing back at Cass.

"No. I mean, we did, but—"

Reuben drops his gaze. "You should leave. I'm busy with an assignment."

"It wasn't my idea. He tricked me!"

But he walks into his room without a backward glance. Somehow, it's worse that he closes the door quietly and doesn't slam it. Disappointment always hurts so much more than anger.

"Shall we go?" he asks, quirking an eyebrow at me. He's wearing a smug smile, arms crossed over his chest as he leans back on one foot. The epitome of someone having a rip-roaring good time.

"Asshole!" I throw him the finger, glaring at him as I storm over to the door and let myself out.

Everyone around here is crazy.

As I walk back to my room, my dirty clothes bundled against my chest, Alice in Wonderland plays on repeat through my head.

We're all mad here.

We're all mad here.

We're *all* mad here.

"Come."

My heart flutters uneasily at Gabriel's command. I tug at the waist of my dress before letting myself inside. The dark, long-sleeved dress—a creation that would have better suited Wednesday from the Adams family—sits tighter than I like it. I even considered opening some of the buttons that run down the front, but I was afraid I'd end up looking like an eighteenth-century prostitute. Mom bought the dress for me about two years ago and I guess I've filled out since then.

The smell of cigarettes and wood smoke wash over me as I open the second door leading into Gabriel's living area.

He's wearing a button-up shirt tonight, sleeves rolled up to mid-arm, and a pair of dark slacks.

"Good evening," he says, turning from the fire to greet me.

I smile and lift my hand to wave.

He comes over, spreads his arms, and draws me into a hug. When I don't hug him back, he hurriedly steps back and releases me.

"Is everything okay?"

Wet concrete pours into my stomach. "Yeah, of course," I manage, although my voice is anything but steady. "I'm just a little tired. I haven't been sleeping well."

"When would you like to eat? Sister Miriam mentioned that you weren't at lunch today, so I'm guessing—"

*Is he keeping tabs on me?*

He cuts off as if I'd asked the question out loud.

I guess if anyone's going to notice I'm missing, it'll be Miriam. And I'm much easier to spot than one of the hundreds of boys in this place.

*You're jumping at shadows, Trinity.*

"I'm okay." I force myself to move closer, pretending to warm myself by the fire. I'm already starting to sweat, but if I keep my distance, he might become suspicious. I can't have him wondering if I have an ulterior motive for being here tonight.

Someone slipped another note under my door a little less than an hour ago. It wasn't Cass's handwriting, thank God. I assume it was Zachary's.

*Keep him busy until eight.*

*You'll have 15 min alone.*

*Good luck.*

It's half-past seven. I should have asked for supper if only to pass the time, but I can't eat when I'm this nervous.

The drive is hidden behind the elastic of my underwear. The dress's fabric is too thick for it to stand out, but to me it feels like a massive, ticking bomb you'd have to be blind to miss.

"How was your…trip?" I hazard. It's as good a question as any right? I have no idea where Gabriel's been the past few days, so—

*Checking in on the children he has holed up in a basement somewhere of course—children like Zachary and Reuben and Apollo and Cass. Maybe the Keepers in his newest hidey-hole fucked up and he had to go sort some shit out. Or maybe he brought some new Ghosts through for a tour of the premises.*

*These are the bunk beds our little sex slaves sleep in. Here are their chains. This is where we feed them, but only if they've been good little boys.*

Jesus *fuck*, Trinity. What the hell is wrong with you? You're here to prove Gabriel is innocent, or did you forget?

Still, I hear myself blurting out, "Where *did* you go?"

Gabriel lets out a soft laugh. "Nowhere interesting. I had a last-minute meeting with the construction company fixing up this old place." A rueful smile touches his mouth. "I truly hope their estimate is accurate. I can't have them gutting the school's finances."

Repair estimates and finances? Pointless. I have to get him talking about something personal. So I ask him the first thing that pops into my head.

"Were my parents good people?" I ask.

He frowns at me, and then slowly sinks into his chair. His eyes never leave me as he nips at the tip of a cigarette from his box and draws it out with his teeth to light it.

"Sit, child."

I obey without thinking. Thankfully there's already a chair near my ass else I'd have ended up on the floor because I obey without thinking.

"Would you like a drink?"

I nod. Gabriel sits forward in his armchair, twists to the side, and pours out two glasses of wine. One is little more than a splash in the glass, the other is close to the brim.

The sissy inside me wants to refuse his offer, but I push aside Trinity the Wimp just as she starts yelling about how wrong this is.

"Why didn't you attend Father Quinn's counseling session?" Gabriel asks.

I had just brought the glass to my lips, but I snatch it away again. "He told you?"

Father Quinn replaced Gabriel when he'd left Redmond. I'd never liked him—he stank of Fisherman's Friend sweets because he somehow thought it would cover up his halitosis.

I don't remember much about the week after my parents were killed. I *do* remember hearing words like "shock" and "therapy" bandied around everywhere I went.

I'd also forgotten that he'd offered counseling. More than once.

"I couldn't talk to him," I say truthfully.

"Can you talk to me?"

I look up. He's watching me with a most familiar look in his warm, brown eyes.

Patience.

Sympathy.

And with the wholehearted belief that whatever sins I had committed, we could overcome them together.

How the hell can a man like this possibly be involved with Ghosts and Keepers?

I almost want to tell him everything, just so we can have a good laugh about it and the world can go back to normal.

But I know my life will never be the same again, so does it matter what degree of fucked up I land on?

*We're all mad here.*

No, we're all fucked up crazy here.

"Trinity?"

My eyes snap back into focus. I take a tiny sip of wine, and then another because I barely tasted the first. It's not as brutally sour as the one the Brotherhood poured for me.

"I don't know how much you can help," I say hesitantly before taking another sip. "You weren't there at the end."

Gabriel looks down, and shadows darken his eyes. For a

heart-wrenching moment, I think I've already blown my cover and pissed him off. I fully expect him to toss me out of his room. Instead, he lights himself another cigarette.

"You don't smoke, do you?" he asks.

"No."

"You're right to sound disgusted," he says through a faint laugh. "It's a disgusting habit." A thick plume of smoke jettisons from his lips. He sips from his glass, and then sits back in his seat, his eyes on the fire.

"I often wonder if they would still be alive if I'd stayed at Redmond," Gabriel says.

The wine glass clicks against my teeth as I turn to face him. I hurriedly lower it into my lap. "Why would you say that?"

"The same reason you wonder if you'd be dead had you been in the car with them." He drags hard at his cigarette, his voice tight as he speaks without expelling any more smoke. "One of Satan's many games, keeping us fixated on the past." Finally, he empties his lungs and then takes another sip of wine. "So easy for him to slip in without you noticing when you're so busy replaying events over and over to see if there ever would have been a different outcome. Like a spider crawling in under the door."

The longer he speaks, the tighter my chests grows. I've never heard him talk like this. His sermons are dry—all repetition and loosely connected anecdotes taken out of context—but this?

If this is how his conversations went with my parents, then no wonder they'd stay downstairs for hours after I'd been sent to bed. Our house had thick doors. Even with my ear pressed to the wood, all I heard was the murmur of low voices.

"Your parents are dead, Trinity. That's not something you can change or control. What you *can* control is how you feel about it."

"I'm angry," I say, without waiting for him to ask.

"At them, or yourself?"

I squirm in my seat. "Both." Then I shake my head. "No. Just myself."

"Because you didn't go with them to church?"

I nod.

"And why is that? Why *did* you stay at home that night?"

I run my finger around the rim of my glass. It's practically empty, but there wasn't much of it to begin with. I don't dare ask for more. I need Gabriel to see me as the same girl I was when he left Redmond—sweet and innocent and naive. Definitely not the undercover spy I turned into.

"We had a fight. They left without me."

"What did you fight about?"

My cheeks warm-up, and I know it's not from the heat of the fire, or the sip of wine.

"Something stupid. Something really, *really* stupid."

Silence settles between us. The fire pops, shooting a spark onto the hearth. It pulses like a dying heart before it fades to nothing.

There's a distant rumble. Is it starting to rain?

"No one alive is a good person, Trinity."

My eyes snap to him.

He smiles faintly, but without looking at me. "You asked if your parents were good people."

Suddenly I don't want to know the answer. Instead, I absently sip at my wine before remembering it's empty.

Gabriel holds out his hand. I give him the glass. This time, he fills it. But when he passes it over, he doesn't let it go straight away.

We lock eyes over that forbidden wine, and I can see his hesitation from the way he frowns at me.

"It's probably better if I don't—" I begin, releasing the glass.

"They shouldn't have treated you like that," Gabriel says. His warm brown eyes are cold now, a muscle in his jaw ticking.

My heart claws its way up my throat.

Oh my God.

He knows.

He fucking *knows*.

I only realize I've gulped down a mouthful of wine when it scorches the back of my throat. I blurt out a hoarse, "How did—?"

But Gabriel doesn't let me finish. "The way they confined you?" He glances away as he shakes his head. "Keeping you from the world like you were a sin?"

What the hell is he talking about?

His gaze touches me again, hot and livid, before jumping back to the fire. "I never wanted that for you, child. I told them time and time again that you had every right to lead your own life, but they refused to listen."

"My...parents?"

"An immune system must be exposed to bacteria and viruses for it to build a resistance against them." He waves a hand in my direction but without taking his eyes from the flames. "They left you defenseless."

Why is he so upset? Did bringing up my parents hit a nerve? I know he was close to them, but—

"If no one's good, does that mean everyone's bad?" I ask.

He turns to me, blinking as he focuses on my face. "We are all born into sin. Only through confession and penance can we cleanse our souls."

"I haven't confessed in a long time."

"Not since your thirteenth birthday."

I swallow hard, and wish I could look away. Mom made me do it. She made me climb into that cubicle and confess my sins to Father Gabriel.

"Don't let such silly things plague you," he murmurs, a ghost of a smile coming back to his mouth. "There are worse things in the world."

Worse than having to admit you'd been discovered touching yourself? Worse than feeling such overwhelming shame at your changing body that you swore never ever to even *look* down there again? And you've kept that promise ever since.

So worse, maybe, but not for me. Not back then.

Except, quite possibly, this moment. Because all that shame just came crashing back like a fucking tsunami.

"I should go," I mumble, wine sloshing up the side of the glass as I push to my feet. "You're busy, and—"

He's on his feet next. He grasps my wrist, and gently takes away my wine. "I'll never be too busy for you, Trinity. Please. Sit."

But my body feels like it's constructed from rusted metal.

He urges me down, but instead of taking his seat again, he goes to stand in front of the fire. His body blocks the heat, and for that I'm grateful. But it also blocks the warm light. I feel lost in his shadow.

"There's something you should know, child," Gabriel murmurs. "Something I've been meaning to tell you since you got here. I probably should have told you a long time ago."

Gabriel turns to face me. With his face in shadow, I can't make out anything in his eyes. But his voice is low and deep when he speaks again, filled with…what? Regret? Shame?

"It's about your father. I—"

A cell phone rings. I yelp at the unexpected sound, and

Gabriel lets out a soft chuckle that sounds forced. "Sorry, dear. Let me just take this."

The fuck? No!

I whip my head around to stare at him as he walks away, already putting his cell phone to his ear.

My eyes latch onto the big wall clock hanging beside his window.

Eight o'clock.

*Right* on time.

## 23

## ZACH

"I'm starting to think you don't like me anymore." The mischievous gleam in Cass's eyes belies the questioning tone in his voice.

"What tipped you off?" I pull the rope tight and give it a yank for good measure.

Cass gags theatrically before slipping the noose off his head. "I'd say forcing me to fake my own suicide, but we both know it goes back further than that."

We laugh. It's sad that we both sound genuinely unfazed.

I sent Reuben and Apollo to watch Gabriel's hallway. They'll message me as soon as he leaves his room. Then they'll keep an eye on both stairwells to make sure Trinity isn't surprised halfway through her scavenger hunt.

"Ready?"

"To die? Yeah, I guess. I mean, I'd hoped for another few years or so, but fuck it." Cass sends a toothy grin my way and climbs up on the chair. "Tell Mom I love her and Dad that he's a cunt."

We chose to stage this shit show in his English class. He hates

Sister Sharon anyway, and I don't agree with her disciplinary methods, so it's a win for both of us. It's been difficult doing all of this with nothing more than the glow of a cell phone screen to work with, but we didn't want anyone to happen to look out a window and see a fluorescent lamp shining in a classroom that should only have souls in it tomorrow morning.

"May I state again, for the record, that there were easier, less lethal ways to create a diversion?"

"Cass—"

"I mean, we could have pulled the fire alarm—"

"Dorm doesn't have one," I cut in.

"Or flooded the bathroom—"

"Then I'd have to phone Miriam, not the provost. Keep up, Cass. It's this or broke. Why the fuck else would I be calling him, and not one of the other staff?"

"I could snap my neck, you know."

I snort at him. "I doubt it. But just in case—" I hold out my hand, and he glares at me before clasping it. "I can't say it was a pleasure knowing you, but at least we both know you'll be happier in hell."

"Damn straight I will," he says, showing me his teeth as he holds onto the rope and rocks the chair back on its legs. "Lucifer had me at succubus."

I check the time on my cell phone. "Thirty seconds."

"Jesus, just make the call," he grumbles as he slips the noose around his neck again. "Gonna take the old geezer like a century to get down here, and that's if he doesn't break a hip on the way."

I hop onto a nearby desk and peer out one of the small windows set into the top of the wall. "Fucking storm's turning the lawn into a swimming pool."

"Hope fuck face can swim."

"Making the call," I say, ignoring Cass's bored voice behind me.

I time his answer with my feet landing on the floor. "Gabriel! F-Father. Please, hurry!"

"Zachary? What's—?"

Cass starts making gagging noises. I whirl around, waving at him to stop.

"It's Santos!" I yell. "He said he's going to, to—shit, father, he says he's going to kill himself!"

Cass starts choking again. This time, he mimics sucking a giant dick to accompany the suggestive gagging sounds.

I wave him away and hurry out the door before Gabriel can overhear.

"Did he tell you where he was?"

"English. Sharon's class. Uh, room 2C."

"Are you nearby?" Gabriel's voice rises several octaves. I hear a door slam and his voice grows choppy, as if he's started running. "Can you see him?"

"No! I'm in the garage. I just got his text. Father, I'm not going to make it!" I tamper down a near-hysterical urge to start laughing. I've never pulled a prank before, but I understand why kids do it. The adrenaline rush is insane. My heart's hammering so hard it feels like it's denting my ribs.

"Call Brother Timothy! Tell him what's happened. I'm on my way." I hear his feet hitting the ground, and it feels like he's stomping over my chest.

I end the call with a trembling thumb.

It's now or never, Trinity.

Now or never.

## 24

## TRINITY

I watch open-mouthed as Gabriel disappears around the corner. I called out to him a few times, but I might as well have been mute.

Eight o'clock.

*15 minutes.*

*Good luck.*

Shit. What the hell just happened? I could barely make out anything from just hearing Gabriel's side of the call. But I know it was Zachary who phoned. The thought makes my hair stand on end.

There's no time for this shit. Start looking, Trinity.

I hurriedly close the door and race back into Gabriel's apartment. I don't bother with the kitchen or study area. If this laptop is filled with as much incriminating evidence as the Brotherhood says it is, he'd hide it somewhere a quick search wouldn't locate.

Damn it.

I throw open his closet and flick through his clothes. I search the bottom by his shoes and then I move onto his shelves. The scent of his fabric softener fills my nose as I worm my fingers all the way behind his sweaters.

Nothing.

I climb up on the shelves and burrow my arms between his luggage bags. I gag at the stink of mothballs coming off of them.

Nothing.

The clock back in the living area seems to have doubled in size. All I hear is that watch hand clanging through each second like a death knell.

Closet is a bust.

I haul open the drawer in his nightstand. A bible, a spiral-bound notebook, hand lotion, condoms—

I freeze.

Condoms.

*Condoms?*

What the fuck—?

*There's no time, Trinity!*

I slam the drawer shut, and try to will the sight of that black-and-gold packaging from my mind. I shove my hands under his mattress and shuffle all the way around the edge, grunting at how heavy it is.

Nothing.

I stick my head under his bed, and then crawl under when I realize it's too dark for me to see.

I try not to imagine that there's someone already under here, all the way at the back, reaching for me like I'm reaching for them.

Condoms?

*Fuck it, concentrate!*

Nothing. Bed's a bust.

I'm about to crawl out again when my hand brushes against something.

A thousand spiders burrow into my hair. I let out a strangled scream and have to force myself not to cannon out from under the bed, yelling.

It's just a bag, Trinity.

A bag *hidden under his bed.*

Jackpot!

I ruthlessly suppress the part of me that wants to wet itself and grab a fistful of the cloth bag, dragging it out with me as I crawl backward.

The closer I get to getting out, the more convinced I am that Gabriel is already standing in the room, waiting for me.

My heart is seconds away from exploding. I clear the last few inches and throw myself onto my back, clutching the bag to my chest like a shield in case Father Gabriel decides to pounce on me.

The room is empty.

No spiders in my hair.

*Just condoms in the drawer.*

I shove away the thought as I roll onto my knees and zip open the bag.

Gloves. A soft hat. A carton of cigarettes. A moleskin journal. Rolled up cables. A laptop.

A laptop.

I rip it out and flip it open. It doesn't look new, but since I've only ever used the library's clunky old desktop computers before, I wouldn't wager anything on my knowledge of this shit. But to compare it to the sleek, black machine Apollo was setting up yesterday? Yeah, this thing is ancient.

The screen is blank. I hunt around the machine, finger raised, until I spot the power button.

I stab it.

The machine remains dead.

Tick-*fucking*-tock, Trinity.

I drag my fingers down my face and stab the button again.

Nothing.

Dad had a laptop too. Never used it, but heard him swearing at it all the time.

*Dead battery.*

Battery died.

*Gotta plug it in.*

Cables.

The cables!

My hands are shaking so hard that I drop the bundle of cables twice as I scramble over the floor to the nightstand.

There's a lamp on it—has to be a power outlet nearby.

Tick. Fucking. Tock.

I yank the nightstand away from the wall, rip out the lamp's plug, and shove in the laptop's charger.

What time is it? How long has this all taken?

Don't look at the time, it'll only slow you down. They always get it wrong in the movies. Always looking back to see how far they've run, then—BAM! Dead.

*Don't die, Trinity.*

I fumble with the other end of the charger, but I can't get that tiny plug in that teeny little hole.

Stop.

Breathe.

Calm down.

Now try the fuck again.

It clicks into place.

"Fucking hallelujah." My voice sounds hoarse and broken.

I stab the power button. The screen switches from black to gray.

"Oh God, please. *Please.*" I hike up the side of my dress and fumble in my underwear for the drive.

It's not there.

I spin around, my eyes going wide. No. No! Did I drop it? Did it fall out while I was wriggling around under the bed?

*PING* goes the laptop.

My heart's about to give out, but then my fingers brush the plastic cover. It shifted, but it's still there.

The laptop's whirring, but nothing else is happening. How slow is this thing?

I can't stop myself.

I turn and look at the clock.

It's five past eight.

I deflate like a balloon, my shoulders sagging as I let out a relieved sigh.

*What the fuck are those condoms doing in the drawer?*

I squeeze my eyes closed. What did Apollo say about this device? Did the computer have to be on all the way, or just powered up? He said I didn't have to do anything, just plug it in, but *when*?

I guess it doesn't matter. Sooner rather than later, right?

My fingers have turned into foot-long sausages. I drop the cap and spend several billion tick-fucking-tocks trying to get the stupid fucking drive into the stupid fucking slot.

When it finally slides into place like a greased pig, I glare at it.

No wonder people throw computers and shit against the wall. I'm stinking of sweat, never mind those fucking mothballs.

The screen starts spitting out letters.

Shit.

Shit!

Was this a virus or something? Was that the Brotherhood's plan all along? But then I actually read the messages, and calm down a little. The computers in the library would spout shit like this too. Checking this, allocating that.

Normal. It's all normal.

My gaze is inexorably drawn back to the clock.

Seven minutes past eight.

Fuck.

I drum my fingers against the laptop's plastic frame. The Windows logo pops up, accompanied by a too-loud set of chimes that I'm sure Jasper heard back in our room.

Christ, I'm breaking out in hives.

Ten past eight.

This is ridiculous. There's no way a computer can take this long—

A bright blue desktop pops open. Twenty or so folders and files scream for my attention.

I have no idea if the drive is doing its thing, but I can't be bothered with it right now. I have about three minutes before I need to shove this thing back in its bag.

Three minutes to prove that Father Gabriel is a good guy.

Three fucking minutes.

# 25

# ZACH

My timing was off. Instead of the five to seven minutes I'd thought it would take Gabriel to make his way down to the classroom. He gets here in three minutes.

*Three* fucking minutes.

Did he run track or some shit?

I think I'm hearing things when his shoes thump up the stairs. I barely get to the other end of the hall before he clears the stairs. My heart beats so loud in my chest, I'm shocked Gabriel doesn't first stop to investigate the sound.

He races down the passage, a dark shape against the shadows. I've left the lights off to make it seem no one's been here yet except Cass.

Hopefully, Cass heard him coming.

Muffled voices reach me. I make my way down the stairs, race across the downstairs hall, and then come up the other side where Gabriel entered.

By the time I skid to a halt outside class 2C, I'm panting.

I flick on the light, flooding the classroom white.

Gabriel is on the floor. The chair Cass had been standing on lies on its back a yard or so away.

"Father?"

Gabriel shifts at the sound of my voice, but he doesn't look up. My chest is so tight, I can barely breathe. I like to think that I'm intelligent and cautious, but I just realized I'm an impulsive fucking idiot.

Cass isn't moving.

With the lights on, the ligature marks around his neck are too bright, too red, too fucking real.

"Did you call Timothy?"

Of course I hadn't. Cass was supposed to tip over the chair *as* Gabriel walked in. He'd be hanging for seconds before Gabriel brought him down.

Unless he slipped.

Unless he actually did break his fucking neck.

Unless the sick fuck let him choke to death as he watched, because he's known all along about us, known we were watching, and he was waiting for just the right moment, the perfect opportunity to—

"Brother Zachary!"

I flinch, tearing my eyes from Cass's slack face.

"Call Timothy." Gabriel doesn't shout. In fact, he sounds calm as fuck.

My fingers are numb as I slide my phone from my pocket. I make the call, and speak the words, but it's as if it's all happening to someone else.

Gabriel lays Cass on the floor and starts doing CPR. When he presses his mouth to Cass's, something inside me snaps.

"Don't!" I snarl, falling to my knees beside Cass's limp body. I shove Gabriel away, dimly aware that I'm doing this all wrong, *so* fucking wrong, but I can't stop.

This wasn't supposed to happen.

I close my mouth over Cass's and breathe into him, feeling his chest rise under my palm.

Once. Twice.

*Start compressions.*

Ten.

Twenty.

Thirty.

Gabriel sits back on his heels. His phone is out. He's talking to someone, but fuck knows who.

It's all over.

He knows.

And I don't give a fuck because I'm losing Cass.

Already lost him.

Fuck.

*Fuck!*

"Stay with me," I yell before breathing into his mouth again. Once, twice. "Stay the fuck with me!"

My ears whine like a buzzsaw. Cass's chest feels too spongy under my stacked palms, like I'm pushing down on a mattress and not my brother's chest. I will the force of every push to draw air back into his lungs, to massage his heart, to do whatever the fuck it was CPR is supposed to.

"Breathe!" I yell.

Gabriel's hand comes into view. For a sickening moment I think he's going to pull me away, to tell me I have to stop, that Cass is already dead. But instead he simply grabs the edge of Cass's t-shirt and draws it down his stomach.

Covering the countless cigarette burns scattered over his skin.

Marks *I* made.

Pain *I* inflicted.

My cheeks are wet, and I know I shouldn't be crying for some random student in front of Gabriel, but fuck knows how I'm supposed to stop.

I'm sorry.

I'm so fucking sorry.

I wish I could take back every nasty word I ever said to you, every fucked up thought, everything.

Every-fucking-thing.

"Zachary."

I'm staring at my meshed fingers as I shove down Cass's ribs. Twenty-five, twenty-six, twenty-seven—

"Zachary!"

I look up Gabriel, my face twisted with rage, with pain, with defeat. His eyes narrow, and his mouth thins into a stern line. "Stop."

"Fuck you," I growl out.

Gabriel's eyes dart up to his hairline. "Brother Zachary—" he says, reaching for me.

"Fuck, stop," someone croaks. A hand slaps weakly at my wrist. "Stop!"

I sit back and end up falling the last few inches onto my ass. Cass rolls onto his side, wheezing and gagging like I'd stuck my fingers down his throat. He puts a hand on his chest where I'd been doing the compressions and moans like a gutted pig.

"I heard something give," Gabriel says quietly. "You might have cracked a rib."

Jesus fucking Christ.

I scramble up, whipping my hands through my hair. The skin of my face is cold, tingling, two sizes too small. "I'm sorry," I hear someone say. "I'm so fucking sorry."

"Go wait outside, child," Gabriel says.

Blood whines as it races through my veins. "Cass—Cassius, I'm so sorry."

"Zachary!"

My eyes dart back to Gabriel. His face is pale, his mouth a

hard, trembling line. He points at the door. "You've done enough. Go and wait outside."

It feels like I'm dragging my legs through concrete to get to the door.

I'm barely outside a moment before I hear running feet. Brother Timothy shoves me aside when I don't move, and falls down beside Cass, a paramedic's jump bag dropping to the floor by his knees.

"Cassius, can you hear me?" Timothy demands, grabbing Cass's shoulders and shaking him.

"Yes, fuck. Stop that, would you? It hurts. *God.*"

I step back further and further, until I can't hear Cass's voice.

I broke him.

I brought him back, but then I *broke* him.

The fuck is wrong with me?

My shaking hands curl into fists as I turn and force myself to walk away. There's nothing more for me to do here.

Like Gabriel said, I've done enough.

I've done enough.

# 26

# TRINITY

A green light starts blinking on the device. I should take it out and shut down the laptop so I can put it back under the bed, but I can't. I'm frozen to the spot—faced with an email my brain doesn't seem capable of processing.

D*earest Gabe,*
      *I wish you had never left Redmond.*
      *I know it's been months since we last spoke, and it seems I only ever contact you when I need something, but I truly hope you understand my reasons.*
      *I know you are busy at the school, and you made it very clear that I shouldn't contact you again…but Keith needs your help.*
      *We need your help.*
      *Things have progressed to a stage where I'm not sure I can keep this marriage together any longer.*
      *My intention is not to guilt you into replying. I understand that there's a chance you might not even see this email. But I hope you do.*

*You've saved my marriage countless times before. I hesitate to ask,*
*but can you save it again?*
　　*Can you bring us back to God's glorious light?*
　　*We need you, Gabe.*
　　*Keith most of all.*
　　*Please.*
　　*Monica.*

T he fire pops, breaking me from my trance. I whirl around
　　to look at the clock. Quarter past eight.

I press the laptop's power button. It starts shutting down as I
yank out the drive and hike up my skirt to slip it behind my
underwear again.

A noise reaches me from the passageway outside Gabriel's
room. So faint, it could have been my imagination, but I'm not
taking any chances. Whether the drive had enough time to copy
everything it needed, I don't know.

I slam closed the lid and pull out the cable, shoving the
laptop back in the bag before winding up the cord as I trace it
back to the power outlet.

Was that a door opening?

My heart knocks against my breast bone. I'm seconds away
from puking with nerves.

I break off the tip of my nail when I pull out the power cord.
I kick the side of the nightstand, shoving it back against the wall
with my foot.

Tossing everything in the bag, I zip it up and crawl under
the bed.

I can't bear going all the way to the back.

You're taking too long!

Fuck. I crawl out again, jump to my feet, and spin to face the
door on the other side of the apartment.

Then I remember to breathe, and let out a massive sigh of stale air.

I tug my dress straight as I hurry back to the fireplace, glancing back over my shoulder to make sure the bedroom is in the same condition I found it.

I hiss in pain when my ass hits the chair. Despite the cushioning, I felt that impact all through my body. I shudder as I try to ignore the pain, and gently shift into a more comfortable position.

*What were you doing while I was gone, Trinity? Who, me? Just been sitting here the whole time. Sitting here, watching the fire.*

God, my heart's pounding. I wipe the back of my hand over my forehead, and then use both hands to swipe the sweat from my hairline.

Crackle, pop, grumble.

Caught between a hungry fire and an angry thunderstorm.

Shit, it's hot in here.

I get up again, scanning the bedroom again as I pass. Dear Lord, I hope I didn't fuck this up. I open the window and stick my head into the wet, chilly air.

Better.

Lightning fractures the sky, and a few seconds later a muted crack rumbles around Saint Amos.

I check the clock.

Twenty minutes past eight.

Damn it! I could still have been going through his emails. It only took me a minute to find the one my mom sent. Father Gabriel—*Gabe?*—is super organized. His emails were all sorted into folders. Accounts, Personal, Redmond, Bishop, To-Do, Unsorted, Spam, Sent, Deleted.

Mom's letter had been the tenth one in the personal folder. I guess it says a lot that the entire folder only contained a little over thirty emails. But although Gabriel likes to pretend he doesn't have a personal life, judging from my mom's email, he's had his nose stuck in our family's affairs for a long time.

His *guidance?*

If she only knew the shit the Brotherhood was accusing Gabriel of.

Oh, wait. She'll never know. She's dead.

There's no warning. One minute I'm glaring out at the black thunderstorm—the next everything blurs with angry tears.

I push away from the window sill and stalk back to the fire. Trinity the Wimp is yelling at me to stop, but I shove her in a mental closet and lock the fucking door.

Wine sloshes over the rim of the glass when I rip it off the side table. I tip my head back and swallow it all down in one go. Then I pour myself another from the decanter.

I even stare at Gabriel's pack of cigarettes for a moment, wondering if they'd help suppress the sudden swell of immutable fury roaring through me, but I dismiss the thought.

*Weed.* That's what I need.

I drain my glass, and press my hand to the back of my mouth as I pause, waiting for everything to come right back up again. It's red wine—what a fucking mess that will make of this pretty carpet.

A bitter laugh bursts out of me instead. I consider drinking straight from the decanter but then I remember I'm not a fucking animal so I pour myself another glass.

"That's enough, child."

I gasp in shock, spilling wine over my hand and—*yup!*—ruining the pretty fucking carpet. Spinning around, I stare at Gabriel with a slack mouth as he comes closer.

He takes the glass from my hand and urges me into the chair before perching on the arm. His head dips as he massages the back of his eyelids and lets out a long sigh.

"What's wrong?" I blink up at him, my hand reaching for him before I can snatch it away again.

That doesn't go unnoticed. Gabriel's eyes latch onto my hand where I keep it pressed into a fist in my lap. The shadows on his face seem to deepen.

"I'll have to reschedule tonight's dinner."

For a second, I have no idea what the hell he's talking about.

"Oh, this?" I nod, licking my lips. "Yes, of course." My tongue feels like it's growing thicker inside my mouth. Starting to regret the wine now, even if it did put out the fire raging inside me.

You can soak shit in alcohol, but ultimately that just sets the stage for a world-class explosion.

"I know I allowed it, child, but you shouldn't drink in excess. Or at your age."

Irritation flickers inside me, threatening to ignite my earlier anger.

*Yeah, and a celibate priest shouldn't have condoms in his fucking drawer, but here we are.*

I think I'm going to puke.

I stand, making contact with Gabriel on my way up. In an effort to veer away from him, I stumble over my own feet. If he hadn't caught onto me, I'd probably have fallen into the hearth.

His hand is on my hip. Strong fingers dig into my flesh.

Into the drive hidden behind my underwear. He frowns, and moves his thumb over the device. I twist away from him, blinking furiously as I try to sober the fuck up.

"I have to go," I state, holding up a finger. "But can—may? —I use your bathroom first?"

He frowns hard, and reaches for my hip again as he gets to his feet. "What is that?" he asks.

"Bathroom!" I yelp out, and then hurry away from him. I saw another door leading off his bedroom—it's either a walk-in closet for the hundred-plus clerical robes he needs, or it's the bathroom.

It turns out to be a bathroom.

I slam the door shut behind me, and because of that I don't make it to the toilet. Instead, I puke into the basin.

This is a new record for me. The most I ever puked was that time Mrs. Brady undercooked the hot dogs at the church fete for handicapped people back when I was sixteen.

I half-expect Gabriel to come inside and hold back my hair like Reuben did.

But he doesn't.

I spend a few minutes making sure there's nothing left to come out, and then a minute more splashing cold water on my face.

Unfortunately, the purge did nothing to sober me up. I stumble out of the bathroom and have to hold onto the wall as I study the back of Gabriel's head.

He's at the window, staring into the darkness.

He turns his head a little, but then straightens again. "Do you need me to help you back to your room?"

My spine stiffens.

*We need your help.*

"No," I say icily, crossing my arms over my chest despite how that makes me sway. "I'm p'fectly fine."

Besides the slurring, of course.

"I like to think I'm blameless, child."

It takes me a second to focus on him. "Wha'?"

He sighs, closes the window and turns to face me. There's a cigarette in his hand, and he drags at it till the coal glows red as Satan's horns.

"You asked if your parents were good people. And they are, Trinity. Truly...they are."

He walks up to me, a sad smile on his face. "But they're not blameless, and neither am I."

His hand is on my shoulder. I don't like it there, but I don't want him to stop talking. "What are you sayin'?"

He takes another long drag at his cigarette. Although he ducks his head to blow out the smoke, it piles up between us and still hits my nose. "Why did you go through my things?"

My eyes widen. "I didn't. I promise."

He looks to the side, drawing my gaze with his.

The bag I'd shoved under the bed is on top of the mattress, contents spilled out. The laptop is open. Even from here, I can see the email program is open.

It didn't shut down properly.

He knows I read the email.

But is that *all* he knows?

"I'm so sorry." I press my hands to my face, trying to hide behind my fingers.

"Shh," he murmurs.

An arm slides around my shoulder and draws me close.

I shudder against him, my hands still covering my face. "I'm sorry."

"I understand. I left before I could answer your questions."

He strokes my head and for some reason that's all it takes for me to surrender. That, and the half a bottle of wine I'd guzzled before he got back.

For a ridiculously sweet moment, *nothing* has changed. I'm sixteen, and I've just admitted that I don't believe in God. At least, not in the same way my parents do. And Gabriel's holding me, just like this, letting me sob into his shoulder.

But the moment is only that—a single moment. Fragile as a wine glass. And it shatters as soon as he speaks.

"I would ask you not to judge me, but—" his lips quirk into

a smile that's warm, but so fucking sad. "You're a better person than I am, so you would have every right."

I lean back from him, my fingers sliding down my face. He cups my face with one hand, the other at his side, a half-finished cigarette dangling from his fingers. His touch causes my legs to lose their strength. I throw my arms over Gabriel's shoulders, holding onto him to keep myself upright.

"I drank too much," I tell him.

"I know, but this can't wait anymore. If you don't remember in the morning, then I'll tell you again. I'll keep telling you, until you find it in your heart to make sense of it."

His words are starting to run together.

Shit! He's about to lay some heavy fucking shit on me, but what. If. I. Don't. Remember?

"Tell me." I grab the front of his shirt, tugging at him. "Tell me what you did."

Tell me about Zachary. About Reuben. Apollo.

Tell me what the fuck you did to *Cass*.

Tell me everything, you sick, perverted—

"Trinity. Child. Look at me." He uses his hand to lift my head. Then he grips my chin and squeezes. The brief pressure brings me back from lolling off into a violent booze-induced daydream where he's crucified at the stake like Jesus, and the Brotherhood are the ones piercing him with spears.

"I had an affair with your father."

# TRINITY

I'm on hands and knees. Technically, *elbows* and knees. I'd staggered out of Gabriel's room what feels like centuries ago, despite him begging me to stay and talk. I might have told him I was too drunk, too pissed off, too over his shit to stay.

I dunno. I just hope I didn't swear too much. Feels wrong, swearing at a priest.

That's not important. *This* is important. I hold up the drive and study it with narrowed eyes. Have to give this back.

But it doesn't fit under the door.

My plan failed because this stupid thing is too big.

I slit my eyes and concentrate on wedging the slim drive beneath the door.

"What are you doing?"

I look up and then sit back on my haunches in front of Reuben like a puppy begging for treats. How'd he know I'd be here? Coincidence…or had he been following me?

I hold up the drive. "Givin' this back."

Reuben watches me for a second and then reaches past me to

unlock his door. Grabbing my elbow, he hauls me up and drags me inside his room. The door closes silently behind us.

I open up my hand, the drive on my palm. "Here."

Reuben barely touches me when he picks it up, and then immediately walks away. "What, no thank you?" I call after him.

I frown and glance around his apartment as he disappears into his bedroom with the drive.

I start nosing around again, but there's not much to see. The single drawer by the coffee station has instant coffee sachets and spoons in it. The microwave is empty. There's a cell phone charging next to the kettle, but when I try and turn it on, it asks for a pin. I try a few random numbers before a massive hand reaches around me, removes the phone from my fingers, and then wraps over my hand.

"You've been drinking," Reuben says.

"And?"

I flex my fingers inside his fist, marveling at how big it is. He could crush my hand without putting any real effort into it.

I hope he doesn't. I like my hand.

"Why would you get drunk around him? Or have you forgotten how dangerous he is?"

I laugh and arch into Reuben. "Hold me," I say, and then try to maneuver his other arm around my waist. But it's too heavy and unwieldy, especially since he's not helping.

"Tell me what happened."

"We spoke. He left." I hold up a finger and glance at Reuben over my shoulder. "That was you guys, right? You did something? He shot right the fuck out of there. I had more than enough time to copy everything."

I have no idea if that's the truth, but I'm not sure how long Reuben will let me hang around if he thinks I'm a failure. He might even send me back to Gabriel.

I flinch at the thought.

Never. I will *never* go back there. Never speak to him again.

He had an affair with *my father*.

"You're shaking."

"It's cold," I say, and try to make myself stop. Then I turn around, ending up facing him with his arm around my waist, still holding my hand. "But you can keep me warm."

His eyes drop to my mouth, then my throat, then my breasts. Every place they pause, the skin there begins to pulse.

"You can't be here," he says, releasing me and stepping back.

I *should* leave. I know that. But I don't want to be alone right now. Being alone would mean I'd have to replay all the shit that just happened, and in my current state, I don't know what to do with that information.

Then again, would I really be better off here? I feel safe around Reuben, but what if Cass or Zachary stop by? I already know I can barely fend off one of them…if they were to gang up on me—

"You're right," I blurt out, pushing my curls out of my face as a wave of cold tingles washes over me.

This is the last place I should be.

There's no safe place in Saint Amos anymore.

Maybe there never was.

I have to get out.

Reuben turns to watch me when I walk past him. "Do you want to know what's on the drive?"

I pause mid-step and peer at him over my shoulder. "You —?" I point to his bedroom. "You found something?"

He shakes his head. "We'll only know tomorrow. But do you want to know what we find, if we find something?"

It feels like a loaded question, and something I'm definitely not equipped to answer right now. So I err on the side of caution.

"Sure. I mean, of course." I nod and head back to the door.

I open it.

A hand slams down beside my head, closing it again. My spine stiffens like someone rammed a pole through my body. "What…what are you doing?"

Suddenly I don't feel that drunk anymore. Maybe it's the adrenaline surging through me.

"I didn't know you liked Cass," Reuben says.

"I…"

I *don't*.

For some reason, I can't say it.

But I don't!

*Still, you enjoy what he does to you. The way it makes you feel. You've always loved the idea of being a sinner, haven't you?*

"I'm not upset," he says in the same monotone as before.

Always so calm, so centered. Makes me wonder what it's like when he loses control.

*Like you did with Cass.*

Shut up!

"I should go," I say again. "Probably can't have anyone see me here."

"Do you still like me?"

"Yes."

Fuck. Fuck!

I shiver when Reuben touches the side of my neck, but it's just to draw a curl away from my ear.

"So you can like more than one guy at a time?"

No.

Yes.

Maybe?

Trick question! I *only* like Reuben.

Don't I?

*What about Zach?*

Fuck.

*Well? What about him?*

"Do I have to?" I murmur, trying to find an easy way out.

"Yes." Reuben's fingers trail down and then caress the ridge of my collarbones. That light touch sends a shiver through me.

"Why?"

"We're too close. Have been for so long."

"If you really thought that, then you wouldn't have kissed me."

He turns me around and gently grasps my chin. "Kisses mean nothing." There's a strange hitch in his voice that belies the words. Because he *does* like me, or because someone told him that a long time ago and he still believes it? "I like kissing girls."

My eyes widen. "Oh," I murmur, heat slowly crawling up my face.

Can I be more embarrassed? I thought Reuben genuinely liked me. But if it's just something he gets a kick from…?

Fuck it—he *does* like me.

I'll prove it.

"Then kiss me," I say. "Kiss me and tell me it doesn't mean anything."

He cocks his head a little to the side, as if intrigued by my suggestion. Then he ducks, scoops me into his arms, and presses me against the door. Just like last time, my legs wrap around him like I've done this a thousand times before.

*Blasphemous little slut.*

I'm suddenly too aware of how close my core is to his body. Pressed to his stomach just above his belt, I can only imagine what it would feel like if he was to lift my skirt so the rough fabric of his jeans could rub against me.

Damn it, I *am* a slut. Is this because Cass got me so hot and bothered earlier? Or is it because when I feel like this, I can't think about other things? Horrible, *confusing* things.

Maybe a little of both.

"Are you sure?" he asks.

"That I want you to kiss me?" I frown at him. "Yes."

"I mean, are you sure you want to test me?"

My frown deepens.

He shifts his grip, pressing me harder against the door. Even through my skirt, that friction is enough to send a host of urgent signals through my body.

Now every part of me is paying attention—from my lips to my nipples, to my center, to my fucking toes.

"You shouldn't treat this like a game, Trinity." Reuben's black eyes harden with the same intense determination he'd worn the day we met. He traces the outline of one of my buttons and then starts popping them open.

"You're supposed to be kissing me," I whisper.

"I am," he agrees calmly. "But you never said where."

Good God, now I'm picturing him kissing my breasts, drawing my nipples into his mouth and teasing each tight bud with his teeth. I start trembling internally. When I grab onto his shoulders, he pauses in his methodical work, his fingers in line with my nipples.

"Are you okay?"

"Yes," I say breathlessly.

He lets out a soft, "Hmm," as if he's not one-hundred percent satisfied with my answer.

God, this is torture. I'm tempted to ask him to hurry the fuck up.

The last button pops open. He slides a hand behind my bodice and parts the two halves of my dress.

But not all the way. Just enough so that I can see the edge of my bra when I glance down.

Then he shifts his grip and holds onto me with one arm— one arm?—while he hunts around in his pocket for something. What is he looking for, a condom?

I know where to find some.

Did Gabriel sleep with my Dad? Well, he'd have to, probably, to consider it an affair.

Dear Lord, I can't handle this shit.

I lean forward, my eyes fluttering closed, fully intending to kiss Reuben just to put an end to the sour thoughts filling my head.

But he moves his head aside so I end up kissing his fucking ear.

I huff impatiently and press the back of my head against the door, glaring up at him as he carries on rifling through his pocket.

I cross my arms over my chest, moving my mouth to the side. "What are you looking for?"

"This."

He lifts a red rosary. My hands fly to my chest, but I touch bare skin. "How did you—?"

"You left it here."

My mind scurries back to the shower I took earlier today. "No I didn't."

He says nothing.

"I must have put it back on."

Still nothing.

"I put it on top of my clothes. It would have been the first thing I saw."

He quirks an eyebrow at me.

"It must have fallen off." I keep brushing my skin and then hold out my hand, palm up. "Whatever. Give it back."

His fingers close over the red beads. "It's mine."

"You gave it to me."

"But you don't believe. What's the point?"

My heart stutters at that. His commanding stare forces me to drop my gaze. What the fuck am I supposed to say to that?

The smell of roses hits my nose. He's rubbing the crucifix with his thumb, intensifying the scent.

I bite down on my lip. I'm such a jerk. It obviously means a lot to him, and I'm demanding him to give it back.

He tenses when I lay my hand over his. I slowly close his fingers over the necklace.

"You're right. There's no point. It's yours, anyway."

But then, as I'm holding him, staring into those pitch-black eyes, a wriggling worm of doubt starts working its way through my mind.

"Wait…" I turn my head, watching him warily from the corner of my eye. "I *know* I put it on my clothes. It…it wasn't there when I got out."

He watches me with the patience of a rock.

My eyes go wide. "You took it."

There's the tiniest flicker in his eyes.

"Oh my God!" I slap a hand into his chest and begin squirming against him so he'll let me go. "You were *watching* us!"

He lets out a soft grunt, grabs my ass, and slams me back into the door hard enough to rattle it.

Shock dips me in ice.

My hands are on his chest, fingers digging into his muscles, but I slowly retract them and hug myself instead.

He lets out a long breath through his nose and then slowly scans my face like he's looking for something.

I don't know if he finds it, but a moment later he slips his rosary over my head and tucks it behind the open halves of my dress. Then he slowly starts buttoning me up again.

"Why?" The word warbles out before I can stop it.

"Why did I watch, or why didn't I stop him?"

"Both!" The anger's coming back, but I force myself to swallow it down.

"I watched because I like you. Because you were enjoying it. Because I wanted to see what you look like when you come."

I should be flooded with horror or disgust. Instead, I stare at Reuben with morbid fascination.

I thought it was *him*. That's the only reason I allowed—

"And I didn't stop him, because I was pretending it was me in there, not him."

His words spear into through me like a blunt knife.

"What?" I belt out, thumping his chest with my fist. "That makes no sense!"

He grumbles faintly as he steps back and lets me slip to the floor. I'm breathing so hard you'd swear I ran a fucking marathon. "That makes no fucking sense, Reuben!" I yell, bashing my other fist into him.

He catches my wrist before I can get off another blow and then closes his arms over me, crushing me to his massive chest. I let out a strangled yell, but fighting him is pointless.

"Can I kiss you now?" he asks.

That knife twists, scraping over my bones and shredding my heart. It takes every ounce of self-control I still have, but I manage a hoarse, "No. Never." I clear my throat and force strength into my words. "Never, *ever* again."

Then I shove at him with all my might.

And he lets me go.

I don't look back when I leave, but I manage not to slam the door. I take two steps before the smell of his rosary hits my nose again.

I leave it hanging from his door handle, blinking back tears as I stalk back to my room.

# 28

## ZACH

**M**y heart almost explodes from my chest when I spot Cass sitting on the couch. I wasn't sure if he'd be here. A part of me wishes he wasn't. A part of me can't be more relieved to see him.

Cass looks up from the latest edition of *Pussy Pounder* as I slip into our lair through the narrow opening in the bookshelves. I can't wait for the day we'll have a space of our own with a proper fucking door. No, fuck that. No doors. Just an archway.

I know exactly where we'll go when this shit's taken care of.

Whenever I go into town on the weekends, I spend an hour or so at the local coffee shop. Their filter coffee tastes like the shit you scrape out of a gutter, but that's not why I go there.

Their Wi-Fi, although spotty, opens up a new world. For an hour, I can escape this shitty school and the decades-long path my brothers and I have been trekking.

For those few precious minutes, I go house hunting. It started as a mental itch I had. We have a game we play. Can't remember the last time we did, but since our answers are always the same, I have that shit committed to memory.

It's called: what would you do, if you could do anything?

Not highly original, but for a bunch of kids trapped in a dark basement who'd never played sports or gone to the mall or even asked out a girl to the prom…it filled a void.

We played it once or twice after we escaped, but it became painfully obvious that we'd be adults by the time we'd had our revenge.

What did it matter, then, what dreams we had as kids?

But those things stuck with me.

Apollo loves the ocean even though he's never set foot on the coast. Before he was taken, he'd watch surfing championships on television and imagine it was him slicing through those waves on some beach in Malibu. Honestly, I think he just secretly wanted to take photos of chicks in bikinis. But who the fuck am I to judge, right?

One day I went to town on a supply run, hungover as fuck after a night of blunts and whiskey, and I decide to get a plate of something greasy at the coffee shop. Only to discover they have Wi-Fi.

In this place?

Shocker.

I had one of Apollo's old laptops with me. He wanted me to send it in, because he swore the on-board graphics card was malfunctioning. I stopped listening after the fifth time he mentioned the driver and took it with me anyway.

They keep forgetting they don't have to repair shit. *Ever*. If it breaks, I'll buy them a new one. Money means fuck all to me.

So, hungover as fuck, I decide to get Apollo's laptop out of the car and go online while I'm waiting for my grub.

I'm guessing the laptop didn't shut down properly because as soon as it boots up, the browser pops open and loads the last website Apollo had been on.

A Youtube video of some surf competition.

Minutes later, I was hunting down coast-side properties in California where I'm guessing—probably incorrectly—that a guy can catch the best waves.

Then I found it.

Six bedrooms, five en-suite. An infinity pool overlooking the ocean. A garage big enough for as big a collection of classic cars as Reuben wants. A game room for Cass, replete with a fucking billiards table. Billiards, not pool, because he's snooty like that.

There's even a fucking dance studio with wrap around mirrors on the walls, perfect for Cass to admire himself in.

I haven't told them about the property.

I also haven't told them I put in an offer on the place on Saturday. I know I'll be getting that call sometime this week— my offer was ten grand above asking.

It's eating me alive, but I have to make sure it's happening before I break out the champagne.

And yeah, I bought champagne. Four bottles of the most expensive brand the liquor store stocked.

"Love the new look," I tell him, pointing at my neck. "Just give me a heads up if you're about to start reciting bad poetry, though."

He's wearing a black turtle-neck shirt and dark jeans. Sullen colors which match the smudges under his eyes.

"I could have died," he says, voice as dead as his eyes.

"I think you *were* dead for a few seconds." I wish there were a power outlet down here so I could brew some coffee. The only other alternative is alcohol or weed.

I choose the whiskey, turning my back to pour out a shot. Fuck the fact that's it quarter past six in the morning.

"But luckily, you've always been a stubborn sonofabitch." I glance at him over my shoulder when I don't hear the rueful chuckle I was expecting.

"It worked," I say.

Cass shifts a little, and then runs his palms down his legs. "Yeah?"

"She took the drive to Rube last night."

"So why aren't they here? Why aren't they going through his shit?"

"You know Apollo has to be in the kitchen before breakfa—"

"You think I give a fuck?" Cass yells.

I set down the bottle of whiskey and turn to face him. He's on his feet, hands bunched into fists at his side. But he's glaring at the floor, not me, as if he can't bear to make eye contact.

"Cass…"

"I risked my fucking life for that shit," he says, finally looking up. Eyes the color of dirty ice stab through me. "I don't care if you have to go drag that little cunt out of the kitchen by his fucking ball sack, you go and—"

"Christ, Cass, I'm here," Apollo says.

We both turn to him as he sidles in through the opening to our lair. He's wearing a baggy plaid sweater with an unraveling collar, sweatpants that have seen better decades, and a pair of tiger-striped gumboots. Judging from his rat tail hair and the damp patches on his top, it's started raining again.

He slides a backpack from his shoulder and collapses on the couch, then glances across at me and groans when he sees the bottle in my hand. "Don't we have coffee down here yet?"

"No power, remember? It's this or warm beer," I say.

"Fuck it," he grumbles, hiking up his sweater as he shoves a hand under the fabric to scratch at his ribs. "I'll get coffee later. Let's get this over with."

I take my usual seat and both me and Cass watch Apollo as he slips the drive into his new laptop.

"So what shit did you make up for Gabriel?" Apollo asks as he starts tapping the laptop's touchpad. "He ran out of there like someone had set his grandma on fire."

My eyes go to Cass, but he keeps his head down, using his thumbnail to push back his cuticles. "Does it matter? It worked."

"Yeah it did," Apollo says through a grin without looking up. "Looked real fucking spooked. That's—"

He cuts off and starts shaking his head.

"What is it?" I sit forward. "Apollo?"

"Shit," he mutters, his eyes flickering as he scans the screen. "There's nothing here."

"What do you mean there's nothing?" Cass growls. He grabs the laptop from Apollo, stabbing the down button as a glare slowly deepens on his face. "There's tons of shit on here."

"Yeah, but nothing useful." Apollo takes back the laptop, scowls at Cass, and then gets up and goes to sit in the armchair opposite us. "Just a bunch of crap."

"You couldn't have gone through everything so fast," I say, wincing around my first sip of whiskey.

Apollo lets out a world-weary sigh. "I'm using keywords and search strings. Either he's code-named the shit out of everything, or he's encrypted the important stuff." Apollo scratches his head and then gathers back his hair from his face. "I'll keep looking, but I have a feeling he's not keeping anything important on here."

"A feeling?" Cass sits back in his seat, crossing his arms over his chest. "How about you actually check first?"

"The fuck crawled up your ass?" Apollo mutters, sending a questioning frown my way before focusing on Cass. "I've done this hundreds of times. I can tell if someone's trying to hide shit."

"I'd feel better if you took a good, hard look."

Apollo lifts his thumbs from the keyboard, throwing me an exasperated look. "Zach—?"

"Do a manual search," I say. "It's the closest we've gotten to him yet. Maybe there's something you're missing."

"Oh, there's something missing all right. She only got like

eighty percent of the drive. Guess she pulled out early." He glances up with a coy grin which none of us return, and then mumbles something under his breath as he goes back to the laptop. "And, he hasn't even bothered to clear his browser history in…" Apollo holds up a finger as he stares at the screen. "Forever. *Literally*, since the dawn of fucking time."

"Or he could have deleted just the shit he didn't want you to see, leave everything else, then it *looks* like he didn't delete anything," Cass says, lifting his eyebrows at Apollo.

"So either he's really fucking innocent, or he's really fucking guilty." Apollo sniffs. "Go figure."

"Apollo, take the laptop with you. Go through it today and make sure. Check every fucking cluster on that hard drive."

He mutters something sarcastic about "clusters" and snaps the laptop closed with ill grace. "Sure thing, Captain." He stands as he slings the backpack over his shoulder again. "But on the off chance I'm right—" a glare for Cass "—what the fuck do we do? If it's not on here, then he's keeping it someplace else."

I study him for a second, and then shrug. But before I can open my mouth, Cass cuts in. "We tell her it didn't copy anything. Tell her she has to do it again."

"I don't know if she can," I say.

Cass turns his glare on me. "Does it look like I give a fuck?"

"Dude, seriously, what's your deal?" Apollo demands, his hand tightening on the backpack's strap. "You have another wet dream about Zach and wake up with a sore ass?"

Cass rushes so fast to his feet, I'm already reaching to stop him going for Apollo. But he doesn't rush him—he just stands there, chin up and shoulders back, as if waiting for Apollo to throw the first punch.

Then he grabs the neck of his sweater and tugs it down.

I squeeze my eyes shut. It's instinct, something I've always done when I'm suddenly faced with a sight I can't—*or won't* —process.

But then I force my eyes open. Force myself to see.

I force myself to become a *witness*.

It'll come down to us versus them, if I get my way. My brothers feel different, of course. They don't want any of this shit going to trial. Their definition of justice is biblical.

An eye for an eye. A life for a life.

And they're convinced that each and every Ghost took a life.

The marks around Cass's neck are swollen and bruised. But he always bruised easily. The Ghosts liked that about him.

Easily damaged, but impossible to break.

Apollo gapes at Cass's neck, the unspoken question writ large in his wide eyes.

"She's going back, and she's getting what we need," Cass says through his teeth. "And this time, there won't be a fucking noose around my neck."

"I hear you, man," Apollo says, putting out a hand as he immediately switches into conflict resolution mode. "But don't you think we're putting a lot of shit on her shoulders? What if she can't do it?"

"She's a smart girl, isn't she? I'm sure she'll figure it out. She just needs the right motivation."

There's a heartbeat of silence before Cass pushes past me. Apollo watches him leave and then turns angry eyes on me.

"What the fuck happened?"

I hold my tongue. I'd been about to spout a whole monologue about how shit got fucked up and it shouldn't have gone down like it did. But none of that matters anymore, does it?

"I fucked up." I take my seat again. I study the glass in my hand and then toss everything into the back of my throat. "I fucked up, and Cass got hurt."

"Yeah, no shit." Apollo sinks down on the edge of the armchair. "Is he okay, though? Like, mentally?"

"I don't know. We haven't had a chance to talk."

I'd gone to his room last night. He hadn't been there. I'd eventually tracked him down in the infirmary, where a grim-faced Timothy was filling up an orange prescription bottle for him.

When I'd tried to catch up to Cass in the hallway, he'd shoved me out of the way without saying a word. I know when I'm not wanted. I didn't try and go to him again. I was hoping he'd have cooled off by now. Guess I was wrong.

I've been getting a lot of shit wrong lately.

"Does Reuben know?" Apollo asks quietly.

"No."

"I'll have to tell him."

"Obviously."

Apollo lets out a sigh. "He's gonna be pissed."

"Aren't you?"

"Yeah, of course. But what's done is done, right? Can't change anything. No reason to start yelling and shit."

I go over to refill my glass.

"Don't you have class?" Apollo asks.

I set the bottle down again. "Yeah. Fuck."

"Smoke a blunt," Apollo says, coming up behind me. He lays a hand on my shoulder and squeezes my muscle. "It'll help more than the whiskey. Want me to roll—?"

"Don't you have shit to do?" I snap. "Reuben, the data, breakfast? Sounds like a busy fucking morning."

Apollo withdraws his hand. The sigh he lets out as he leaves takes me back.

*Fuck*, it takes me back.

I'm losing my shit again, and he knows it. Cass probably

knew it before anyone, but he loves playing with fire just as much as the rest of us.

But no one, *no one* likes to get burnt.

# 29

# TRINITY

Instead of going to morning prayer, I hide out in a restroom stall staring at the freshly painted door. From the faint marks shining beneath the white paint, it looks like someone had gone to town on the thing with a Sharpie. Wish I knew what they'd written.

My appetite hasn't been back since I puked last night so I don't bother going to the cafeteria when the breakfast bell rings. Instead, I head back to my room and try and get in an hour's sleep.

The next bell rings me from a death-like sleep I don't remember falling into.

Time for class.

Thankfully, I only have Calculus and Sociology before lunch. It gives me half the day to work up the courage to find a way to excuse myself from Psych with Brother Rutherford.

Despite my nap, exhaustion weighs down my limbs and fogs my mind.

*I had an affair with your father.*

I. Can't. Even.

I thought I'd wanted answers from Gabriel, but I changed my mind.

Now that the shock's worn off, all I'm left with is a weird mix of disgust and anger. Not disgust over the fact they're two guys, but because Dad cheated on my mom. And with our fucking priest, of all people.

But that's not what's eating me alive.

If Gabriel is capable of having an affair, then what *else* is he capable of? And since he's openly admitted that he has sex with men…

I cover my face with my hands and rock forward on my bed. Class starts in a few minutes, and I'm still dressed in last night's clothes.

I came to Saint Amos to be with the man I thought of as a friend.

But I was wrong. There's nothing here for me. No friends. No support.

Come the weekend, when all the other students transfer over to Sisters of Mercy for spring break…

I'll be going with them.

When I enter the dining hall at lunch, finally peckish for the first time today, I immediately regret my decision when I spot my tray with its pink post-it note.

TRIN

There's a heart over the I again. Thankfully, the actual food inside looks like everyone else's. If anything had been cut into the shape of a heart, I'd have bolted.

Jasper tries to get my attention, but I ignore him and head

for the back of the room. When I walk past the kitchen doors, I spot Apollo through the window.

I ignore him too, even when he beckons me with a flick of his hand.

The Brotherhood has what it wants. I'm sure Gabriel's computer was stuffed full of all sorts of incriminating evidence. It's time they realized I'm not useful anymore and left me alone.

Apollo doesn't leave the kitchen or try and attract my attention again. I sit and eat my sandwich, pretending not to notice the way the boys around me stare as if expecting me to start doing somersaults.

Then Sister Miriam comes up to me, stopping right beside my bench during her usual rounds.

I pause mid-chew and look up at her as my mouthful of cheese-and-tomato sandwich dissolves on my tongue.

My stomach flips over when she hands me a folded note. "What's this?"

"It's a note, Miss Malone." Miriam's voice could have fixed our little issue with the melting ice caps.

"Thank you?"

But she's already gone. The boys around have me have all transformed into spotted barn owls. I'm itching to fold open the note and find out what it says, but then anyone at the table could read it.

It looks just like the notes the Brotherhood slips under my door. Same paper, same fold. Probably just a coincidence.

More likely, it's a note from Father Gabriel.

*Gabe.*

I twist my mouth to the side and shove the note into my pocket. The dress Sister Ruth made for me feels softer after it's gone through the laundry a few times. I'm grateful for the thick fabric now. It's been raining pretty much nonstop since last night, so the temperature inside the dorms has plummeted.

I leave the other half of my sandwich uneaten, and take my tray to the rack filled with empty dishes. I spot Apollo in the window again, but I pretend not to see him beckoning me.

Did they find something on that device? Is that why—?

No, fuck it.

Curiosity killed the cat, hung the monkey, and drowned Trinity Malone.

I'm done looking for answers.

I get as far as the prayer room down the hall from the cafeteria. Glancing around, I duck behind the pillars shielding the alcove's door and tug the note out of my pocket.

*I apologize sincerely for my behavior last night. I was out of sorts, and I shouldn't have handled such a delicate matter the way I did.*

*Please join me for dinner tonight.*

*I am sure you have many questions.*

*I would like to answer them.*

*Gabriel.*

My heart is thundering like a waterfall by the time I reach the end. Did Miriam read this? There'd be no way for her to decipher such a vague letter, but I'm still convinced she knows everything.

*I had an affair with—*

Fuck!

I crumple up the letter and hurl it away from me, tears blurring my vision. I storm off as fast as my whipping skirts allow, wiping furiously at my eyes as more tears build up.

Why can't I just be normal?

A normal girl, with a normal family, attending a normal school, with normal friends.

*Is that too much to ask, Universe?*

Rain batters my face. I glare up at the sullen clouds stretching from horizon to horizon. In their dull light, Saint Amos looks more like Dracula's castle than ever before.

I spin around and give Saint Amos the finger. Then I stalk over the lawn, heading for the classroom block. I'm early for my next class, but if a brisk walk through the drumming rain can't clear my head, nothing can.

I was going to skip out on Zachary's class. I'm pretty sure he wouldn't have reported me. But I can't bear the thought of being stuck alone with my thoughts one second longer.

Halfway down the slight incline, my shoe hits a patch of thinning grass and I slip in the mud.

I sit for a moment like that, rainwater soaking through my dress, before I push myself up and carry on walking.

*Fuck you, Universe. I've had worse.*

Don't have your notes, Trinity. Textbook's still in your room.

And so what? Let Zachary write me up for detention.

The rain should be steaming off my skin, that's how mad I am. But all it does is pound down, wet and relentless, until I finally step under cover of the eaves. I shove open the door and storm inside, heading for Zachary's class.

Breathing hard from climbing the stairs, I pause a second outside his door before going in.

I come to a stop as soon as I'm inside.

He's at his desk, hand cupping his jaw as he stares at nothing. When he looks up at me, the heavy frown on his face clears in an instant.

He gets to his feet, watching me expectantly.

"What?" I snap. "Did you also forget how to thank

someone?" My skirts whisk around my legs as I storm up to him. "It's easy. You say, 'thank you,' and then I tell you to go fuck yourself, because it wasn't a pleasure."

His frown is back. "What?"

"The files." I wave my hand. "The things I copied. You got it back, didn't you?"

"Yes, but—" he begins, stepping around the desk.

"But *nothing*. The least you owe me is a thank you, and I'm still fucking waiting." I grab my hips and start tapping my foot. "Well?"

"Well *nothing*." He rushes forward, grabbing the side of my dress before I can move out of reach. "Did you even *find* his laptop?"

"Wh-what?" I splutter.

"How did this play out in your head, hmm?" He drags me with him as he heads for the door.

And then he locks it.

I go stiff a moment before the panic hits.

"Let go!" I yank at his hand, but he's holding on so tight I'd probably tear the fabric before I could peel off his fingers.

Instead of releasing me, he slams me into the wall beside the door. Even if someone were to look through the frosted glass, they wouldn't see either of us.

I open my mouth to scream, but he slaps a hand over my lips before I can get a sound out.

Fuck.

I try and knee him.

He kicks my legs open and wedges himself between my thighs, inadvertently hiking up my dress to a rather inappropriate height. When I go for his eyes with clawed fingers, he grabs my wrists and slams them into the wall above my head.

Fuck!

"Listen carefully, Miss Malone, because I'm only going to say this once," he hisses in my ear. "There was *nothing* on that drive."

I yell against his hand, but of course he can't understand me. And all my protest earns me is him slamming his body against mine and driving the air out of my lungs.

I collapse against him, wheezing.

"You're not listening."

I try and say "I'm sorry" through his hand. Some of it must come through because he eases up ever so slightly on my wrists and pulls back so he's not crushing me to the wall.

For some reason, my body responds with despair at the sudden loss of pressure. Like I somehow *enjoyed* the fact that he was suffocating me.

He puts his mouth by my ear again. "You seem to think you can just do whatever the fuck you want. Let me assure you, little girl, that's nowhere near accurate."

My eyes are squeezed shut, but he stays quiet for so long that I dare to open one just to peek at him.

He's watching me like a jungle cat.

"We need that data." He squeezes my wrists, grating the bones together. I mewl against his hand, nodding furiously to convey just how ready I am to listen and obey.

"You will go back to him tonight. Do you understand?"

Another furious volley of nods.

The fury on his face subsides a little. He studies me again, his gaze tracing every contour on my face.

"And you will bring it to us the moment you have it, not a minute later. Do you understand?"

I nod and then push a vehement, "Yes" through his fingers.

His lips quirk into a smile that's as cold as the ruthless gleam in his eyes. "Good girl."

It shouldn't, but even his backhanded praise sends a sensuous ripple through me. Perhaps it's just relief that he's decided not to slit my throat.

I squirm a little, trying to convey to him that I would be happy to comply even more if he stopped pinning me to the wall like a maniac.

His eyes grow hooded. Slowly, he slides his fingers off my lips. They settle around my throat, which isn't much better for my health, but at least now I can talk.

Which means I could try to persuade him that I'm on his side.

*Their* side.

It doesn't have to be true. Fuck it, it *definitely* isn't true. But I like to believe I'm getting better at lying. Or, at least, warping the truth to my advantage.

But first, I need to figure out why he seems dead set on the fact that I didn't do my job.

"I did what you said." I keep my voice soft and low, not wanting to provoke the beast that's only now starting to retreat. "I don't know why it didn't—"

"Think we give a fuck about your excuses?" he rasps. My eyes fly shut as he starts squeezing my throat. "We don't!"

"But I did everything you said." Despite my best efforts, frustration builds as I force my voice to stay calm. "I found the laptop under his bed, and I put the drive into the—"

"I don't want to hear it, little girl."

Boiling hot anger pours into me. I've had just about enough of everyone in my life telling me what the fuck to do. How the fuck to feel. What I can and cannot control. Which version of the truth they think they can get away with.

My father and I were never on the best terms, that's a given. He ruled our house with an iron fist, and I always resented him for that. But I obeyed, because it's what my parents expected from me. Because the bible said so.

Honor your parents somehow became shorthand for blindly obeying every single rule. For letting them tell you what to believe and how to behave.

*They shouldn't have treated you like that.*

No, Father Gabriel—fucking Gabe—they shouldn't have. But they did.

*Everyone* did.

Everyone still does.

Will it never end?

Or has it only gone on this long because I've let it? Because I submitted where a normal, sane human being would long ago have thrown off their shackles and stormed the plantation?

My veins thrum with sullen rage as Zachary carries on talking, his mouth an inch from my ear. "I don't care how you do it, but you *will* get us that data, and you *will*—"

My eyes fly open. "No!" I yell. "If you want it so bad, get it yourself!"

His fingers tighten even more as he grinds his hips into me. "Did you just shout at me?"

I freeze when his hard-on presses into my belly.

Oh my God. He's enjoying this!

I almost laugh at the thought. Of course he's enjoying this—his dick was twice this size when he was *spanking* me, what the fuck am I expecting? He gets off on other people's pain, so I guess humiliating them, torturing them, it's all the same.

"Gabriel's busy." I swallow and try not to let the feel of his cock distract me. "He told me so last night. He'll be busy this whole week."

He rakes his gaze over my body, and then glances to the side. Curiosity, of course, gets the better of me.

It's ten past one.

His class starts at half-past.

We both look back at the same time. He moves against me

again, and this time it's obvious he wants me to feel his erection. My heart spasms with panic while my inner thighs contract with the urgent need to close and deny him access.

Dear Lord, all he has to do is dip down, and he could be inside me. If we were both naked of course. But he's wearing slacks, and I'm in this monstrosity of a dress, so—

"I know what you're thinking," he murmurs. His mouth twitches, and then he's biting down on his lower lip, drawing that tender flesh through his teeth. "But as much as I'd like nothing more than to fuck you against this wall, we both know this isn't how it happens."

A heatwave crashes over me. I let out a mangled, "What?"

He releases my throat, dragging that hand over my breast. He squeezes so hard that I yelp in pain, and then catches his lip between his teeth again.

"I've been thinking about it," he murmurs, crushing me with his body again. His hand coasts down my belly, and I feel him move his erection aside so he can burrow his fingers between us.

"Fucking you."

He wriggles his fingers through the folds of my dress. I quiver when he makes contact with my bare skin an inch above my underwear.

If he hadn't been pressing my wrists to the wall, I might have ended up on the floor. The lower his fingers move, the more strength leeches from my body.

"You know where it will happen, don't you?" His voice drops low. Rough, guttural. He barely sounds like himself. "In our special place, down there in the dark."

His mouth touches the side of my neck and despite everything, a shiver dances over my bones. He slides his lips over my skin, and then grazes my jaw with his teeth. I twist my head away, terrified at how hard my heart is pounding.

His lips follow, and he nips at my jaw again. A moan slips

out of me before I can stop it, and in response he groans and dips down.

"That place where no one can find you. Where no one can hear you scream."

I gasp and jump onto my tippy toes when the crown of his cock presses against my underwear. A hard, aching throb pushes into me, almost as if he'd already broken through that flimsy barrier. He grabs my jaw and wrenches my head back to face him.

"And trust me, girl, we'll make you scream," he whispers, a malicious light dancing in his eyes. "Because it always hurts like fuck the first time."

He devours me.

When I close my mouth, he forces it open with his tongue. When I try to move away from his cock, he slides a hand over my entrance and squeezes me so hard that I whimper into his kiss.

"Christ, we're going to enjoy making you bleed."

Shock finally battles through the confused blur of emotions roiling inside me. I bite down on his lip and buck my hips against him as hard as I can.

I taste blood in my mouth a second before he falls away from me. Staggering to the side, I barely find my feet before his hand is around my throat again.

Lights dance across my vision as he slams me against the wall.

"I like it when you fight. Playing with dead things isn't any fun."

He laughs at me.

And then he kisses me.

Blood and mint-sweet saliva mix in my mouth. He shoves his hand up my dress. Before I can slam my legs shut, he strokes me through my underwear with his knuckles.

That feather-light caress is so at odds with his kiss that for a long moment I'm lost.

His kiss slows, but becomes harder. Somehow more urgent. He strokes me again, sending a deep ache through me.

Instead of pushing him away, I claw my fingers into his chest.

His breath hitches.

He rakes his nails against my inner thigh, leaving a trail of fire behind. I gasp and rear back, and whatever had been keeping me at bay snaps.

Zach steps back, dragging a hand over his mouth. There's a cut on his bottom lip, smears of blood around his mouth, but it doesn't look like he's bleeding anymore. He gives me a quick, condescending scan with his forest-green eyes, and then points to the classroom door.

"Clean up before someone sees you," he grates.

And I move to comply without a thought. With my back turned, I stop.

"No." I don't turn back. I don't look at him. If I see him, I'll falter. "I'm not your puppet anymore. I'm not *scared* anymore." I hear movement behind me, but I simply curl my hands into fists and refuse to let fear take root.

"Things have changed. I can't go back there again. Not tonight. Not ever. And if you contact me again…if you threaten me again…"

I swallow hard and force myself to turn around.

Zachary's watching me with a cocked head, face unreadable, body slack. As if his mind became disconnected from his body. It's the most terrifying sight I've ever seen but somehow, I push through.

"If you or any of your brothers come near me again, I'm calling the police. Or the church, or something. Someone."

Fuck it, Trinity, stay strong.

"Stay away from me. And stay away from Gabriel."

The last is as much a surprise to me as it is to Zachary. He straightens his head with a snap, eyes boring into me like a physical force.

"Or I'll tell him everything."

I should have led with that. Zachary's face slowly pales, but I know it isn't with fear.

It's anger, or rage, or a dirty-bomb of the two. I back up, and feel behind me for the door.

I turn the lock.

Then the handle.

I keep my eyes on him like I would a wild animal, just in case he decides to pounce on me before I'm in the clear.

The last thing I see before I close the door is Zachary's face.

He looks like he's seen a ghost...and he's planning to murder it.

I barely make it to the downstairs restroom. I puke into the basin, my stomach contracting so painfully, I'm shocked there aren't chunks of blood in the sink when I rinse it out.

It takes a few seconds before I can convince myself to look in the mirror.

My hair is mussed and my dress isn't sitting right. But it's the blood on my chin and around my mouth that makes me force down a dry retch.

*Trust me girl, we'll make you scream.*

I have to get the hell out of this school.

## 31

## ZACH

Reuben doesn't bother to knock. It's not that he doesn't respect my privacy or any of that shit. The four of us never need permission to speak to each other, or even just to be in the same room. If we'd had to put up with pleasantries like that back in the basement, we'd all have gone stark raving mad.

"I came as soon as—" he begins.

"Sit."

He takes the foot of the bed, perching picture perfect like always. Straight spine, chest out, chin up.

I watch him for a second, and then reach over to my drawer and take out a joint I'd rolled just for this occasion.

"It's the middle of the day," Reuben says. "Someone could—"

"What?" I snap. "Ex-communicate me?" I glare at him from the bed where I'm sprawled on my back.

As part of my pious disguise, I took a room more befitting a first-year student than a teacher. That's Zachary fucking Rutherford for you. Groveling would-be priest who couldn't swat a fly.

*I'm not scared of you.*

But she sure fucking looked it. Trembling like a newly born foal. It had taken every atom of self-control I still possessed not to pin her to my desk exactly like in Cass's drawing, and fuck her into submission.

Monsters breed monsters.

Rube shakes his head when I pass the joint to him after lighting it up.

"I insist," I say, pushing the words through my teeth.

He could have argued. He might have won. Instead, he takes the joint, studies it, and hits it like a champ.

That's what I love about Rube. He knows when to say yes, and when to say no.

That's how he stayed sane with his Ghost. That evil motherfucker broke him over and over again. Eventually Rube stopped fighting. Every "no" turned into a "yes". He taught himself to submit.

We'd all have been a lot better off if we hadn't fought so hard. But then everyone except Cass would be as broken as him. Days like today I don't know how Reuben can stand to look at himself in the mirror.

He hands back the joint without making eye contact.

"She won't do it," I tell him before taking a drag.

"Why?"

"Because sometime in the last twenty-four hours, she decided we're full of shit and Gabriel's a fucking saint."

"She said that?"

"Pretty much." I study the tip of the joint, and then move my focus to Rube's face. He's staring at nothing again—most convincingly. "He got in her head."

Rube lets out a soft sigh through his nose before leaning back to dig in his pocket.

He exchanges a piece of mangled paper and his red rosary for the joint.

I read the note and then toy with the rosary while Rube helps himself to the rest of the joint.

She was lying to me. Not only is Gabriel not busy, he *asked* to see her tonight. I'm not sure I like this version of Trinity. It takes a special skill set to manipulate people with backbone. I don't think I have the energy to play that game.

"Guess we should have seen it coming," I say.

"So we're back to Plan A?" Rube exhales a plume of smoke.

"Not yet."

He looks across at me, frowning hard. "Then what?"

I wriggle my shoulders under me, pressing my head into my pillow. "I'll go."

"To see Gabriel?" Reuben sounds uneasy.

"She told me where he hid his laptop."

"How will you get in?"

"I'll figure out a way." I wave my hand at him. "Leave it to Beaver."

"Cass should go instead." Rube should have taken my glare as a warning, but he just keeps going. "He's got a reason to talk with Gabriel."

"So do I."

"Yeah, but—"

"He's sacrificed enough." Rube goes quiet, but I can sense he wants to say something. "What?"

"Cass. He was—"

"What, Rube?"

But Reuben shakes his head. "It doesn't matter. You're right —you should go."

I frown at him. "What were you going to say?"

He turns to me, a faint smile on his mouth. "We're getting close. Can you feel it?"

Is it the weed, or is he being weird on purpose? "Close to what?"

His smile inches up, but it doesn't grow warmer. "To the end."

I shove my hands under my neck and massage those suddenly tight muscles. "You excited or something?"

He takes a moment to consider. "Eager."

"For vengeance?"

His dark eyes latch onto mine. "You know what you'll have to do?"

I blink, thrown by his sudden change in direction. "What, tonight?"

He nods.

Yeah, I fucking know. I'll have to do whatever it takes. Just like Cass.

"Like you said, we're getting close. Can't fuck it up now, can we?"

He grabs my ankle and squeezes. I wince, but the pain I feel is ephemeral. He keeps his thumb there, digging into the sensitive spot behind my Achilles tendon. It doesn't seem intentional, but I learned a long time ago that Reuben does everything for a reason. He puts other psychopaths to shame.

"Then do whatever it takes, brother, and let's finish this."

Gabriel's door is open. I stand in the hallway for a moment, my face slack and my body non-responsive no matter how hard I try to force it to move forward.

*He knows you're coming. No need to postpone the inevitable.*

I wrap my hands over my chest, grabbing my elbows as I step inside. No use going in like a warrior in a battle charge—I must be the epitome of calm-as-fuck Brother Zachary. I can't let my mask slip for even a second.

Not like it did last night with Cass.

*I broke him.*

But he's still alive.

*For nothing.*

We don't know that.

*Shut the fuck up!*

The argument in my head ceases. For now.

*Let's get this over with.*

I announce myself with a weak, "Father?" as I step through the antechamber and into his apartment proper.

I've only been here once before, and then too briefly to remember much. The fire is lit but smoking heavily, as if the logs he put on were damp.

The laptop isn't under the bed like Trinity said it would be. It's right in front of Father Gabriel on the four-seater dining table.

White light bathes his face and reflects off a pair of glasses I've never seen him wear. I know I didn't make a sound getting here, but as if he senses my presence, he looks up from the screen.

The jolt he gives when he sees me couldn't have been faked and suddenly I'm questioning every fucking thing that's led me to this point.

"Son," he says, hurriedly taking off his glasses and standing as he closes the laptop lid. "I'm so sorry, I didn't hear you come in."

*Son?*

I suppress a disgusted snarl before it can reach my lips. "It was open." And then I add a belated, "Sorry, I should have knocked."

"No, no." Gabriel moves around the table, lifting his hands. "It's perfectly fine. I was just..." He looks toward the fire. "Is it too warm? I thought with the rain it would be colder tonight."

He's wearing a t-shirt and jeans. With his glasses off, he could have been in his late thirties.

*Keeps himself buff for a priest. Vain much, Father?*

My eyes narrow as I study his back. What fucking game is he playing, pretending at some saintly priest who needs glasses to read and gets so easily caught up in his work he wouldn't notice the knife plunging into his neck until it was too late?

Now I'm wishing I had a knife on me. Wishing I'd crept up behind him and used it.

But I could never forgive myself for doing such a selfish thing. My brothers deserve to take his life as much as I do.

We made a pact.

Their vengeance is mine. Mine is theirs.

If we can't find the Ghosts, if we can't get Gabriel to confess and give up their names, then we agreed to kill him together.

Gabriel's voice wrenches me back to the present. "I'm glad you came to see me."

"It's about Santos—" I begin, eager to get this shit show on the road.

"Yes." He waves a hand to one of the armchairs. "Please, sit."

My skin crawls at the thought of being closer to him.

*Coward.*

I take the seat he offers and risk another glance around his room. With my back to it I can't see much, but at least I have a good view of the bedroom area from here. His bed looks roughly made. Did he just draw the sheets up and plump the pillows?

Was he sleeping before he decided to turn on his laptop? Or has he not tidied since he woke up this morning?

*Perhaps he never went to sleep.*

I'd love to know what happened here last night. What he and Trinity spoke about. What he said to turn her against us.

Or had we done that ourselves?

"I know this would have been discussed at length during your seminal training, but after last night, I feel you may need a refresher."

I frown up at Gabriel. "About what?" And then add a reluctant, "Father."

"Celibacy."

I look away, my lips writhing in an attempt to smile. I transform my bemusement into confusion so that when he turns to face me, he'll see nothing suspicious. "I don't follow."

Gabriel's face is anything but warm and kind. There's a hardness to his mouth, a chill in his eyes.

*There* he is.

Is our Guardian coming out to play?

I slide my hands along the arms of the chair and sink my fingertips into the cushion.

We stare at each other until he breaks the frigid silence. "When did you and Cassius meet?"

My eyelashes flutter before I can widen my eyes in surprise. I don't even have to fake it.

"When he enrolled?" I grimace inwardly when I hear my words come out as a question and not a statement.

Gabriel's mouth curls up at the edges. "This is a safe place, child."

A safe place?

My fingers dig deeper, and I let them. It's either that or they'll be digging into his fucking throat.

"What is it that you're insinuating—?"

He lets out a soft huff of a laugh, a sad smile touching his mouth. "God sees everything." He lifts his hands for all the world like he's preaching a sermon. "*I* see everything."

Cold shock flashes through me. I'm on my feet, hands balled in fists. Gabriel doesn't seem surprised by the sudden vehemence in my voice when I say, "And what is it that you see, Father?"

He steps closer, until there's barely a foot between us.

"I see a lonely young man who turned to a friend for comfort."

His hand lands on my shoulder, but I dip away from him and stumble back. My jaw clenches so hard, I don't think I could have spoken if I tried.

"It's something I've seen a hundred times, if not more. And while it's perfectly understandable, it's still a sin."

Is he talking about the basement? Back then we only *had* each other. Where else could we have found comfort but in each other's arms? There was nothing wrong with it.

There *is* nothing wrong with it.

Nothing.

Gabriel follows me, face neutral but his cast with deep shadows.

Cunning, shrewd, *cautious*.

So careful not to reveal anything.

"I know you, Zachary."

And there it is, bare and naked. He knows me. Gabriel's known about us *all along*.

"Then you know I've known *you* for a long time too," I growl, no longer bothering to disguise any element of my true self. "So why do we keep playing these childish games?"

Suddenly, there's hesitation in Gabriel's eyes. And when I step closer, it's his turn to step back.

Dancing with each other.

Parrying. Attacking.

Like we've practiced this altercation in our minds for years.

I know *I* have. Why wouldn't he?

They say strangling is an act of passion. I can't agree more. I'm in love with the thought of snuffing out the Guardian's life with my bare fucking hands. So much so, my fingers itch to be around his throat.

He lifts his chin, his gaze wavering before his mouth sets in a hard line. "You don't know anything, child. You're dealing with malevolent forces you can't *begin* to understand."

Too fast, he grabs me. We're against each other but with bodies bristling—repelling each other like same-pole magnets.

"I know exactly what I'm dealing with," I grit out as I scour his eyes for the truth. For his *genuine* self. But before I can find anything, he grabs the back of my neck and digs his fingers into my flesh.

A shudder courses through me, and I hate myself in that moment more than I ever have before.

I used to think I was a sadomasochist. That I enjoyed both inflicting and receiving pain.

But that's not the case.

I simply *endure* pain in return for others allowing me to inflict it on them.

His hard grip rouses a sexual tension in me—not because I enjoy the pain he inflicts, but because I know that soon—so much sooner than I'd thought—he'll be at *my* mercy.

A mercy his Ghosts eradicated from me years ago.

"Don't act like you hate me," Gabriel murmurs. "I *am* you. And you are me."

"I'm nothing like you!" I yell. I fist his t-shirt in my hand. "I'll *never* be like you!"

He tsks me as he searches my face, a fond smile stretching his mouth. "I'll let you in on a little secret, child." He licks his lips, and on instinct I lick mine. "You can only hate yourself for so long. Then there's nothing left to do but forgive."

I should have seen it coming, but I'm so wrapped up in my own hateful thoughts that his mouth is against mine before I can push him away.

Though that contact is brief, the outrage of his unsolicited touch rips through me like an electro-magnetic blast.

"The fuck?" I stagger back from him, wiping my mouth with the back of a shaking hand. My disgust is mirrored on his face.

He tilts his head to the side and blinks slowly at me. "So you can fuck a man, but you can't bear to kiss one?"

He walks up to me. I fall back with a warning growl he ignores.

"It might feel like less of a sin, but trust me, son, it's not."

My back hits the wall.

Gabriel stops a few feet away, sliding his hands behind his back.

"God has already condemned us both to hell."

# 32

# TRINITY

I should be in the laundry room doing chores, but with four days left till the end of term, I doubt anyone's going to lay down the law on a rainy Monday afternoon.

So instead I'm in my room, considering sneaking into the shower room.

I feel dirty after what Zachary did to me.

How he made me feel.

And while there's nothing I can do about my filthy mind, the least I can do is wash the feel of him off my body.

After what happened yesterday with Cass in the shower, though…

That delicious tightness and tingling had stayed with me for close to an hour, maybe a little more.

Today? It's been three hours since Zachary touched me, and I can still feel him stroking me through my underwear.

None of it makes sense, of course. I should be horrified—disgusted even—by what he did.

Scaring me like that.

Forcing himself on me.

I thought my heart had been beating with panic…but now I'm wondering if it hadn't been excitement instead.

Maybe if your life is as boring as mine, anything is exciting.

It's seriously messed up to think that my body is capable of confusing fear with lust, or pain with pleasure.

God, when did I turn into such a sexual deviant?

I realize I'm stroking my hip bone through my dress and hurriedly snatch away my hand.

*Not going to happen, Trinity.*

I wouldn't be able to bear the guilt. The shame.

*Don't let such silly things plague you.*

Gah, I knew it!

My mind keeps going back to Gabriel or Zachary.

Gabriel feels the need to answer my questions. About how my father was gay, or the fact that he cheated on my mom?

The Brotherhood will hurt me in the worst way if I don't find the data they're looking for. I may have bought myself some time today with Zachary, but how much?

There was an announcement about the end of term in prayer today, Jasper told me. The buses are arriving on Thursday morning to take everyone through to Sisters of Mercy.

Can I hide from both sides of this war until then?

I grab my pillow and shove it over my head, muffling a frustrated yell.

"Need a hand?" Jasper asks from the doorway. "I'd be more than happy to oblige."

I whip away the pillow and glare at him. "Fuck off," I snap.

He pushes away from the door with his shoulder. "Geez, what's got your panties in a bunch?"

"Nothing." I watch as he rummages in his side of the closet and pulls out casual clothes. "Hot date?"

Maybe he's meeting Perry. I can only hope he won't go down to the library again.

THEIR WILL BE DONE

"Gross," Jasper says.

"Why gross?"

"Because I'm going to see Father Gabriel, you sicko."

"How was I supposed to know?" I call after him as he exits our room.

I shrug my shoulders into the mattress, wincing when one of the many lumps dig into my back. Why is he going to see Gabriel? Maybe he's going to confess about liking Perry. About the things they did.

Great. Now I'm reliving *that* saucy interlude in my head.

Is this what being horny feels like?

Maybe it's hormones or something. My cycle's due to start any day now...I always get a little cranky before. Except this time I'm craving Reuben's pecs, Cass's mouth, and Zachary's fingers, not pepperoni pizza.

Oh, Lord. I'm *still* hot and bothered. I throw my arm over my eyes, letting out a huff of annoyance.

For fuck's sake.

The worst part is, I know exactly what will help. But ever since Mom made me confess, it's been impossible for me to get myself off. Soon I was pushing away the urge the moment it arrived.

Not what I'd consider healthy, but there you go.

I'm rubbing my hip bone again.

Damn it.

I jump up and go close the door, peeking out into the hallway first to make sure there's no one around.

What I wouldn't do for a lock on this door.

I plop back on the bed and skim my fingers over my dress until I'm hovering an inch or so above my clit.

Then I wait for the shame to drive me back like it always does.

Except...it doesn't.

My fingers creep closer. My core constricts in anticipation the closer I get to my clit, as if more and more nerve endings spark into action.

I make a soft noise in the back of my throat when I finally touch myself through the thick fabric. It's so subtle, I can barely feel the pressure, but fuck it if anticipation isn't eighty-percent of the thrill.

Quickly I lift my knees, letting my dress slip down my thighs and pool at my waist.

I grab the hem of my skirt and tug it up my stomach—

"Am I interrupting?"

*Are you fucking kidding me?*

I sit up in a rush, cheeks glowing as I shove my skirt into my lap to cover my underwear.

Is it just me, or does Apollo's grin stretch even wider when I glare at him? "What the hell are you doing here?"

He stands to the side, one arm holding open the door, the other beckoning me with a flick of his fingers. "Come with me. I want to show you something."

"Wait. Wait!" I push the words between heaving pants. "You're going too fast."

"You gotta work on your stamina, Trin," Apollo says. I don't have to look at him to know he's wearing a fat grin. "We still have a flight to go."

"Do I look like an athlete?" I ask, straightening with a wince and forcing myself up the stairs after him.

He laughs as he disappears around the corner of the landing. I arrive a few moments later, blowing like a racehorse. Okay, maybe not that bad, but I definitely have a stitch. I guess I didn't have to run after him when he loped up the first flight of stairs, but he had me so curious I couldn't help myself.

He hasn't answered a single one of my questions. Hasn't told me where we're going. But I realized about halfway up the tight corkscrew stairs that we must be going to one of the towers dotting the four corners of the dormitory. That, or the bell tower.

I was kinda freaked out taking the stairs. While I won't go as far as to say Saint Amos is cozy and inviting, the dorms are a far sight homelier than this staircase. Here, there's nothing to dress the rough brick wall, and the only natural light comes from small square windows filled with thick panes. Of course, with the overcast sky, it's practically night outside already. That leaves the job of illumination to the handful of naked light bulbs sticking out of the walls every few yards. They're so far apart that I have to step through deep shadow to reach the next one.

Someone could break their neck.

"You made it," Apollo says, sounding genuinely surprised.

"Screw you," I mutter, and then stop talking so I can concentrate on getting air back into my lungs.

We're standing next to a thick wooden door that Apollo unlocks with a key from his pocket.

I half expect to hear bats take flight when the door swings inward.

The bell tower.

It's so much larger than I'd thought. The bell hangs a few yards away from where we're standing. A wide ledge circles it, opening to balconies.

"It's…"

"You should see it during the day. The view I mean. The bell's nothing special."

Apollo moves inside. When I don't immediately follow, he grabs my wrist and hauls me after him. "Come on. We don't want to be here when the bell goes off. It's super fucking loud."

He leads me past the bell to a much smaller door set off to one side. The metal door makes it seem like some kind of maintenance area.

The door opens to black nothingness.

Then Apollo turns on the light, revealing a tiny room with nothing more than a desk and a rickety-looking office chair, fabric unraveling on one corner of the cushion.

There wouldn't be enough room in here to swing a cat. Possibly not even a small guinea pig. Not unless decapitation was on its bucket list.

Less than a yard away from me is a blank wall.

Well, it *used* to be blank. Now it's covered with sheets of paper board glued together to form a massive canvas.

I step forward on automatic.

I'm dimly aware that Apollo's still holding onto my wrist, but instead of letting me go, he comes in behind me and shuts the door.

"This is everything," he says.

He's not kidding. The wall is covered with photos, news articles, and pink post-it notes. Lengths of blue string join seemingly random objects together, forming the type of web only a spider on LSD could make.

"There's so much…stuff," I murmur as I step to the side to try and find a starting point.

Apollo uses the grip on my wrist to lift my hand. He carefully forms my fingers until I'm pointing, and then moves my fingertip over the collage.

He stops a foot or so away from the middle. I'm pointing at an old photograph—color, but edging toward sepia and slightly out of focus. It's a school photo showing a small class of about twenty girls and boys dressed in school uniformed lined up on sports benches with two adults.

Behind them rears the majestic turrets of Saint Amos.

. . .

# F riends of Faith Children's Home
## CLASS OF 1991

My heart sinks like a stone tossed into a deep well. It still hasn't hit the black bottom when Apollo says, "Recognize him?" and drags my finger to one of the boy's faces.

"I do."

But it's not the only face I recognize. I swallow hard and then glance at Apollo. He's looking at me, not the board. "Why are you showing me this?"

"They told me you don't want to help anymore," he says. "But I think you should."

I rip my hand out of his. "Zachary told you to bring me up here?" My voice is tight, my hands balling into fists.

"No." Apollo shakes his head. "He—they…" He lets out a long sigh and pinches the bridge of his nose before looking back at the hysterical matrix of evidence scattered over the wall. "They'd kill me if they knew this was here."

"*Kill* you? Bit dramatic, don't you—?"

"Don't tell them. *Please*." He turns to me, grabbing hold of his elbows. "We're not supposed to keep stuff like this around."

"So why do you? Why is this here?"

"I had to put it all together so I knew it made sense." He waves a hand at the photos and clippings, shaking his head. "I mean, it's easy for them. They're all so fucking smart. They just keep this shit in their heads. You ask any of them which year the fire broke out on Rhode Island, how many orphans apparently died in it, they could just tell you straight off the bat."

Fire? Orphans? What the hell is he babbling about?

"Me? I get it all confused. So I made this. It helps me keep track. Helps it all make sense."

I find the clipping he's talking about.

# 1 4 DEAD IN FIRE

My eyes swivel back to him. "And it all leads here?" I ask, pointing at the photograph again.

"Yeah, in some way or the other." He runs his palms carefully down the wall, smoothing everything in his path. "I thought, if you saw this, you would know it's not just four guys talking shit. It's real, Trin." He cautiously moves closer. "Can you see how real it is?"

"Where did you get the photo?" I force myself not to look at it, even though I'm itching to snatch it off the wall and burn it.

"High school yearbook. Tracked it down in a library a few years ago."

"How old is he?" My voice is hoarse now. I'm barely holding back...what? Anger? Fear?

Apollo is right. This changes everything. This photo?

*It. Changes. Everything.*

"So will you do it?" he asks. "Will you go back and try again?"

"I don't know." I have to crane my head to look up at him when he steps closer still. "I'd need more time, I think. Or maybe I did it wrong. Zachary said—"

"He lied." Apollo's eyes narrow. "He wanted you to think you'd fucked up so you'd try again."

My mouth falls open. "That's—"

"Why I brought you here." He squeezes my arm. "But please,

don't say anything. Not to anyone. Understand? No one can see this."

I nod mutely, wishing my skin would stop tingling where he touched me. Maybe it was our proximity, or my brain trying to cope with the next-level shit it had just been dealt...but suddenly I want nothing more than to kiss him.

He must see something in my eyes because his gaze drops to my lips a second before he ducks down and presses his mouth against mine.

Wanting and doing are two very different things, of course. No matter what I want, I shouldn't let him kiss me. I mean, what does that say about me?

*Blasphemous little sl—*

You know what? Fuck it.

I arch into him, tangling my fingers in his hair. If this is going to happen, then for once I'm going to be in charge of it fucking happening. No more being bullied. No more unwanted fingers in my yoohoo.

Apollo huffs out a laugh as we totter back from the force of my kiss. But instead of pushing me away, or laughing harder at my pathetic attempts at seduction, he slings an arm around my waist, hoists me up, and plops me onto the desk behind him.

The cold metal starts seeping through my dress.

But cold is the last thing on my mind.

I'm focused entirely on Apollo's mouth. But, also, how silky his hair feels as I twine it through my fingers. Then there's his intoxicating taste, and the way he urges my hips closer to his with both hands on the small of my back.

Okay, fuck it, my mind is going in fifty different directions. But just like that web on his board, everything leads back to him.

His kiss grows deeper. He slides his tongue into my mouth, cautiously curious, until I give him unrestricted access.

Then he kisses me so hard my core starts to ache, and I can't help but moan against his lips.

"Fuck, you taste good," he murmurs, a volley of hot pants brushing my skin as he pulls away. "I thought they were making that shit up."

Wait...*what*?

I shove him away. Stare open-mouthed.

He grins, rakes his hair out of his eyes, and pounces on me again without a word of warning.

They told him what I *tasted* like?

I thump a fist into his chest, but he just grabs my wrist and moves it off to one side without pausing his kiss.

It's ridiculous to attack him, especially since I'm still kissing him back. Fuck...kissing him back? I'm barely holding my ground. He's so passionate, so enthusiastic, my heart starts fluttering in my chest like a moth trapped in the tub.

But still I try and pound him with my other fist.

And then he snatches that one too. Now they're both at the small of my back, and he uses both hands to keep them there while he urges me forward, closer to the edge of the desk.

He tips his head forward, leaning his brow against mine. We're both panting, and this time it has nothing to do with climbing stairs.

"I could kiss you all day," he breathes, and then brushes his lips over my nose, my cheek, my ear. "But that bell's going to go off in a minute."

And then the craziest words fall out of my mouth. "Can we go back to your room?"

Hormones.

That's my story, and I'm sticking with it.

He grins against my mouth, and a happy huff caressing my lips. "I'd love to, but I can't. Raincheck?"

I nod, biting the inside of my lip hard enough that I'm surprised I don't taste blood.

He lifts me, twirling me around once before letting me slide to the ground, kissing me on the way down.

Then he herds me out of the tiny room, allowing me a precious second to stare at his media mural before he shuts the door and locks it.

When he turns, I force a wide smile onto my face and desperately hope he can't see through it.

That photo is going to haunt me. Those faces...

I push the thought out of my mind. It's pointless trying to understand, especially when the answer is but a question away.

Gabriel wants to see me? Well guess what...?

I *do* have questions for him.

## 33
## TRINITY

I spend a good half hour fussing with my hair as I stare at my reflection in the restroom mirror.

Stalling.

Trying to convince myself that going to see Gabriel is for the greater good, even if I'm not sure I actually want him to answer my questions.

Eventually there's nothing left to do but to start climbing those stairs.

I'm so deep in thought that I don't notice his door is open until I'm about to walk through.

I pause.

Should I announce myself or just go in? He did invite me and I doubt he'd leave the door open if he didn't want me to come inside.

The antechamber's door is partially closed. I step up to it and touch my hand to the worn wood before I hear their voices.

Thank God I stop to listen.

"I'm nothing like you! I'll *never* be like you!"

I flinch and snatch back my hand. What is Zachary doing

here? I back up, intent on turning tail and getting the hell out of here, but then I hear Gabriel's voice.

Compared to Zachary's outburst, his soft reply is barely audible. I move closer to the door and put my ear right by the crack.

"…only hate…for so…"

*Speak up, damn it.*

I move closer and push gently at the door so it swings a little wider. Zachary stands in the middle of the room, silhouetted by the fire.

There's a hand on the back of his neck.

"…nothing more to do but forgive."

I slap a hand over my mouth when Zachary twists away with a grimace on his face. Had Gabriel just tried to *kiss* him? I stagger back, but I can't bear to take my eyes away from them.

"So you can fuck a man, but you can't bear to kiss one?" Gabriel moves closer but Zachary retreats until his back is flush with the wall.

"It might feel like less of a sin but trust me, God has already condemned you to hell."

*What the fuck?*

My heart's in my throat as they glare at each other. The tension from whatever argument they were having before I arrived presses down like gravity on steroids.

I half-expect them to break into a fight, and the thought has my chest so tight I can't breathe.

My brain works overtime as I try to piece together what might have happened.

Is this because I told Zachary I wouldn't come back here? Did he decide to get the data himself? I turn, scanning the room through the door crack. The bed looks rumpled, and my stomach sinks.

Did they…?

*Oh my God.*

But then I spot the laptop on the dining table, lid closed, plugged in. I put a hand on my dress pocket. Apollo gave me back the drive just before we went our separate ways. He said I'd done everything right, but that the copy wasn't complete. Luckily, it wouldn't start from scratch—the device would check which files were already copied.

Five minutes, Apollo said.

Five minutes should do it.

I turn back to Zachary and Gabriel. They're both so tense, it's impossible to tell who's mad at whom. Seeing them side-by-side, I can't say which one would win in a fight. Gabriel has a good fifteen years on Zachary, but he's much more muscular than the younger man. I know Zachary's strong but is he strong enough?

If they started fighting…could I slip in and copy the files while they were distracted? I could hide under the tablecloth—it almost reaches the floor.

That's a big if.

Especially since now they both seem to be relaxing a little. Weighing each other up.

I can't imagine what's going through Zachary's mind, facing his nemesis like this.

I'd be terrified.

I don't know if I moved at just the right moment, but something makes Zachary look straight at me through the crack in the door.

His eyes flicker, but that's literally the only reason I have to think that he saw me.

"You're right," he says, pushing away from the wall. Gabriel stands his ground as he comes closer. My lungs are about to burst how I'm holding my breath. "I'm a sinner, Gabriel. Just like you."

Oh, God. What is he doing?

Zachary grabs Gabriel's shoulder. Gabriel doesn't even flinch.

"I guess even penance couldn't change that."

Zachary makes as if to walk past Gabriel, his hand slipping from Gabriel's shoulder. The priest turns to follow.

Putting his back to me.

Crap!

Zachary must have come to the same conclusion I did. But now I'm too terrified to move.

*Do it, Trinity. Do it!*

Just a few yards, then you're under the table cloth. Gabriel won't see you—he's completely fixated on—

Zachary's eyes slide past Gabriel and his lips twitch with what I've come to recognize as suppressed anger.

Wondering why I'm not moving. Why I'm wussing out like the pathetic wimp I am.

Despite what Apollo thinks—what I *made* him think—I didn't come here to steal Gabriel's private files. I came to confront him about that photo, the one that's been plaguing me since I laid eyes on it.

But now it feels like stealing the files is the *only* reason I'm here. Like this was fated from the moment I set foot in Saint Amos.

Gabriel must have seen Zachary's gaze shift. He turns to look behind his shoulder.

Zachary snarls.

My stomach folds in on itself like a poor attempt at a souffle.

*No. No! Don't—*

Zachary grabs Gabriel's jaw and wrenches the older man's head back to face them.

And kisses him.

My skin goes ice-cold, but the jolt of panicked adrenaline that spikes through me is enough to get me moving.

I push open the door, slip through, and pause just long

enough to close it again. Then I'm scampering silently over the carpet. I rush under the table cloth and almost knock my head against one of the table legs in my hurry to conceal myself.

I squat there for a moment, trying to muffle my too-fast breathing.

I shouldn't have bothered.

There's a soft sound a few feet away. Something whisking against leather, maybe.

I squeeze my eyes shut.

What the hell am I going to see when I emerge from this table cloth?

I push away the thought before it can debilitate me. I take the drive out of my pocket and uncap it, then steel myself with an unsteady breath.

One.

Two.

I slowly peek out from under the tablecloth. I'm close to the wall. Zachary and Gabriel were at least a yard or so behind me, to the right. I peer around the side of the tablecloth trying not to disturb it.

I see their legs and hurriedly retract into the safety of the tablecloth.

Shit. They're too close.

But I can't wait any longer. If I can slip the drive in without being seen, then I can probably just leave. Maybe Zachary can pull it out when—

*He's done fucking Gabriel?*

I squeeze my eyes shut.

*Fuck it, Trinity.* Focus.

When he's *done.*

Breathe in. Out.

*Much better.*

I duck out from under the tablecloth, letting it drape my

shoulders as I go to my knees. The chair Gabriel was using is in my way, so I have to twist awkwardly to get at the laptop.

Would it work with the lid closed? It'll have to, because I can't open it. That's something Gabriel would definitely notice.

I peek up over the top of the table and almost immediately latch eyes with Zachary.

Oh. My. God.

My lips part as a quiet shock rifles through me like wind through a discarded newspaper.

Gabriel sinks to his knees in front of Zachary, who's propped against the back of one of the armchairs on the other side of the room, his back to the fire.

There's a clink of a buckle as Zachary yanks open his belt.

But his eyes aren't on the priest in front of him.

They're on me.

Hot and livid.

*Look what you made me do, Trinity. Look what you* fucking *made me do.*

Guilt wracks me. My hand trembles uncontrollably as I try and push the drive into the slot on the side of the laptop.

Gabriel wrenches down Zachary's fly. I force my eyes to stay on the laptop, but those two bodies are stuck in my peripheral vision. Even blurred, I still know what's happening. What they're doing.

The drive twists, falling on the floor. I almost don't catch the hiccup of frustration that claws up my throat. I drop down, panicked tears filling my eyes.

Zachary groans.

Even that sounds angry.

*Look what you made me do.*

I snatch up the drive and straighten, not bothering to duck my head anymore. Gabriel has his back to me, and he's so focused on servicing Zachary's dick that I doubt he'd notice if the rapture happened.

Despite my trembling fingers, I force the drive into its slot.

Zachary's next groan drags my gaze back to him.

This time, I can't look away.

His head moves back, mouth parting. His Adam's apple bobs as he swallows. Then he grabs Gabriel's head, his fingers sinking deep into the man's dark hair.

He grunts as he forces Gabriel to move faster over his cock.

All the time glaring at me from across the room, lips parted, his whole body moving with each furious breath.

His jade eyes glitter with hatred. But none of it's focused on the man giving him head.

Every ounce of that rage, that revulsion…that disgust…

*Look what you made me do, little girl.*

His eyes flutter as he lets out a deep moan. As if that sound triggers the memory, his promise fills my head.

*Christ, we're going to enjoy making you bleed.*

I don't dare stay any longer in Gabriel's room, so I creep out while they're busy. I can only hope Zachary manages to take out the thumb drive without Gabriel noticing.

It shouldn't have been possible, but somehow—despite everything—I manage to fall asleep a few minutes after I get back to my room.

And not only do I sleep…I dream.

In my dream, Zachary's stalking me down the halls of Saint Amos.

I know it's him because when I turn my head fast enough, I

catch a glimpse before he ducks away behind a column or an open door.

When I try to run away from him, I quickly realize my top speed maxes out at a fast walk.

Which means it's only a matter of time before he catches up with me.

When I face forward again, Gabriel is waiting at the end of the hall for me. I come to a stop but the hallway keeps moving as if I'm standing on a conveyor belt.

Whether I like it or not, I'm headed straight for him. He opens his arms—a handsome, charismatic, modern-day Jesus with his short hair and dark eyes. His clothes flicker—priests robes, jeans, slacks—and then he's just wearing a loincloth.

His body gleams. Sweat? Oil?

A crown of thorns appears on his head.

They pierce deep. Draw blood.

A hot breath warms the back of my neck. I turn around. Now the hallway streams backward and it's Zachary I see. But I'm racing away from him, and he's reaching for me.

*I'm a sinner.*

I hear his voice even though his mouth doesn't move. In the blink of an eye, his face contorts into that of a maniac's—mouth twisted in a sadistic laugh, eyes wild—before smoothing into the mask of a saint.

*Just like you, little girl.*

Terrified, I spin around and start running away. The hallway zooms past in a blur.

Gabriel streams toward me. Dark, wet blood masks his entire face, the whites of his eyes too pure in contrast.

*He tends to his flock like a shepherd. He gathers the lambs in his arms and carries them close to his heart—*

I try to scream, but the sound stays lodged in my chest, burning.

*Burning.*

Gabriel's skin catches alight. He doesn't seem to notice. The only thing he cares about is holding me.

Comforting me.

Bringing me to the light. But if I so much as touch him, I'll be consumed in flames.

Zachary breathes on the back of my neck.

I spin around, body convulsing with horror.

He reaches for me, face flickering from saint to demonic sinner a thousand times a second, until it's nothing but a smudgy blur.

A hand clamps over my mouth, and muffles my terrified yell.

My eyes fly open.

A dark figure ducks down and slowly transforms into Apollo.

"Shh," he murmurs, putting a finger over his mouth. "It's just me, pretty thing."

I watch him with my heart thundering away in my chest.

He crouches beside my bed and puts his head close to mine, nuzzling the side of my throat.

But I can't shake the feel of Zachary's hot breath on the back of my neck, and that leaves me paralyzed.

"About that raincheck?" Apollo whispers into my ear.

## 34
## TRINITY

Maybe I'm still dreaming. I must be, because Trinity the Wimp would never follow Apollo anywhere in the middle of the night.

Never in a million years.

Right?

Because rational me knows that he's trouble, despite the cheeky grin he keeps sending my way, despite how he looks like he's bursting to tell me something juicy.

So I'm dreaming then. Which makes all of this much easier to process. Like when he says he hears someone coming, and suddenly presses me against the wall like we're in a spy movie and this is just an excuse for him to kiss me?

Well, don't think I don't know what he's trying to pull. His lips barely touch mine before I'm convinced this whole thing is an elaborate ruse.

But then I don't care anymore, because he's kissing me, and fuck my life, he's a good kisser.

We're partially hidden in one of the alcoves on the ground floor. I think he was leading me to the kitchen courtyard, even though I'm sure it would have been way too cold to be out in the open this time of night.

He barely gave me enough time to grab my slipper-boots, and all I've got on is a thin sweater and a pair of yoga pants that have started wearing out at the hems how I've stepped on them countless times before.

"I didn't hear anything," I murmur in lieu of a protest when he starts kissing my neck. "Are you sure there's someone—?"

He presses two fingers against my lips, silencing me as he grins down at me. "Nah. Just wanted to kiss you."

My tummy flips over at that. I bite the inside of my lip, and he must take it as a sign, because he ducks down again and captures my mouth with his.

When he kisses me, it's as if we only have seconds left to live.

His hands slide down my hips, caressing my ass through my thin pants. But he never squeezes, never gropes, never shoves anything anywhere. It's like he's exploring a foreign new land he's only ever heard of in fairy tales, and is determined to drink it all in.

But despite the fact that all we're doing is kissing, despite how I'm sure that's all he wants, my body responds to him like he's announced he's going to pop my cherry.

When his hands skim up my waist and begin exploring my breasts, my nipples instantly harden to tight buds.

He stops kissing me and leans back, staring down at my breasts like he's never seen a pair in his life.

Right—and he never looks through any of those porno mags in the Brotherhood's lair. As if.

His warm breath chases shivers through my body as he slips his hand under my sweater and scoops my breasts into his hands, weighing them in his palms.

My head falls back. I sigh as he strokes my skin and moan when he ducks his head and sucks one of my nipples into his mouth. But as soon as it disappears into his hot, hungry mouth, he pulls back and glances down the hallway like a double-agent sure he's been caught in the act.

"In here," he whispers, and drags me into the small prayer room where I first met Reuben.

I'm sure Reuben told them what had happened—they tell each other everything, after all—and my suspicion is confirmed when Apollo stops in his tracks and glances back at me with a sheepish grin on his face. "Is this cool?"

I don't know what comes over me. Maybe it's the fact that these four boys have been toying with me since the day I arrived. Maybe it's all the fucked up shit that's been circulating through my head the past few days.

It makes no sense, but suddenly I want nothing more than for Apollo to descend on me like a bird of prey on an unsuspecting rabbit.

I surge forward, grab his face in my hands, and kiss him as hard as I can.

In response, he circles my waist with his arms and spins me around and around until we bump into the altar.

He lifts me. My ass thumps onto the hardwood a second later. I wince into our kiss and he must suspect that he hurt me, because he darts back almost a yard and holds out his hands, palms out, like he's trying to fend off arrest.

"I'm so sorry. Shit. That was so stupid of me. Did I—?"

I'm almost fucking panting, and he has the nerve to run away? I shift closer to the edge of the altar and deliberately spread my legs.

He just stands there, looking like he's trying really hard to remember if he left the stove on.

So I beckon him like he's beckoned me so many times before. That works.

He surges forward, smiling into our kiss. But then he

deepens the kiss and urges me backward. I expect a hard wood floor beneath me, but he grabs one of the pillows reserved for pious knees and tucks it under me.

My heart wants to burst open at that simple gesture. When it seems everyone only ever wants to fuck you or spank you, someone giving you a pillow seems like the kindness of the century.

He lays on top of me, light and wiry compared with his brothers, but he more than makes up for it with passion. His lips scour mine, his tongue eager and demanding and gentle all at the same time.

When I start panting against his mouth, my body working overtime to try and process the delicious sensations he's wringing through me, his lips skate over my cheek and brush my ear, the side of my neck, my collarbones.

"Fuck," I murmur as my hands disappear into his hair.

I forgot how silky it was.

He grazes one of my nipples through my sweater, and I arch from the pillow. The fabric is already damp from his mouth, and when he moves to my other nipple, it grows cold in the tiny chapel's brisk air.

So I slide my hands over his shoulders, trying to keep him close so I can absorb the heat cascading from his body.

Which is when I feel his hard-on pressing into my leg.

And for the first time, that feeling doesn't freak me the fuck out. Instead, it flabbergasts me.

How can I do that to him? Does he really find me that sexy, that hot, that…fuckable?

I squirm under him, willing him to touch me somewhere other than my breasts. My nipples are already as tight as they can go—that pleasure turns into almost-pain.

When he doesn't move, when he keeps nibbling at my

nipples like we have all night and he's existed without sleep for centuries…well, I guess I feel I just have to take charge for once.

I grab his hand and mesh our fingers together.

Somehow, he takes that as a signal to start kissing my mouth again. He presses our interlaced hands above my head, pinning me as he forces his tongue between my lips and steals my breath away.

Which is all fine and well, but his kisses are only aggravating the now heavy throb emanating between my legs. I clamp my thighs together, but that doesn't help.

So I open my legs again and wrap them around his waist.

That, *finally*, gets his attention.

Apollo stops kissing me. He pops up onto his hands like he's doing push-ups and stares down at me with a look akin to panic on his face.

"No, shit, Trinity…"

"What?" Wow, why is my voice so hoarse? "What is it?"

"We can't do that, pretty thing."

"W—what?" My head's spinning from his kisses, and it takes a second for me to realize what he's saying. "You don't want to… you don't want to have sex with me?"

"No."

And then it's as if he's stomping on my fucking ribcage.

My legs fall away from his body, my feet thumping on the altar's wooden floor. I pull away from him and immediately start wriggling out from under his body, my cheeks on fire.

I don't think I've ever been this embarrassed in my whole fucking life. And I had to tell Father Gabriel that my mother caught me masturbating in the bathtub, so the bar's pretty fucking high.

"Hey, wait now, I didn't mean it like that."

"No, really, it's fine," I mutter. I stumble to my feet, pushing him out of the way when he jumps up and tries to stop me from leaving.

"You don't understand," he calls out. "I can't!"

I come to a stop, head low and curtained by my disarrayed curls. "Can't, or won't?"

And then I wait for whatever vague, bullshit excuse he expects me to accept. Because that's how it is with the Brotherhood. They're so caught up in their own shit, they don't realize that the people around them have a right to know what's really going on in their heads.

Even if it's tragic. Or horrific. Or downright psychotic.

You can't trust a stranger. And they'd always be strangers to me until they actually started telling me the—

"It's…kinda complicated."

And there it is.

"Yeah, well, I've had enough *complicated* to last me a lifetime, thanks," I call out behind me without turning around. I storm to the little prayer room's door, fumbling for that special spot—

Apollo grabs my shoulder and turns me around. "But if you have a minute," he says quietly, "I can try and explain."

It takes longer than a minute, but fuck does he do a lot of explaining.

I sip at my hot chocolate as I peek at Apollo from under my lashes. He brought me to the bell tower after fixing me the drink so we could talk. He's wearing a puffy bomber jacket, and I'm cuddling into a blanket.

One of the things he told me was that he wasn't allowed to fuck me.

Girls, sex, money, clothes, parties, sports, movies, games—
they were all distractions.

The Brotherhood had sworn an oath to each other. And
nothing—*nothing*—was as important as that oath.

"So…none of you have ever really dated anyone?"

I'm more than a little tired. It's exhausting just *kissing* Apollo
—having him explain the intricacies of the relationship between
four friends who met in a sex dungeon when they were kids…

I'm too scared to tip my head to the side in case all that
information pours out of my ears.

At least he made me hot chocolate. And it's fucking
delicious. And at least, tonight, we can see the view. Which is
fucking spectacular.

But the Brotherhood's personal life?

I. Can't. Even.

"I guess." He tugs at his cigarette and exhales a plume of
smoke into the black night. "Although, Cass once brought home
this chick—"

"Home? Where?"

He flicks ash from his cigarette. "Virginia. Zach rented us a
house. We only stayed six months or so." He takes another drag.
"But it was home while it lasted."

"How old were you?"

He lifts the hand holding the cigarette and squints as he
scratches his head. "Shit. I dunno. Sixteen? Seventeen? Zach
might have been nineteen already. But anyway, Cass was still
getting fucked up back then, and when he went out to go score,
he picked up this random chick. Think she was fucked on
heroine too, I can't remember. Anyway, he brought her home,
back to us."

My body goes rigid. I'm not sure I want to hear what
happened to the fucked up girl. And Cass did drugs? It's like I'd
need an encyclopedia to keep track of these guys.

"…and then she was all like, you don't have to pay me, I'll just take the dope—"

"But Cass tried to fuck me," I cut in. "More than once." I turn to look at Apollo. "Why do you let him get away with it?"

Apollo flinches, maybe because I sound so fucking bitter, but what? Am I supposed to be nice about the fact that Cass can assault me when his brothers aren't even allowed to touch me?

"He can't help himself," Apollo says.

I laugh. "Are you for real?"

"He has impulse issues."

I frown over at him. "What's that supposed to mean?"

"You take psych, don't you?" Apollo shrugs. "We all got our issues. Cass can't keep it in his pants. It's like he blacks out or something." He waves a hand, smoke trailing erratically behind his cigarette. "Zach can explain it better than me."

"So that's it? He has issues, so he can get away with whatever he wants?"

"Yeah, no," Apollo murmurs. "On that count, you're very fucking wrong." He stands. "Anyway, you have school tomorrow. You should get back to bed."

I stand and quickly drain the last of my hot chocolate.

"Just leave it there," he says, waving in the general direction of the cup as he walks past me. "I'll come fetch it tomorrow."

My eyes skip past him. The door he took me through yesterday is hidden behind the massive bronze bell. If I had X-ray vision, I would have been able to see that incriminating photo through the bell and the wall.

I hurry to catch up to Apollo. "Did you find anything?"

"Hmm?" He flicks the butt of his cigarette over the balcony and glances down at me a second before he slides his arm over my shoulder and hugs me closer. "Oh, yeah. Fuck. I totally forgot to tell you."

I stop walking.

He turns, frowning curiously as he faces me. "What now?" he asks through a laugh.

"What did you find?"

"You sound surprised. Did you think we wouldn't?"

"Apollo!"

He shrugs. "We found what we were looking for, Trin." When I scowl at him, he uses a thumb to smooth down my brows. "Sorry, but it's not my place to tell you."

"Then whose it is?"

Another shrug. "Speak to Reuben. Maybe he'll tell you."

"And if he won't?"

Apollo bops my nose with a knuckle. "Then I guess you'll just have to keep asking until you find what *you're* looking for."

# 35

# TRINITY

R euben isn't in morning prayers. I wolf down my breakfast and hunt around the campus for him, but without being able to ask anyone where he is, it's no surprise when I turn up empty-handed.

Gabriel said he was the same year as me, but I haven't seen him in any of my classes. I could see if he's attending one of the others this morning. So I head out early to the classroom block and stalk the halls like a petite, poop-colored version of Death.

But either he has a free period this morning or he's playing hooky, because I don't spot him anywhere.

Cass looks up when I walk into English class five minutes late, and sends the kind of wolfish grin I've come to expect from him my way.

Because I'm late, Sharon gives me a rap on my knuckles that stings well into the rest of the lesson. It's impossible to miss how much Cass enjoys my punishment—I'd be shocked if he doesn't have a boner.

A few minutes into the lesson, a teacher comes to speak to

Sister Sharon. She instructs us to read from our textbooks while she's gone before slipping out of the classroom.

"Morning, slut," Cass whispers into my ear before the door's finished swinging closed. "Hear you've been sticking your nose where it doesn't belong again."

I sit forward, crossing my arms over my chest and pretending to ignore him.

If I can't find Reuben, then the alternative is asking Zachary or Cass. But screw that, there's no way I'll be asking Cass anything.

I'll find Reuben, even if I spend all day looking.

Thank God it doesn't take me the whole day. A few minutes before lunch I pass the little prayer room. The hall is empty, so on impulse, I decide to slip inside and check for Reuben.

He's kneeling on one of the cushions, head bowed, hands meshed in prayer.

"Hey," I call out, and then do a double take.

Is that the same pillow—?

Nope. *Push that thought right out of your mind, Trinity.*

Walking closer, I brush my collarbones. Is it weird that I miss his rosary? I'd gotten into the habit of toying with it—I had to go back to playing with my hair instead.

I stand for a minute or so behind him, but he doesn't acknowledge my presence. If my business with him hadn't been so urgent, I'd have taken the hint and left.

But I have to know what they found. If they have actual evidence against Gabriel…

I go to kneel beside him, grabbing another cushion for my

knees. I glance at him and then mimic his pose.

And I manage to stay that way for a whole ten seconds before my patience runs out.

"I'm sorry to interrupt you—"

"Then don't," Reuben says.

Wow. Cranky much? I shift on the cushion, glancing at him again.

His red rosary is tangled in his fingers, the crucifix dangling down between his wrists.

I have to get him to talk to me. If not him, then who? Zachary? Cass?

I'd rather poke a fork in my eye.

"I'm sorry about…the other night."

"Which one?"

At first I think he's playing it cool. He'd have to be, pretending my rejection didn't affect him.

But what if it truly *didn't*? What if he's moved on? Apollo said they all had complicated relationships with, well, relationships in general. Sex was even more complicated.

"I was upset, okay?"

Reuben stays silent.

"After what Cass did—"

"What's this got to do with him?" Reuben asks, finally straightening and turning to look at me.

"W-well, he tricked me." I frown up at Reuben. Even with both of us on our knees, he's a foot taller than me.

Just tell him, Trinity. What's the worst that can happen?

"I thought he was you," I blurt out.

Reuben frowns. "What are you talking about?"

"The shower?" My cheeks start heating up, but I forge ahead before I can lose my nerve. "I only let him touch me because I thought he was you."

Reuben watches me, expressionless, silent.

"My eyes were closed."

Nothing.

"Because of the soap."

You'd swear he was a marble statue, not a living, breathing man. Although I'm only guessing that he's breathing right now, because it's definitely not apparent.

"I just...you've got to see it from my perspective, right? You guys...you tell each other everything. Share everything. It's... kinda weird for me, okay? It feels like you're ganging up on me."

And then I stop, because honestly I've run out of words.

He tilts his head a little. "Don't good friends tell each other everything?"

"Not like that," I say through a laugh, but I cut off the sound prematurely.

How the fuck would I know? My best friend used to be Gabriel.

The thought sends a wave of shameful heat coursing through me.

I realize now I was the only one of us who thought that. To him I was his lover's daughter. A member of his flock, nothing more. I bet the only reason he ever spoke to me was at the request of my parents. They probably begged him to get me more involved in the church.

In God.

Reuben grabs my chin and lifts my head back up, forcing me to look at him. "I'm not angry with you, Trinity."

For some fucked up reason, that admission makes my heart flutter. "Oh. You just seemed—"

"But I wouldn't want to expose you to anything that makes you uncomfortable."

He releases me, and I wish he hadn't.

"I realize it's asking a lot, probably too much, for you to accept us the way we are."

Something in his tone makes my chest grow tight. "You mean…?"

He waits for me to finish, but I have to swallow down the lump in my throat first.

"You mean…you *want* to go out with me?"

The edges of his mouth quirk up.

He shakes his head, and grabs hold of one of my curls. His eyes shift to his fingers as he winds it around his digit. "It's not that simple."

I try and pull my hair free, but he's got it good and twisted.

I let out a confused chuckle. "But…then I don't—"

He pulls me closer. "And even if I asked, you'd never say yes."

"Of course I would." My eyebrows flinch into a quick frown. "That's what…I mean, I just said—"

He laughs, but without humor. "Are you sure?"

I nod, and then wince when the movement tugs at my scalp.

"No backing out," he warns, moving closer still.

My heart's beating faster the closer he comes. "Why would I want to?"

"Because," he murmurs, his lips brushing mine.

My eyes flutter closed and my mouth parts, fully expecting a kiss. "Because why?"

"I'm not sure you can handle it."

"Only one way to find out."

"I guess."

Oh my God, is he never going to kiss me?

"So do it." Find out, kiss me, whatever the hell. Just do it.

"And what about them?"

"Who?" My thoughts are already evaporating like fog.

"My brothers?"

"Fuck 'em." I murmur.

"That's just it, Trinity."

Despite it tugging my scalp again, I move back so I can look into his eyes. I don't like the tone in his voice. And when we lock eyes, I like the strange gleam in his even less.

"That's what? Stop going in circles. I know it's complicated." Suddenly, my mouth doesn't seem to have an off switch anymore. "Apollo told me. Sex, girls, whatever—too distracting. No relationships. But you're all big boys now, I'm sure you can multi-task." I lean in again. "Now are you going to kiss me, or what?"

He laughs and slides a hand around the back of my neck. But he still doesn't close the distance.

"So he told you everything, did he?"

"Yeah."

"Hmm. Then I guess you really *are* sure," he says. "Trinity Malone…will you go out with us?"

Yes!

"Yes!"

Fucking finally.

His eyes light up with a smile. He presses his lips to mine, but we barely touch before my mind finally catches up with me.

Will you go out with us.

*Us.*

"Wait…" I push away from him and hold up a finger. "Hold on. Did you say—?"

"I thought Apollo explained it?" Now he's looking…not upset, but maybe a little impatient. Or frustrated. Maybe he really wants to kiss me as badly I want to kiss him.

"I think, maybe, he might have left some stuff out," I say quietly, my shoulders sagging.

Reuben nods. "We're a package deal, Trinity."

My brain instantly rejects the thought. "But—"

He puts a finger on my lips. "That's why I didn't stop you when you left. It's always too complicated. Girls like things simple." His dark eyes flash. "We're not."

Understatement of the fucking century.

He stands and gets ready to leave, putting his rosary around his neck, buttoning up his shirt again.

Well fuck this. I'm not leaving empty-handed.

"Apollo said you found something in Gabriel's files."

Reuben pauses as if considering my statement, and then nods just once.

"Can you tell me what it is?"

He goes to his haunches in front of me and watches me for a moment as if he's trying to figure out how sincere I'm being.

"That's the thing with us, Trinity. You're either with us, or you're against us." He smiles, not unkindly, and traces my bottom lip with his thumb. "There's no in-between."

# ZACH

My last student files out of the door seconds before
Reuben steps into my class. I happen to glance up, and
do a double take when I see him.

"What the hell are you doing here?" I widen my eyes at him
as I hurry past to force the door closed faster than the hydraulic
normally allows. "Did anyone see you?"

Reuben doesn't have a class with me, and I've made a point
of not associating with him in the dorms. Cass being the hallway
monitor gives us a little more leeway, but this…?

"You weren't checking your phone," he says, not even
seeming apologetic for contravening our strict guidelines. "It's
important."

"So what is it?" I ask, and then duck my head forward when
nothing changes on his stony face. "Well?"

"Trinity came to see me. Wants to know what we found."

"And?" I cross my arms over my chest. "What did you say?"

"What you told me to." He shrugs. "But it's been hours. I
don't think it worked."

"Of course it did," I tell him, pushing the words through my teeth as I head back to my desk. This was my last lesson of the day—I was on my way to pack up and head back to my room. I shove my handbook in my drawer and remove my cell phone. There are a handful of notifications on the screen—so many that most of them are crowded out. The last few are from Reuben. "So what's so urgent it couldn't wait?"

"We're running out of time for your games. Why can't we just tell her about—?"

"Why are you risking everything coming here to argue over something we've already discussed?" I shove the phone in my pocket and head for the door. "The decision's been made. Now get out before someone sees you."

I turn, my hand on the door handle, to see if he has any last words before we exit the classroom. His eyes narrow, but that's the extent of irritation he ever shows.

Reuben's like an iceberg, though—what you see on the surface is only a tenth of what's lurking below. If he looks this annoyed, he's close to a meltdown.

"We have until Friday," I tell him, my words exiting with a sigh. "Trinity will come around by then."

"But if we just told her—"

My hand tightens on the handle, but I force my voice to remain at the same level. "Then what, Reuben? She'll *trust* us? Trust requires proof, belief doesn't. You want her to trust us? I want her to have *faith* in us like she should have from the beginning."

"Blind faith?" he asks.

"Best kind there is."

He opens his mouth, possibly to carry on arguing, but cuts off when the door opens under my hand. I take a hasty step back so it won't crash into me, my heart doing acrobatics at the thought of who was about to walk in on Reuben and me.

Apollo's blond head peeks around the door, his eyes going

wide when he sees me, and then wider still when he sees Rube. "Thank fuck I found you," he says.

"The hell are you doing here?" I whisper furiously.

"It's important, and you weren't answering your—"

I grab him by his shirt and drag him inside, closing and locking the door behind him. "Christ, what the fuck has gotten into you two?" I turn on them, but don't get a word out.

Apollo's very rarely serious, but right now he could be running for fucking president.

"What?" I bark out.

"I started searching manually through everything Trinity copied. I just found a bunch of emails," he says, voice wooden. His mouth twitches as he starts nibbling on the inside of his cheek. His eyes flicker to Reuben. "You're not going to believe this."

# 37

# TRINITY

The church goes quiet when Father Gabriel climbs onto the altar. I'm sitting right by the door of the chapel, hoping I can be the first to get out of here at the end of morning prayers.

I still have no idea what I'm going to do. As much as I want —*need*—to know what the Brotherhood found, Reuben's words keep going through my head.

*You're either with us, or you're against us.*

But I can only decide which side I'm on once they tell me what they have on Father Gabriel. They could be bluffing. Trying to get me on their side so they can use me for their own nefarious purposes.

And then there's the other thing Reuben said. How they're a *package* deal.

He wasn't talking about their war, or their oaths, or any of that shit.

He was talking about me and him. Or…I guess…me and *them*.

Definitely not the sort of stuff I should be contemplating in a house of worship. I might just catch on fire and I doubt any amount of Holy Water could put me out.

The hall shushes as soon as Father Gabriel walks onto the stage. I study him as circumspectly as possible as he leads us through a prayer. Usually we go through announcements and read a bible verse before ending on the Father's Prayer and being dismissed. But this morning, everything feels like it's taking a thousand times longer.

So, like always, I zone out.

And I'm only wrenched back to the here-and-now when everyone inside the hall breaks out into cheers.

My heart pounds in response to the unexpected ruckus as I hurriedly scan the hall to figure out what I'd missed. Some students even have the gall to stand up, but they hurriedly sit when Gabriel lifts his hands to silence the crowd.

"The buses arrive at seven tomorrow morning. Please ensure you are ready to depart so we don't have any delays."

I sit back, shoulders sagging in relief. The last I'd heard, the buses taking us to Sisters of Mercy were supposed to arrive on Saturday—now they'd be here tomorrow. Three days early.

But that relief evaporates a second later.

What am I going to do?

I need to find out what the Brotherhood knows. I thought I'd still have a few days, but now…?

My mind is made up about Sisters of Mercy. I don't belong here anyway—I can finish my senior year over there. At least I can make some friends there.

But I can't leave without knowing.

Guess I'm going to have to bite the bullet. Much as I didn't want to, I'll have to track down Zachary and speak to him. I'll probably have to trade a few spanks for the info, but I survived those last—

"—nity Malone, please come see me after assembly."

Shock flashes through me. Did Gabriel just call my name?

A few of the boys sitting in the pew in front of me glance back in my direction.

Shit. What does Gabriel want with me?

Oh, right.

He wants to *talk*.

I cross my arms over my chest and hug myself hard, my mind like a kicked-over anthill as Gabriel runs through the last announcements.

I don't join in for the Father's Prayer, and that gets me more than a few scandalized stares from the boys around me.

Let them stare.

Gabriel knows I'm not a believer. It wouldn't surprise him in the least to hear I sat this one out.

When kids stream past me on their way outside after assembly ends, I consider for a full minute what the repercussions would be if I just left but I'd just be delaying the inevitable. Plus, Gabriel would never let me climb on a bus tomorrow without talking to me.

I wait for the majority of the boys to leave, and then make my way to the front of the hall, fully expecting Gabriel to be waiting in the small room just off the stage.

He's not.

So I head to the only other place he could be.

I've been knocking on a lot of doors lately. Would be excellent practice if I ever decide to become a missionary like my father.

There's a grim smirk on my face when the door opens.

I stand there for a second, speechless, before I lower my

hand. If Gabriel had been here, I'd have expected him to ask me to come inside, not to answer the door himself.

"I wasn't sure if you'd come," he says. His eyes dart past me, and then he waves me inside his apartment. "Let's talk inside, child."

I scrape up every spare bit of courage I still have left after his miraculous appearance. "No."

He frowns. "I'm not going to talk to you out in the hall," he says, his eyebrows drawing together. "This is a personal—"

"You're right, you're not going to talk to me." I push back my shoulders and hold up my chin. He's so much taller than me, but somehow it helps. "Honestly, I think you've said enough."

He tilts his head a little, eyes flinching as if I caused him actual pain. My chest tightens at that, but fuck it. I'm not the one in the wrong here. Not even a little.

"I came because you're the Provost, and I'd probably get detention or something if I didn't. But I'm not here to talk, and I won't listen to anything you have to say."

*Thump, thump, thump* goes my heart in the sudden silence following my statement.

For a moment, I think he's going to ignore everything I said and just drag me inside anyway. But then his eyes drop, and he lets go of the door handle.

"I'm sorry you feel that way." His eyes fix on me again, studying me for a second as if wondering how far he can push my moratorium. "But I didn't mean to hurt you, Trinity."

I lift my chin a little higher. "By sleeping with him, or telling me about it?"

"I know what I did was wrong. I should have stopped it. No —I should never have let it happen in the first place." Again, his gaze drops. "But your father is a very persuasive man."

I go from an imperious glare to a confused frown. "What do you mean—?"

"I—" Gabriel's mouth tightens, and then he steps back. "Please. At least just let me close the door."

I shouldn't show him any quarter, but for some reason I do. For some fucked up reason, I step forward and let him close the door behind me. We stand in the small antechamber, both stiff and uncomfortable and looking away from each other.

"I should have stopped the affair before it began, but I was… weak. And every time I broke it off, all it would take was one email from Keith, and I'd be back."

I squeeze my eyes shut as my cheeks start heating. "Please stop. I don't want to know."

But he doesn't. He just keeps telling me things I don't want to hear.

"I told your mother we had to tell you, but she said it wasn't any of your business. And that hurt me, Trinity, because I believe you had every right to know."

My eyes flicker up to him, my mouth going dry. "Mom…*knew*?"

He nods. "Yes. It was…she…" Gabriel clears his throat. "Are you sure you won't—?" He twists to grab the handle of the door leading into his room.

"No. You said one minute." I hug my chest and try to will myself to leave. I guess it's morbid fascination keeping me here.

"It was her suggestion," he says.

An incredulous laugh tears through me. "Oh my God, do you honestly expect me to believe—"

"In an effort to keep their marriage intact, she suggested we—"

"No!" I yell out, lifting both hands to ward him off. "Fuck no. You are *not* trying to convince me that my mom has anything to do with this!" There's laughter in my voice, but it's far from pleasant. I take a step closer, stabbing a finger toward him. "And because they're both dead, I'll never be able to confirm or deny any fucking thing you tell me, anyway. So why not blame everything on her, right? Make it out as if my dad was the one who—"

I cut off with a disgusted sound.

"You're not fooling anyone," I whisper as my eyes start filling with tears. I step back, fumbling behind me for the handle without taking my eyes off Gabriel. I grab it, wrench it open, back up.

"Especially not me." I swipe at my wet cheeks, shaking my head as I scowl over at him.

He hasn't moved, hasn't tried to get another word in. And thank the Lord for that, because I might have physically attacked him if he'd tried.

I point at him again. "They were right all along." The world blurs, but I blink hard to jar those hot tears from my eyes.

"Who?" Gabriel demands evenly as he steps forward. His expression is neutral, but there's anger in those brown eyes.

I step into the hall, my lips twisting so hard I almost can't get the words out. But when I do, they echo down the hall.

"Burn in hell, Gabriel! You fucking burn in hell!"

## 38

## TRINITY

W eed and cigarette smoke taint the air. I shouldn't be here, but I couldn't keep away any longer. My curiosity is stronger than my fear, and it's what compelled me to slip out of bed as soon as Jasper fell asleep.

It's what has kept me moving down the stairs and across the lawn and through the crypt.

It's what is keeping me here now.

I would have come sooner, but I told myself I'd wait. With each passing hour, the certainty that I had to come here, that I had to do this, grew and grew until I couldn't think of anything else.

I want to know what they found.

I want to know what Reuben meant.

I want to know…what it *feels* like.

And I'm hoping, dear Lord I'm hoping it will make the pain in my heart go away. Because after I yelled at Gabriel like that, it's as if someone's spent the rest of the day carving a hole in my chest with a red-hot poker.

Digging, and digging.

Fuck knows what they're looking for, but if it's sympathy or forgiveness…spoiler alert—they won't find any.

My fingers brush the drape disguising the entrance to the Brotherhood's lair. It's quiet out here—so quiet I'm starting to wonder if I'll walk into an empty room like last time.

*Like last time? You mean when Zachary was here and he spanked you until you almost had an orgasm?*

Yeah, fuck, like last time.

I didn't want to wander down here in my pajamas, so I slipped on one of my church dresses before climbing into bed. But now I'm regretting it, because the more modest of the two dresses hasn't come back from the laundry yet, and this one ends at my knees.

I feel naked.

When I pull away the curtain, orange light cascades into the dimly lit library. If someone is inside and facing the exit they could probably see my hand jutting through. But no one announces my arrival.

I haven't yet decided if I *want* them to be here, or if I want the place to be empty. I'll never have the courage to come back. But will I have the courage to stay if they're here?

When I sidle through that opening and come out on the other side, the decision is taken away from me.

The Brotherhood *is* here. And from the looks on their faces, they were expecting me an hour ago.

Zachary's on his wooden chair, Apollo lounging in the duct-taped armchair. Cass and Reuben share the couch like they have each time I've been here. A joint is making the rounds. This time, everyone takes a drag before passing it on. When it reaches Apollo, he stands and comes over to me with it, holding it out.

I take it. Study it. Smoke it.

It's strong enough to make me cough, and Apollo looks like he's holding back a smile. When I try to give it back to him, he shakes his head and his eyes move back to it, then to my mouth. A silent command for me to take another hit.

I'd only be fooling myself if I thought I had a choice in the matter, so I take another drag and hand it back. This time he takes it, hitting it on the way to Zachary.

He takes a last drag and then extinguishes the burning tip between his fingers.

Then there's silence.

Just four men watching.

Waiting for me to speak.

I step closer, hugging myself. It's colder down here than I remember. Probably because it's past midnight already. There's no heat down here—the room is brisk, despite their body heat.

"I want to know what you found," I say, staring at each of them in turn, but landing last on Zachary and holding his gaze. "I have a right to know."

Zachary laughs.

Just once.

Roughly.

And with not a trace of humor.

Suddenly the room is a lot colder.

"I can't argue with that," he says, and slowly gets to his feet. "In fact, I think it's downright impolite for us to keep anything from you anymore, right guys?"

There's a muted, "Right" from the others.

Impolite?

I sense danger in the air, and it has nothing to do with the way Zachary's stalking over to me like he has all day to pounce.

Something's happened.

Something's changed.

But what?

"So go on then." My hug intensifies, until I start losing feeling in my fingertips. "Tell me."

Zachary tuts me. "First, I feel we owe you an apology, Miss Malone."

I don't like the way he says my name.

I don't like it one bit.

"For what?" When I frown at him, a faint smile touches his mouth.

"For treating you so poorly. For withholding information. Withholding...our *affection*."

My eyes dart to Apollo, but he looks away. When I turn to Reuben, his face hardens.

What the hell is going on?

Maybe I *am* too late—a bottle of whiskey and several joints too late. The malevolence seeping out of these men feels like it's all directed at me.

Just your imagination.

Just your—

"So I think it's time we righted some of those wrongs, don't you?"

I shake my head. "Stop with the games. Just tell me what you found and then I'll leave."

Zachary snatches my wrist, moving so fast that I don't have time to step back. "No, see, Miss Malone...we *insist*."

Trinity's pulse flutters like a hummingbird's heart under my thumb. She's not terrified, but definitely unnerved. I guess it's a good thing I went ahead and smoked as much as Apollo said I should. The last thing I want is to accidentally break this pretty little thing.

Not when there's still so much pain to wring out of her.

And pleasure, of course, but that has always been secondary.

"Cass," I call out. "Get ready."

Trinity's amber eyes open a touch wider. She tries to peer around me, but I move to the side and block her view. "Let's not spoil the surprise."

From behind me comes the sound of someone's belt being removed. The metallic clink of the buckle sends a rush of blood to my cock. She has no idea what's coming...but I can see she's already convinced herself she knows exactly what will happen next. Meanwhile, I'm getting a semi just from the thought of what we have in store for her.

I cup her face in my hand. "We made a deal a few days ago, do you remember?"

Her face turns a shade paler. When I take a step back, urging her forward, she digs in her heels instead. "No," she murmurs, shaking her head.

"You don't remember?"

"No, Zachary, please. I…" Her brow furrows, and she darts to the side to see past me again.

With another smooth step, I block her view. I grab her chin, wrenching her head back and forcing her to look up at me.

"That's not how this works, girl. You want something, and so do we."

She flinches at the pet name. "I've changed my mind. I don't—"

I dig my fingers into her chin, feeling her jaw move as she snaps her mouth closed.

"Of course you do. Stop denying it."

I'm holding her too tight for her to nod but I take the widening of her eyes as agreement.

"Good. No use wasting our energy on fighting." I turn my head a little. "Ready, Cass?"

"Yeah." He sounds too serious. Grim, almost.

Goosebumps break out on my bare arms, and it has nothing to do with the chill air down here.

We're used to the cold, my brothers and I. That basement was cold and damp and disgusting—so it's no wonder. Trinity's little dress doesn't seem to be keeping her very warm taking into account her trembling lips and cool skin.

But it could also be fright.

Because when someone behind me snaps a belt those bright, amber eyes dull, dread replacing her uneasiness. She even stops shivering for a second as she turns those terrified eyes to me.

Yeah, keep your eyes on me, little girl. Because if you happen to look down, you'll get an idea of just how much I'm enjoying this.

Which is exactly what she does. She rips her face out of my fingers, leaving red marks behind, and tries to peel my fingers off her wrist.

"Let me go," she murmurs. "Please, Zach, let me go."

"So now it's *Zach*?" I jerk her into me, grab the small of her back and grind my dick into her stomach. "And when exactly did we become such good friends?"

Something akin to a whimper escapes her lips. She starts struggling against me, another breathless, "No!" slipping out of her trembling lips.

"Jesus, is this happening or not?" Cass demands behind me.

Guess I go out of my way to be cruel sometimes, even to those who don't deserve it.

I grab Trinity's arms, fumbling with her when she tries to rip free, and turn her to face my brothers. She tries to step back, but I keep her in place with my body.

We don't have the kind of props and equipment down here that we had in the basement. No wire-framed beds with handy straps. No suspended rails and butcher's hooks.

But we have Reuben.

He's sitting on the couch, feet firmly planted. Cass is kneeling on the floor in front of him, buck naked.

When Trinity goes rigid in my arms, Cass glances up at Reuben and gives him a barely perceptible nod.

Reuben breaks eye contact, and his usually emotionless face turns to stone. He grabs Cass's upper arms and wrenches him forward.

Tonight, Rube will be our brace *and* our straps.

Cass folds over Rube's lap, burrowing his head into the couch beside Reuben's hip, baring his already bruised ass to Trinity.

"Who did that to you?" she gasps.

Aw, fuck. Ain't she the cutest?

Trinity hurries forward the instant I release her. While she falls to her knees beside Cass for all the world like a fucking mother hen, I walk past Apollo to fetch the belt he's holding out to me.

"I did," I say.

Cass lets out a soft grunt when my belt slams against his flesh.

Trin yelps in surprise and falls back, flashing me her white panties and a horrified expression as she scrambles away.

I expect her to start crying.

Maybe even run.

Instead, she bolts to her feet and shoves me hard enough to make me take a step back.

"Stop!" she yells, putting herself between Cass and me. "Stop hitting him!"

"Hear that, Cass?" I ask, absently snapping the belt as Trinity shows me her teeth. "She wants me to stop."

"Jesus, fuck," Cass groans, which is surprisingly articulate for him at a time like this.

I try to keep my eyes on Trinity, but it's impossible with Cass busy having a fucking apoplexy behind her.

She doesn't have a fucking clue. Not a single goddamn clue.

She's hurting him more than my belt ever could.

"Put it down," she says, holding out her hand. "Just…put it down."

It must be the weed, because I legit want to humor her, just to see how far this goes before she realizes what the hell's going on.

I can see why Rube likes her so much.

Fucking adorable, she is.

I haven't met something this innocent since my parents tossed Cass down those basement stairs, nearly breaking the poor kid's neck. That didn't happen again, of course, not after his first Ghost saw the scratch he'd gotten on his pretty fucking face.

Oh no.

After that, *nothing* touched his face.

Or Rube's.

Or Apollo's.

I wasn't there because I was pretty, so they felt they could hit me wherever the fuck they wanted. One of them even broke my nose.

Luckily, I don't scar as easily as Cass.

Luckily, mine wasn't the first nose the Ghosts broke in that basement, and by the time they broke mine, Rube had experience in straightening broken bridges.

"You think I want you to watch me belt him?" I ask Trinity, genuinely intrigued.

"I don't care what you want," she says. "Just give it here, okay?" She flicks her fingers, but doesn't look at the belt. Keeps her eyes on me. Like I'm a wild animal bound to attack as soon as she breaks eye contact.

I guess I am, at that.

Her eyes flicker when I hand her the belt. "Okay," she murmurs. Then she glances at Rube. "Now how about you let him go? Please?"

"Why are you sticking up for him?" Apollo asks as he collapses into his couch, a freshly rolled joint dangling from his lips. "Thought you had it in for him?"

"I didn't say that," she says, frowning briefly at Apollo before looking at me again. "Can Reuben let him go?"

I lean my weight back on one foot. "We're not done here yet."

"Please, Zachary. Whatever he's done…he doesn't deserve this."

The smirk falls right off my face.

She shakes her head, those amber eyes glowing with naivety.

"No matter what he's done, you can forgive him. You're friends, aren't you?"

A soft laugh huffs out of me. "You think he deserves forgiveness?"

"Yes." She nods firmly. "Definitely."

"Fine. We'll forgive him. But on one condition…"

Her eyes become wary, searching my face as if she can try and spot where I'm headed. But if she hasn't figured it out by now, it's not gonna happen.

"What?" she asks reluctantly.

Apollo lights the joint. A haze of weed smoke fills the space between.

I smile at her as I lean forward. She flinches when I touch the belt in her hands, but since I don't try and take it away, she doesn't fight me.

"You take his place."

I'm about ready to pee myself. Of all the possibilities I'd dreamed up, Zachary belting Cass while Reuben held him down and Apollo watched…

Yeah, that never came up.

I wince as Zachary tightens his grip.

I don't want him hitting Cass, but…I don't want him hitting me either.

At least, not with a fucking belt.

I don't know where I summon the courage, but perhaps it's because I've managed to convince myself that this is the lesser of two evils.

I move the belt to the side. "You can use your hand."

Surprise or irritation flickers in Zachary's eyes. He rips the belt out of my hand and grabs the front of my throat.

"You get the belt, or Cass gets the belt. It's that fucking simple."

He's not choking me, else I'd have fought him. Maybe I can still reason with him. "What did he do to you?" I murmur, trying to keep my voice for Zachary's ears alone. "Why do you have to hurt him?"

But this place is too small, because Cass hears me.

"What did I do?" Cass says.

Unwilling, my eyes drop to where he's still kneeling a few feet beside me. And no matter how hard I try, I can't look away.

It's not just that he's beautiful. And I mean, holy hell, he's the kind of handsome where if you saw him in a movie or in a magazine, you'd spend a good few minutes wondering about him. What his life was like, where he lived, if he had a dog, how much he was paid and whether that was a lot of money to someone like him.

Even naked, bruised, and wearing a condescending smirk, my stomach flips over at the thought that someone as gorgeous as him is speaking to me.

Me.

Trinity Malone.

A no-fucking-body.

Somehow, I hold his gaze. Hell, I even manage to study him a little.

Countless circular scars dot what would have been perfect abs. Pale, nearly invisible scars along his ribs and thighs. More burn marks there. Most so old and faded, it's no wonder I didn't notice them that day in the shower when they—

"I sinned," he says and sits back on his haunches, stretching his arms like a cat getting up from a nap.

Thankfully, he doesn't stand, else I'd have been able to see everything. Instead, his dick is hidden in the shadows pooling his lap.

"Sinned how?" I ask.

"I touched you without your permission. More than once." Cass's smirk transforms into a smile that's anything but repenting. "Apparently, I should be punished for shit like that."

My skin suddenly feels two sizes too small. I can't turn my head, so instead I swivel my eyes to look at Apollo. "You told them?"

He shrugs as he takes another pull on the joint. Smoke billows from his mouth, clearing to reveal a Joker-like smile. "We tell each other everything."

"I didn't mean—"

"Fuck it," Zachary growls. "Offer's just expired."

He rips the belt out of my hand and shoulders me aside. Grabbing the back of Cass's neck, he pushes the top half of his body onto Reuben's lap.

I stumble back before I can catch my balance. I don't know who would win in a fight between Cass and Zachary and I never want to find out. But there must be some unspoken agreement between them, because although Cass's muscles go taut as if he's resisting Zachary, he ends up right where Zachary wants him.

Which is when Reuben grabs hold of him again, holding him still.

"No, Zachary, please!" I reach for Zachary, but I'm too scared to grab him in case he *does* turn that belt on me.

"You had your chance," Zachary hisses.

Cass tenses when the belt whistles through the air. The crack of it meeting his flesh is too loud. Too violent.

My heart breaks when Cass's entire body ripples with pain. He's gritting his teeth—spittle dotting his lips as he grunts through the blow—

*Crack!*

And the next.

"Zachary!"

And the next.

"Stop!" I grab Zachary's elbow, but he shakes me off with a growl.

*Crack!*

"Enough!" I yell.

My brain is obviously misfiring, because then I do the most idiotic thing in the world. I slip between Zachary and Cass, turning my arms up so the belt would land on my forearms and not on my face.

Zachary freezes, arm upraised, a wild snarl on his face. "Move," he says.

"No! That's enough!"

When Zachary doesn't move, when no one tries to get me out of the way, I start babbling in self-defense. "I'm the one who said he has to pay, right? Well, it's enough. I forgive him. For everything. Okay? So…enough. It's *enough*."

Zachary slowly lowers the belt. "You don't get to decide the sentence."

"Of course I do." I straighten, reluctantly dropping my arms. "I'm the one who charged him."

"This isn't a fucking court, girl."

"I don't care."

Hooded green eyes study me for a long moment. "There're still two lashes left." His voice is rough, but his face is a wooden mask. "Move out the way, or you'll be getting them on his behalf."

I glance over my shoulder at a shaking Cass.

Tear tracks shine wetly on his cheeks. His skin is virulent red and purple now. Tiny dots of blood have come to the surface where Zachary's belt landed.

He won't last another two lashes. He'll start bleeding, and it will all be because of me.

I turn back to Zachary, swallow hard, and force my voice not to shake.

"Then I'll do it," I say, holding out my hand. It quivers a little, but when I concentrate, it stills. "Give me the belt."

Zachary laughs. "What, so you can tickle his ass? This is punishment, girl, not fucking foreplay."

"I'll hit him as hard as I can. I swear it."

Cass would never last another two lashes from Zachary's muscular arm, but mine is like spaghetti in comparison.

Lesser of two evils, right?

I narrow my eyes a little. "Reuben said I'm either with you or against you. No in-between. Right?"

"That's right," Reuben says.

"Well, I'm with you, Zachary." My eyes dart to Apollo. "Apollo." I glance behind me. "Reuben. Cassius." I turn back to Zachary. "I'm *with* you."

I duck forward and wrap my fingers around the belt.

"Now give me the damn belt."

# 41

## ZACH

I don't know who's more shocked out of the five of us. Trinity asks for the belt, and I give it to her. I fucking *give* it to her. I expected begging, perhaps finally some tears, maybe even her going to her knees and sucking me off in exchange for Cass's hide.

I'm *with* you.

And fuck, for a second there, I believed her.

I step back so that I don't lunge for her instead.

I almost forgot why we allowed this girl in here. Why we're humoring her.

Why is it so easy to forget that she's the enemy? It's not like it's news—I've known from the moment I laid eyes on her that she was some kind of trouble.

I just didn't realize how deeply enmeshed in all this she is.

But that all changes tonight.

When we're done with her, she'll be as broken as we are. Useless.

Trinity folds the belt in half and readies herself.

She thinks she can get one over on us? I know she's going to go easy on him, and we'll punish her for it.

That, and everything else she's done to us.

Luring Reuben with promises of romance and love and all that bullshit. Acting all surprised when Apollo turned down her pussy.

I'll admit—we were idiots for not spotting the snake in the grass.

But we're wiser now.

We've caught onto her little games. Her little tricks.

She's in our territory now. Until we decide she can leave this place, she belongs to *us*.

And I, for one, plan on using her until she begs me to stop.

But I won't. No matter how hard she begs.

Because *they* never did.

Our Ghosts never let our curses or our pleas touch their cruel hearts. We thought it was because they were impervious to our pain.

Until it became obvious they didn't *have* hearts.

Guess they traded them to the Devil in exchange for fulfilling their sick desires.

Just like each of us has given ourselves over to the Devil too.

For a chance at retribution.

For revenge.

Tonight we seal that pact.

Tonight, Trinity becomes our sacrificial lamb.

I smirk as she lifts her arm, a mix of sympathy and utter reluctance on her face.

Oh, she plays her role so well. But I see right through her.

Trinity grits her teeth.

The belt whistles down.

Cass grunts and squirms against Reuben's grip.

A cloud of weed smoke creeps around me like a nefarious

fog. Behind me, Apollo murmurs, "Fuck me," with the utmost respect.

My admiration is fleeting, and leaves me feeling hollow inside.

I watch deadpan as she strikes the final blow, only mildly surprised it doesn't make Cass come or bleed.

Then she hurls the belt away from her like it's a viper and spins on her heel.

Her cheeks are red. Her eyes bright, zealous.

"There," she says, pushing the word through her teeth. "It's done. Now tell me what you found."

Trinity Malone isn't the innocent little girl we'd all assumed she was.

Does that mean we won't enjoy breaking her?

Not at all.

It just means we don't have to hold back.

# 42

# TRINITY

It's obvious Cass is in pain, but he's not acting like someone who's just been punished. In fact, the longer he stays as he is, breathing hard and holding onto Reuben's waist as if he'd fall over if he let go…the more I'm starting to wonder about all of this.

I know they were waiting for me, but why? Just so they could show me words have consequences?

And even after all of this…I have a feeling Zachary is still not going to tell me what I need to know.

"Zacha—"

He lifts a hand, the first two fingers raised, for all the world like a priest about to bestow a blessing.

"There was a file," he says. His lips part, but then he hesitates. "Apollo, you tell her."

"He hid it in the system directory," Apollo says.

Ice blows over my skin and settles deep in my bones. I'm dimly aware of Cass moving behind me, making soft, pained sounds as he dresses. I can't imagine how much pain he's in—I only got a handful of lashes from Miriam and I could barely stand the agony.

How long has Zachary been beating him? Why do Reuben and Apollo allow it to happen? Do they always watch like tonight? Does Reuben always hold him down?

Suddenly I don't want to be here anymore. Not surrounded by these four twisted men.

I thought I liked Reuben. Hell, I thought I could learn to *love* him, even, but not if he lets Zachary push him around like this. But can I blame him? I wouldn't want to be on Zachary's bad side either.

And that's not the only reason I want to leave. As much as the Brotherhood terrifies me…it's also the look in Apollo's eyes.

Sympathy. Pity. I'm not sure.

He feels sorry for me and I'm not sure why.

"Clever, but not clever enough. He encrypted it, renamed it, and hid it around a bunch of other system files so it would blend right in."

Apollo slips off the couch and stands to his full height. When he comes closer, I have to crane my head back to keep his gaze.

"See, he disguised it so well that I almost gave up. But I got a hunch. Ran a system check. Replaced all the standard files. All except a handful were overwritten. That file of his, it was one of them. One of the outliers, the ones that didn't fit."

"Any of this sound familiar, my little slut?"

I nearly jump out of my fucking skin when a hand lands on my shoulder. Cass's voice is right by my ear. I want to slap away his hand, but…it was because of me that he was punished. And more brutally than I'd ever have considered necessary. I could at least hear him out.

Hear *them* out.

Even though I just want to run out of here with my hands over my ears.

Because even now, after I'd yelled at Gabriel and told him I believed the Brotherhood...I don't *want* to be on their side. I want to be on *my* side. I want to live in a Utopia where there's no such thing as pedophiles and sex trafficking and men with psychological issues caused by the kind of trauma normal people can't even wrap their heads around.

I guess that stopped being an option after Lucifer was thrown out of heaven. Not that I ever believed in God and the Devil. It sounds like a story used to drive home common sense in a world where it's somehow not obvious that you should love thy neighbor.

But after meeting the Brotherhood?

I don't know if I can afford *not* to believe.

"What was inside it? What—?" I swallow hard to dislodge the knot from my throat. "What was he hiding?"

"We don't know," Reuben says.

His hand is on my shoulder too, now. Warm and big compared to Cass's smaller, cooler hand. But both grip me equally tight. Both hold me just as firmly in place.

"It needs a password," Zachary says. My eyes flicker to him as he steps closer.

Now that I'm surrounded by three of the four brothers, the room isn't that cold anymore. Apollo stands a little way off still, watching.

"I'm running a decryption program on it, but unless I get my hands on a server farm or some shit, it could take months to crack."

"So you don't know," I say, and the words come out with a laugh of relief. "It could be anything."

The hands on my shoulders tighten. Cass begins stroking the side of my neck with his pinkie finger.

Zachary takes my chin, but almost gently this time, tipping

my head up. "We don't have to know what it says to know it's what we want. What we've been looking for."

I grab his wrist and slowly, carefully, pull his hand away from my face. "Gabriel's not perfect." I nod a little, glancing at each of them, even the two standing behind me. "But neither are any of us. We're all sinners, right?" I face Zachary again. "What if it's all in your head? Maybe it's time you stopped looking for ghosts in the shadows."

The moment the words leave my mouth, I know it was the wrong thing to say.

Zachary twists his hand, grabbing my wrist and tugging it down.

Before I can pull away, he's forcing me to grab his hard cock right through his jeans, his fingers folding over mine. He makes me squeeze him, and that only makes him harden even more.

"Does that feel real to you?" he says.

I try to pull away, but he just grips me tighter. I can feel him pulsing beneath my hand.

"Stop," I whisper.

"Never," he says, his lips peeling back in a snarl. "We'll never stop. Not for you, not for Gabriel. No one can stop us, Trinity."

He presses against me, sandwiching me between him and the men behind me. Apollo stalks closer, for once not looking like he finds anything about this situation remotely humorous.

"Not even your father."

I can't fight one of them. Definitely not four. Begging has proved useless. So, instead, I scream.

But that just makes them laugh.

And then everything goes to shit.

Reuben's hand slips around the front of my throat. The other, around my waist. He drags me over the floor and sits on the couch, pulling me onto his lap.

When I try and kick his shins, he wraps his legs around mine, pinning them to the couch.

And then drags them apart.

My skirt dips into that space, thankfully retaining some of my modesty, but that doesn't give me a shred of relief.

Not when I'm faced with three men who look ready to rip every last stitch of fabric off me with their fucking teeth.

When Apollo darts forward, I let out another useless scream. A scream he silences with a kiss as he climbs onto his knees beside Reuben

Now I can barely breathe, never mind fill my lungs for another scream. I tear my lips away from Apollo, but Zachary steps forward and grabs my jaw in his strong, unrelenting grip.

"That's not how it works, little girl. If he wants to kiss you, then you'll let him fucking kiss you."

I only realize he's holding a belt in his hands when he slaps it against his thigh. I jerk at the sound, and squirm on Reuben's lap in an effort to escape.

Again, futile, but there's no way I'm just going to sit here and take this.

Zachary said he'll never stop?

Neither will I.

*But you wanted this, Trinity,* a sinister voice croons inside my head. *You said you wanted to know what it feels like…? Well, you're about to find out.*

No, not like this! I wanted—

*Flowers and romance and dinner dates?*

Normal.

I wanted *normal.*

Zachary turns my face back to Apollo and releases me.

Apollo's lips capture mine, his kiss going from tentative to violent in a matter of seconds.

My dress, full sleeves and a bodice that reaches my collarbones, opens with a zip in the back. So when Apollo tries to slide a hand behind the fabric, it's too tight for him to gain access. He makes a grumpy sound and shoves a hand between Reuben and me, hunting.

I feel every inch of that zipper coming down. And when I slap my arms over my chest to keep my dress in place, Cass grabs my wrists and wrenches me open again.

So I bite Apollo's lip. Not hard, I mean, I don't even taste blood, but—

"Fuck!" He jumps back, pressing the back of his hand to his mouth. "She bit me!"

I feel as much as hear Reuben chuckling.

"I don't think we've made ourselves clear," Zachary says.

My eyes are drawn reluctantly to him when he drags his chair in front of me. He uses his boot to urge Reuben's legs wider, in turn spreading me open even further. Then he sits down, his legs between mine and Reuben's, and leans in close.

"No one dragged you down here, girl." He puts his hands on my thighs and grips tight. "You came on your own. You'd probably like us to believe it was out of curiosity, but we know that would be a lie."

"What are you talking about?" It's not my imagination anymore. There's something they're not telling me.

Something they found?

My mind instantly goes back to the email I read. The one my mother sent Gabriel. Did they figure out Gabriel was having an affair with my father?

There's no way to stop my cheeks from growing hot, just like there's no way I can stop Zachary noticing my sudden humiliation.

His lips quirk into an unfriendly, one-sided smile. "There she is," he hisses. "Took you long enough."

"I can explain," I blabber out, immediately contradicting myself with a panicked, "I didn't know!"

This makes the Brotherhood laugh.

Cass sits beside Reuben and me, wincing when his ass touches the cushion. He sticks his hand under my skirt and trails his fingers up the inside of my leg. "Really expect us to believe that?" He lets out a huff of a laugh and then strokes a knuckle over my underwear. I squirm against Reuben, trying to get away from his touch.

Which is when I realize something that's been nagging at me for a while.

Reuben's got a hard-on. And every time I move, he gets harder.

Fuck.

"I didn't know!" My voice wavers. "Please, you have to believe me. I only just found out."

"And you didn't think to tell us?" Zachary says. His fingertips dig into my thighs as he leans close enough to kiss me. "Didn't think we should know?"

"Does it matter?" I shout. "Does it change anything?"

At this, they're silent. Zachary even draws back a little. I squirm again, but hurriedly stop when I realize that's a bad move.

Zachary drops his gaze to my lap. And then I can't help but shift because it's as if I'm stark naked.

He looks up at me without lifting his face, staring at me through thick lashes.

"It changes everything, girl."

Trinity doesn't like my statement. Oh, she doesn't like it one bit. But there's fuck all she can do about it, isn't there?

Fuck all she can do about *anything* right now. If there'd ever been a good time to stop this in its tracks…well, she flew by it about ten minutes ago.

My brothers are ravenous wolves and she's the little rabbit that sprung the trap. Me? I'm the hunter who *set* the trap, and that with only one purpose in mind—to catch something they can sink their teeth into while I watch.

Apollo rips down the front of her dress, exposing her perky tits to the room. To those rabid wolves.

And they descend on her every bit like a predator on prey.

My fingers slide off her thighs as I sit back in my seat and take out my cigarettes. I nip one out of the box and light it as Cass and Apollo duck their heads and consume her nipples with hungry lips and ferocious tongues.

Thick, warm smoke fills my lungs. Watching them, a surge of blood hardens my cock behind my jeans.

Trinity lets out a whimper of protest and tries to move away from their mouths, but there's nowhere for her to go.

"Stop!" Her yells don't exactly fall on deaf ears. In fact, Cass and Apollo both look up at each other when they hear her. With perfect timing, they grab the sides of her dress and yank it down to her hips.

That's when she really starts thrashing.

But with Reuben holding onto her throat, his other muscular arm strapping her waist, she can only wriggle around like a fish on a hook.

Between the three of them, they urge her dress out from under her hips and down her legs.

I lean forward and snag it, slowly dragging the fabric over her knees. That's where it gets stuck—with Reuben's legs twined around hers, I can't take them off.

Lucky for me, I have a knife.

When I flick it open, she freezes. Her pale stomach trembles as she holds her breath.

"You're not fooling anyone," I tell her.

I lean forward, running the sharp tip of the knife over one hipbone, then the next.

Cass groans softly in the base of his throat, and shifts as if the hard-on trapped behind his jeans is giving him grief. That or his bruised ass. Probably a combination of the two because he enjoys pain as much as I enjoy inflicting it.

With her dress tangled around her spread-apart knees, only her panties on, she looks like a doll sitting on Reuben's lap. His thick thighs are twice the size of hers. That arm of his looks capable of snapping her in half if she so much as breathes wrong.

It's impossible to miss Reuben's dick either. Still trapped behind his jeans, that massive ridge looks like it's trying to nestle into her ass crack. No way she can't feel it. No way she can't realize where that dick is destined to burrow itself as soon as we're done playing with our supper.

My cock wants to bust a seam trying to get out of my jeans at the thought.

And tonight, he can't back out either.

We have two cherries to pop.

My knife hitches against the hem of her underwear and then travels straight down between her legs. From where I'm sitting, I have the perfect view of her cunt—if she wasn't wearing these panties.

Trinity sits absolutely still, lips parted, eyes hooded as if in resignation. I pause right above her clit—nothing but a film of fabric between her and the knife. Holding the tip there, I smile at her and slowly drag at my cigarette.

"You keep telling us to stop, but this wet pussy is singing a different tune."

Her tits quiver when she dares to take a breath. "Please, Zachary. Don't do this."

"You've changed your mind?"

She swallows and dares to shift. I guess Reuben's getting harder by the second. That comfy lap ain't so comfy anymore.

"Yes. I…wanted this but not anymore. So please, let me go."

"You're a good liar," I tell her. "One of the best I've met." I glance at Cass, then at Apollo. "Go on, boys." I cock my head at her cunt. "Check for yourselves how badly Trinity doesn't want this."

Cass wastes no time, and Apollo's only a beat behind him. They trail their fingers over her thighs while she starts kicking up as much as a fuss as she dares with my knife tip held so close to her clit.

Their fingers trace the plain hem of her underwear before they each sink a hand behind that filmy fabric. They're both staring at her, as if daring her to look at them, but she's staring straight at me.

She holds her composure for a second longer, and then her lips start trembling again.

"No, no, no, please, stop, stop!"

But they just keep going.

Their fingers inadvertently lift the fabric up as they pass, sending the tip of the knife slicing through.

Her scandalized gasp could either be for the naked blade now teasing the fuzz above her clit, or those fingers sliding over her wet folds.

Because, from where I'm sitting, I can see she's soaked right the fuck through.

Betrayed by her own depravity.

Just like us.

# 44

# TRINITY

I'm light-headed. Confused. Scared shitless. Naked but for my useless underwear, I've never felt this exposed.

Or this turned-on.

As soon as Cass touched me earlier, it was like he'd turned a switch in my brain. Not the part that does the thinking—ha, if only—but the part that controls my body.

Now it's on automatic.

I can't control the way I clench deep inside when Cass and Apollo touch me. Or how tingles ripple through me when Zachary scrapes that knife over my underwear.

And now?

I have their fingers smearing my pussy with juices that leaked out of me because somehow—*some-fucking-how*—it appears that I'm actually enjoying this.

I moan in protest, trying to shift back from their fingers. But that only digs Reuben's dick deeper against my ass.

"No, please, God." My moans turn into whimpers when Cass and Apollo dip their heads and start teasing my nipples with their teeth. While their fingers are still stroking my wet pussy.

"Fuck!" I yelp as Cass bites down hard enough to leave faint marks on my breast.

A warm, sweet breath rifles the hair by my ear.

If Zachary hadn't moved the knife away at just the right moment, I'd have it sticking an inch out of my fucking stomach right now, because without any warning, Reuben sits up straight.

The grip around my throat lessens, but only a little, and then I realize why.

He's unzipping his pants.

"Reuben, no. Please. Please!" I squirm furiously now that there's no knife pressed to my fucking clit to stop me.

Zachary lets out a muffled laugh around his cigarette. Cold metal presses against my thigh.

*Snick, snick.*

Heat flashes over my skin as Cass and Apollo yank off my underwear.

Now there's nothing shielding me from their eyes. Or the warm, hard, cock Reuben releases from his pants a second later.

"P-please," I murmur, blubbering like a little girl as I start to struggle.

"Ssh," he murmurs into my ear. And then kisses my earlobe. The side of my jaw. He slings his arm around the front of my throat, and drags me against him as he sinks back on the coach.

He brings his legs together, and for a second I'm convinced they'll let me close my legs.

Maybe even let me go.

I mean, fuck, they can't actually do this, can they?

*But you want them to, don't you? More than anything in the world.*

I shove the traitorous thought from my head. I said no a

dozen times. I've yelled, I've screamed, I've begged. Why the fuck—?

*Because you love this.*

*You're loving every fucking second of it.*

"No," I whisper furiously.

Apollo and Cass drag Reuben's jeans down his legs and then hold me down while he takes off his shirt.

Now it's just flesh against flesh.

While Zachary's untangling my dress and tugging it off my ankles, I squirm on Reuben's naked lap.

And that's when I realize how wet I am, because I can feel it.

And I'm guessing Reuben can too.

He lets out a low rumble deep in his throat that I feel as much as I hear. Zachary just pulls Reuben's jeans away when I start kicking. Almost absently, Zachary catches my ankle and tucks my leg behind Reuben's.

And just like that, I'm trapped again.

Zachary's cigarette is gone—fuck knows what happened to it. Cass and Apollo are both struggling out of their shirts.

My breath hitches. I start panting, soft and shallow.

Zachary grabs my chin and yanks my head to the side. Forcing me to stare straight into Reuben's black eyes.

His warm breath chases a shiver through me a second before he kisses me.

It's fucked up, I know.

It makes zero sense.

But I kiss him back anyway.

Maybe it's a form of escape. Because when my eyes flutter closed, I can't see the others anymore. And in this moment, no one else is touching me. I can almost convince myself that it's just Reuben and me.

Our first night together.

Just a guy and a girl—

Until Zachary's hands land on my knees. I know it's him, because he's the only one who would grab me hard enough to bruise.

He urges my legs open, for a moment fighting not just me but Reuben too.

I think Reuben won't let him win, but I'm always wrong when it comes to the Brotherhood and this time is no exception.

Reluctantly Reuben opens his legs, in turn dragging mine open too.

Cool air licks over my wet pussy, and I shudder at the sensation. Reuben's kiss deepens, his strong lips bruising mine. I mewl against his mouth, digging my fingers into his arm as I try and pull it away from my throat.

Cass and Apollo descend on my breasts again. This time they use their lips and their teeth. Kissing, sucking, nipping, biting. I start writhing on Reuben's lap and, if his legs hadn't been open, I'd probably have smeared him with my juices. But I'm suspended over the gap between his legs.

And when I feel Zachary's body heat warming my knees, and force my eyes open, I realize why.

Zachary smirks at me for a second and then reaches between my legs. "You'll have to open a lot wider, girl," he says.

The back of his hand brushes my pussy as he reaches past me. I gasp and shift against Reuben, breaking our kiss.

He lets out a low grown a second before I feel the tip of his cock brush my pussy.

I go rigid, frowning as I try to look down to figure this all out.

Zachary's got a hold of Reuben's cock in one hand. And when I look up at him in utter shock, his smile slips away.

Without letting go of Reuben's cock, Zachary goes to his knees in front of us.

Reuben groans again, and shifts under me. Suddenly, his cock is right against my entrance.

My body sparks alight. I gasp, my nails sinking into Reuben's arm as I try to get out of the way but Cass and Apollo grab my thighs, keeping me exactly where I am.

Zachary uses his other hand to grab Reuben's wrist, urging the man's fingers between my legs.

A furious throbbing starts up deep inside me as Zachary shows Reuben where to touch me. How to smear my juices over my pussy until I'm drenched and dripping.

Then he guides Reuben's cock back to my entrance. Together they part me. Someone's finger—fuck knows who—slips inside me.

I gasp as my body goes rigid.

Cass and Apollo stroke my inner thighs, building a crazy hot friction over my skin. I hear zips being pulled down.

For my own fucking sanity, I know I shouldn't…but I do. I look.

They take their cocks out and start stroking them with expert hands and fingers.

I choke back a sob. "Please…"

But this time, I don't know if I'm begging them to stop…or to just end my fucking misery.

The ache inside me is unrelenting. I keep clenching tighter and growing wetter until I'm drenching Reuben's cock and Zachary's fingers.

Reuben nuzzles against the side of my neck, bites my earlobe, and murmurs, "Kiss me."

And I turn. And I fucking kiss him.

Because, obviously, I've lost my fucking mind.

Zachary rubs Reuben's cock through my folds faster and faster, his thumb dipping inside me on each pass. Teasing me until it feels like I'm already coming undone.

Hands grab my wrists. Cass and Apollo urge my nails out of Reuben's muscles. And I let them, because Reuben's kiss is melting every last shred of resistance.

My fingers brush the softest, warmest skin. I hesitate, almost recoil, but then I feel a mouth on my inner thigh.

Oh fuck.

No.

What?

My eyes flutter open and I dare to peek down as Reuben's tongue slips into my mouth.

Zachary's shirt is off. Possibly his pants too—my eyes are blurring with lust and passion and whatever crazy spell they've put me under.

Zachary kisses the top of my knee. My inner thigh. When he leans closer, his body heat sends an electric ripple through me.

I gasp into Reuben's mouth as Zachary grazes the sensitive flesh of my inner thigh with his teeth.

Working his way up.

Closer.

Toward my exposed pussy. My bared clit. All the while stroking me with the dripping-wet crown of Reuben's cock.

So when Apollo and Cass urge me to grab hold of their dicks…

They groan in tandem as I wrap my fingers around them.

Hard. *Fucking* hard.

And just how Zachary guides Reuben's cock over my pussy, they show me how to touch them. How fast to stroke them.

I'm aching and throbbing and panting like a fucking animal before Zachary's mouth even comes close to my pussy.

When he holds Reuben's cock out of the way and swipes his tongue over the entire length of my pussy, I buck against his mouth like a woman possessed.

Yeah, fuck, I *must* have the Devil inside me right now.

What the hell else is there to explain why, when Zachary reaches the top of my pussy and flicks his warm, wet tongue against my clit, I force myself against his mouth hard enough to make myself come?

I'm so lost in my own climax, I barely notice that I'm gripping Cass and Apollo hard enough to make one curse me, and the other come.

Warm cum trickles down the back of my hand when my eyes flutter open a second later.

Cass eases my fingers off his dick, muttering something about keeping me the hell away from him. Apollo, on the other hand, ducks forward and steals my mouth from Reuben. Then he makes my hand move harder, faster.

"Fuck," he murmurs, breaking off our kiss.

And then he leans back from me, a wicked grin sliding off his face as he urges my movements to slow. His gaze flickers to Zachary, and then down to my pussy.

Another silent command.

One I understand when Zachary ducks down and sucks my clit into his mouth.

I gasp as blissful agony shoots through me. I shove a hand in Zachary's hair, only realizing a second later that it's still covered with Cass's cum. But then nothing matters anymore, because I'm pushing Zachary's mouth harder against my clit as I buck up to meet him.

While Apollo uses my hand for his own pleasure. His groan comes seconds before he does, and then that hand is coated with his cum too.

Zachary nips me with his teeth, and another climax comes charging toward me. A gasp rattles through me as I arch my back, fully expecting another spectacular orgasm to tear through me.

Instead, he moves his mouth away and shoves a finger inside me.

"She's ready," he says.

He looks up at me, and for possibly the first time ever, a genuine smile spreads his lips.

"This will hurt more than anything you've ever felt," he says. "But you're going to bear it, because he fucking loves you. Hear me?"

My heart stutters a beat.

Reuben relaxes the arm he's had slung around my throat the past eternity and instead grabs a breast, squeezing it mercilessly in his strong hand. I whimper, turning confused eyes on him.

"I'm sorry," he murmurs, and then nuzzles his face into my hair. "I should have said something."

"You…?"

I can't even.

It doesn't make sense.

We've only…like…

I go limp.

I can't fight this anymore. It would take another three of me to even try. I just don't have it in me.

"Hmm," Zachary murmurs and then goes back to his knees. "I liked it better when you were fighting."

Then he slaps the inside of my thigh with a hand. I gasp, but barely flinch.

"You come once and you're useless after?" he says. "That's not good enough, Trin."

He ducks down, scraping his teeth over my skin hard enough to leave behind ridges. I squirm, but that's all I have the energy for. "Where's your fight. Where's that spunk?"

"All over my fucking hands," I say, holding them up. "And your hair."

There's a moment, this crystallized silence, where it could have gone either way.

I don't know if I'd have preferred us to all laugh it off.

I didn't get a choice.

Zachary snarls at me. "Want me to pity you, slut?"

A cold shiver races through me. "No, I—"

He grabs my face hard enough to bruise and then yanks at his belt.

"Zachary," comes Reuben's voice from behind me.

"You'll thank me later," Zachary says to Reuben as his belt clatters to the floor.

"Zach—"

"You might want to bite down on something, little girl," Zachary says, his eyes on me. But then he looks past, to Reuben. "Hold her down so I can open that pussy up for you."

## 45

## TRINITY

**M**y scream does nothing to stop them. Apollo grabs my hands and holds me down so I can't fight. And Reuben just opens his legs, exposing my pussy for Zachary's cock.

My eyes blur with frightened tears, but I blink them away before they can fall. Zachary wedges his knees between Reuben's legs and leans closer, one hand slipping past us to grab the cushion beside Reuben's head.

Zachary's breath stirs the fine hairs beside my ears when he leans in and I turn away. But then strong fingers make me face him again.

Reuben. The fucking traitor.

Zachary's eyes dart down to my lips. "Want me to kiss you like I love you too?" he murmurs.

He ducks down, his lips brushing mine. No more than the faintest tease.

If I could have turned away I would have, but Reuben's keeping me in place in every possible way—chin, body, legs.

I feel the couch cushions sink down a little as Cass returns from wherever he went to. His fingers trail over my thighs. A second later, so do Apollo's.

Reuben shifts under me, and suddenly his cock is pressing against me again. He groans softly as he grabs his cock and smears it through my pussy, again coating himself. The tip of his thumb slips inside me, and then his cock is pushing against my entrance.

I don't know if Zachary somehow knows what's happening down there, or if they're all psychically linked, but when I gasp as Reuben pushes against me, Zachary kisses me.

Hard.

Passionately.

And yes, like he fucking *loves* me. But in his own twisted, fucked-up way.

It's nothing like he's kissed me before. It feels wrong, but the kind of wrong that makes me wonder why I was trying to stop him in the first place.

Any of them.

Cass and Apollo's fingers stroke over each side of my pussy, and then pull me open even more. I push up into Zachary's kiss, breathless as I try to kiss him back as hard as he's kissing me.

He makes a surprised sound in the back of his throat a second before his tongue forces its way into my mouth.

And then his cock brushes over my clit. He dips down, wetting himself on my arousal, and then comes back, massaging me with the tip of his dick as he tongue-fucks my mouth.

Reuben releases my jaw and instead grabs one of my breasts, squeezing me so hard I whimper against Zachary's mouth.

"Jesus fuck," Zachary whispers, briefly breaking our kiss. "If you had any idea how badly I want to hurt you."

My eyes flutter open.

"Then do it," I say.

I don't know where it comes from, the sudden bravado that rushes through me.

Maybe it's the brief flash of admiration that flickers deep in Zachary's moss-green eyes. Maybe it's the fact that, even for a second, it feels as if I have all four of these men at my beck and call.

Reuben strokes his cock over my pussy and tests my entrance again. And as I'm staring up into Zachary's eyes, panting from our violent kiss, I understand what he meant. Why he wanted to fuck me first.

Because when Reuben pushes the first inch of his cock into my pussy, I let out a low, agonized moan.

He immediately pulls out, stroking me as he nuzzles the side of my neck. All while I stare up at Zachary as if to defy him, only to realize it doesn't work like that.

As much as Reuben wants to make love to me, he can't, because it would hurt me. And he can't hurt me.

Zachary knows it.

If I want to fuck Reuben, I'd have to fuck one of them first. I bite down on my bottom lip as wild thoughts rage through my head.

Slut.

Whore.

*Sinner.*

But I push them all aside.

I keep forgetting, I'm not normal.

I'm *special.*

Zachary's eyes drop to my mouth. I bite down harder on my lip, and let out a small moan.

"Christ," he mutters. But instead of kissing me, he nips at my chin. "Don't just give it to me, little girl." He kisses me once, hard, and leans back as he starts stroking his dick. "I want to *take* it."

So I give him what he wants.

When he drops his hips and touches his cock against my pussy, I start struggling.

It comes easily enough, because I'm fucking terrified.

Not just of him.

I don't know what will become of my life, even if I miraculously don't go through with this.

So I fight him.

When his shoulder comes close enough, I sink my teeth into him. And I get a slap on my pussy for that, which makes me whimper in pain.

And that makes him even harder.

So he slaps me again, groaning as I buck.

"Finger her," he snaps, his eyes only briefly darting up to Reuben.

Two thick fingers tease my opening. And then Reuben shoves them into me.

I arch off him, a gasp rattling in my throat that Cass leans forward and snatches with a kiss.

Fuck my life.

I moan into his mouth as Reuben slowly starts to finger me.

A hot mouth presses to my pubic bone. I'm convinced it's Zachary's but when a tongue tentatively licks my clit, I realize it's not.

Apollo.

My body melts against Reuben under their attention. Reuben fucking me with his fingers, Apollo massaging my clit with his lips and tongue and mouth. Cass stealing my breath with a kiss.

My eyes flutter open the second Cass breaks away.

Zachary's sitting in his chair, stroking himself as he watches me being devoured, a look of utter contentment on his face.

But the spell breaks when a climax thunders toward me. I claw my fingers into Apollo's hair, forcing him harder against my clit, but Zachary grabs his shoulder and wrenches him away.

"Stop."

Reuben's fingers tug out of my tight, dripping pussy. Zachary slips between my legs, drags his fingers through my slit, and licks my juices from his fingers.

"You're wet enough," he says as he leans closer. He puts his mouth by my ear.

He pushes my head aside with his, and Reuben's lips catch mine in a slow, gentle kiss I can feel all the way down to my toes.

Zachary's cock touches my clit and drags down.

He stops against my entrance, and eases himself in the first inch as his breath paints hot lashes against the side of my neck.

"Jesus, you're soaked," he says.

I manage a mewl in response.

Then he goes in another inch. I gasp into Reuben's mouth, and he starts kissing the corner of my mouth instead.

"Don't hold back. I want to know how much I'm hurting you."

A breath rattles through my throat as he eases himself in another inch. I grab hold of his shoulders, and then sink my nails into his flesh.

He hisses through his teeth.

And then slams into me.

I scream, because *fuck* it hurts.

And then I fight, because I want him out.

But he holds me there, pinned on his cock, and pants against the side of my neck.

"So fucking tight," he whispers. "Jesus."

A sob chokes me. I try and move, but I'm pinned between him and Reuben.

"P-Please," I manage.

"Does it hurt?"

"Yes!" I hiss.

"I'm not even in all the way," he says. And then he forces another inch inside me.

Tears slip down my cheeks as I gasp out in pain. Fingers slip between us and touch my clit and then pleasure wars that pain.

Reuben begins massaging my clit as he kisses the side of my neck.

Caught between them, I slowly start to come undone.

Zachary pulls back no more than an inch, and then thrusts into me hard enough to jar a hoarse yell from me.

Reuben's fingers speed up.

I'm clinging so tightly to Zachary's dick, I'm surprised he can move at all. But he does. As soon as he's filled me with every inch of cock, he starts fucking me hard and deep.

Every thrust rips a new yell from me. Powerful at first, and then hoarse and broken.

Reuben massages me even harder.

I'm howling now, scratching at Zachary's chest like a caged animal.

Because that is exactly what I am.

Trapped between them, I have nowhere to go. No way to stop him fucking me, hurting me, making me bleed.

And as he picks up speed, as his rhythm smooths, Reuben bites the side of my neck, and Zachary captures my lips for another kiss, I come.

I fucking come so hard I can't even scream.

And Zachary fucks me through my climax and beyond. I'm still coming down from that impossible high when he grabs my hips and thrusts into me the hardest he has yet.

His cock pulses as he empties himself inside me, bruising my hips with his fingertips.

I don't even have time for a breath. Zachary pulls out of me with a ragged gasp, the last spurt of his cum warming my skin as he comes over my clit.

"Fuck her," he says, not even bothering to look at me. "Get in there and fuck her while she's still bleeding."

Reuben shifts under me. I have time for a breathless, "No!" of protest, and then I'm being split open all over again.

Zachary grabs my hair in a fist and yanks me forward for a violent kiss as Reuben buries himself balls deep in my bleeding, aching pussy.

I might have died. It's entirely possible. Because I remember kissing Zachary, and then suddenly I feel like I've gone to heaven.

I've never felt such mind-numbing pleasure. But the pain is too intense for me to enjoy it.

At least, that's what I think.

But then someone's strumming my clit again, and...

"I'm going to come!" I whisper against Zachary's mouth.

He steps up, his dick bouncing angrily, already erect again as he steps aside for Cass.

"What...?"

Cass goes to his knees. Sits forward. And closes his mouth over my clit.

I throw my head back and gasp.

"Am I hurting you?" Reuben whispers into my ear.

I somehow manage a whimpered, "Yes."

"Should I stop?"

"No!"

"Good," he growls. "Because I can't. You feel too good. So fucking good, my love."

Something invisible squeezes my heart. "Fuck me harder."

"But I don't—"

"Fuck her harder!" Zachary barks out.

Reuben growls deep in his throat, but he obeys. Grabbing hold of my hips, he shifts forward until he's right on the edge of the coach. Cass scrambles back as he wipes his mouth with the back of his hand. By the time Reuben's done arranging me and I look up, Cass is stroking his dick and looking about to come again.

Reuben spreads my legs, reaches past me, and grabs Cass's head. He jerks the man forward, forcing his mouth over my clit. "Fuck his mouth," Rube commands quietly in my ear. And then he puts his hands on my hips and moves me against Cass's lips.

Fuck, but it's too much.

I begin to unravel.

Reuben swipes a hand over my pussy, opens me with his fingers, and rams his cock into me. I buck forward, but he grabs my hair and yanks me back. Keeping me caught between his cock and Cass's mouth, he starts fucking me slow and deep.

It fucking hurts like all hell, and then it doesn't anymore. But still I'm whimpering and mewling because the pleasure is just as agonizing as the pain was.

When I come, it's with a hoarse yell. Reuben grabs my ass and yanks me against him, driving his dick as deep inside me as it can possibly go. Cass follows us, his tongue lapping against my clit.

I shudder as my climax plays out, my fingernails leaving crescent moons in Reuben's thighs. He fills me with his cum, and it leaks out of my pussy when he starts pulling out.

I grab the back of his neck and turn my head to kiss him.

"Stay inside," I whisper just before our lips touch.

So he does.

He stays inside, filling me even when he starts to soften, as Cass keeps licking me and licking me and licking me.

We're still kissing, both still panting, when I feel myself about to come again.

But Reuben doesn't capture my cries this time. The mouth on my clit disappears, and instead I'm staring into the bluest eyes I've ever seen.

As Apollo tears me apart with his tongue on my clit, Cass snatches my breath away with a kiss.

I should feel different. Why don't I feel different? Sure, there's still a faint ache deep inside me, but mentally, I'd have thought I'd feel…

*Like a woman?*

I shrug off the voice and tug in a deep breath. I'm nestled against Reuben's chest and stomach, his arm draped over my waist. We're using Apollo's lap as a cushion while he's propped against a heap of pillows. Cass and Zach are somewhere nearby too, but in the dark I can't quite be sure *where*.

They brought me in here after they were done with me last night. After I couldn't take any more pleasure or any more pain.

My eyes are grainy, and my body's sore. I don't know if I slept for hours or minutes.

I don't dare wake the Brotherhood but I need to get the fuck out of here and figure things out.

Also, I need to pee.

I carefully slide out from under Reuben's arm and creep naked into the living area of their lair. There I find my dress and slip into it as quietly as I can. Thank God Zachary didn't decide to cut it off me along with my underwear.

I hunt around for my shoes. One of them ended up under the couch.

Having to go to the bathroom almost becomes a non-issue when I stand and see Zachary leaning against a nearby bookshelf, watching me.

"Christ," I whisper, putting a hand on my pounding heart. "You scared me."

"Leaving already?" he says, and goes over to a packet of cigarettes tossed on one of the empty shelves. There's a metallic click. A puff of smoke. He still has his back to me.

"I need the bathroom," I tell him. Then I hesitate. "I'll be back after."

Tobacco ignites with a faint crackle as Zachary inhales. "What makes you think we want you coming back?"

My heart stutters. "What did you say?"

"You all had your fun." He turns, exhaling a plume of pale smoke. "It's time for you to fuck off." He comes closer while I'm still trying to process his words, and grabs my chin. That touch hurts more than it should—they bruised me all over last night.

"When the first bus to Mercy leaves this morning, you'll be on it."

I start to shake my head. "Why—?"

Zachary shoves his body against mine, driving me back.

A pained gasp rattles out of me when I thump into the bookshelf, but my lungs seize up a second later when something cold, sharp, and all too familiar pricks the side of my jaw. "Shake your head again, and this'll go straight through your fucking cheek," he says.

My body goes rigid. I swallow hard, my mind reeling as I try to think of something to say.

I thought I'd seen Zachary angry before, but the rage burning in his eyes has nothing on that.

The knife slides down the front of my throat, over the front of my dress. I squeeze my eyes shut when his hand goes up under my dress.

"Look at me, Malone."

My eyes flutter as I reluctantly force them open. The tip of the knife scrapes the inside of my thigh as he brings his hand up…and up…and up. Then it's touching the most sensitive part of me, a breath away from slicing me apart.

In sheer panic, I glance at the curtain separating this room from the next. If I screamed, would they—?

"I know what you're thinking," Zachary says. "But I'm in charge, not them. If I say you leave, they'll agree."

My skin tries to crawl off my body as I slowly pull my gaze back to Zachary. Cold, dead eyes watch me for a second.

"Why?" I murmur, not able to stop the tears welling in my eyes. "Why are you doing this?"

"Because you and that fucking priest take us for fools," Zachary hisses. The knife pricks my skin, but doesn't break the surface.

It doesn't have to—I know Zachary wouldn't hesitate to slice into me. I can see it in his eyes.

"I don't understand," I say.

I saw what Zachary did last night. He has to be bisexual to some extent to have done what he did last night. So why is my father and Gabriel's relationship such a sticking point with him?"

I search his face, trying to find meaning in his words. "You can't blame me for what my father did. It was his choice. I had nothing to do with it."

Zachary's eyes narrow to slits. "Back then, maybe. But now? You expect me to believe this is all a coincidence? You arriving here just before we're ready to strike?"

I frown hard at him. "What does that have to do with—?"

He leans into me, snarling. "I know who you are. Nothing you say is going to change my mind, little girl."

Who I am? He's always known—

"If you're not on that bus when it leaves, I'll come find you, and I'll make you bleed."

He smiles.

Claps a hand over my mouth.

And drags the tip of the blade down the inside of my thigh as I whimper in sudden panic.

"Only this time, I'll use my knife."

# 47

# TRINITY

I barely have enough strength in my legs to drag me up the stairs, but somehow I make it all the way to the fourth floor of Saint Amos. It's still early—the sun hasn't even risen yet—but already I hear the distant sound of doors opening.

Saint Amos is coming to life.

But I'm dying.

It has nothing to do with the shallow cut on my thigh. It was the fear that came after. It has drained my spirit to the point where I'm wondering if I'll live to see sunlight again.

I could have gone to my room. Climbed into bed. And fallen asleep…possibly forever. But I came here instead. I came back to Gabriel.

I know he'll take me back because that's what he does. It's his job to forgive people.

Sometimes, he even does it on behalf of God.

Maybe I should confess. Serve penance. Maybe then my life won't be so fucked up anymore.

Makes sense. This was all my fault. I went there. I slept with them. What did I expect? That I'd wake up to breakfast in bed?

No, I hadn't expected that. I'd *hoped*.

But Zachary made me realize something I should have realized a long time ago.

The men down there in the back of that library? They are mentally unstable. I'd be too if I'd suffered like they had. I don't blame them for that.

But they need help.

I stop outside of Gabriel's door, lift a fist, and bang it on the wood. Then I lean against the wall beside it as the world takes a slow tumble.

Am I in shock? If Zachary had pushed that knife less than an inch up, he would have—

"Trinity, what are you—?" Gabriel cuts off with an angry sound. "Who did this to you?"

Oh.

Right.

The bruises on my face.

The cum stains on my dress.

The blood trickling down my leg.

He's wearing sweatpants and a t-shirt. Glasses resting on top of his head. He looks like my father sometimes did on Saturday mornings when he slept in and would come downstairs at ten o'clock in the morning for his first cup of coffee.

Gabriel and my father had a lot in common, come to think about it.

I straighten, hug myself. Stare at Gabriel.

"There's…"

He holds out a hand. Wants me to come inside. I look past him, into the small, dimly lit antechamber. Past that, to his room.

No fire this morning.

A suitcase, packed.

Ready to leave.

But I thought he was staying? That's what the Brotherhood's entire plan hinged on.

"Please, child. Come inside. I'll make you some—"

"There's something I need to show you," I say.

Gabriel's gaze searches my face. "What is it?" His voice is low.

I swallow hard, and wish I could look away. But his brown eyes have mine trapped, his face blank. "It's…"

His voice is clipped when he says, "Speak, child."

"It's in the bell tower, Father."

# 48

# TRINITY

My heart's pounding like a bongo drum. Father Gabriel holds out a big bunch of keys he'd taken out of a drawer in his apartment and glances at me over his shoulder.

He doesn't say anything. He just frowns, and puts the key in the lock. But when he turns the key nothing happens.

Because it was already unlocked.

He opens the door. A slash of light paints the blank wall inside. Gabriel steps inside, turns, lifts his hands. "What do you want to show me?" he asks.

I rush into the small room and slap my hands on the bare wall.

"It was right here. Pictures, photos, articles." I turn, and stab a finger into his chest. "About you. Everything. It all leads back to you!"

He grabs my wrist and twists my hand. I yell out in pain, my body moving to the side on instinct.

As soon as I yell, Gabriel releases my hand and takes a hurried step back, the metal desk rattling when he backs into it.

His fierce expression dissolves into shock. "I didn't mean to hurt you."

I scramble away from him, my back slamming into the wall.

This can't be happening. Where the fuck did it all go?

*They'd kill me if they knew.*

Shit…Did the Brotherhood find out about this room and take everything down?

"Why did you bring me here?" Gabriel has a hand on his heart, but not clawing at it like he's having a heart attack or something. Just…flat. Like he's counting his own heartbeats.

"It's gone," I murmur. "They took it."

"Who? What?" He looks around. "Trinity, talk to me. Tell me what happened." He steps closer, reaching for me, his eyes darting to my legs, to the blood. "Tell me who did this to you."

But I can't. I mean…what the fuck am I supposed to say? Yeah, so, there's this bunch of guys, they say you're a criminal mastermind. And they have evidence, which was all here, but now it's gone.

I'd sound like a lunatic.

"You can trust me, Trinity."

His one hand connects with my shoulder. Then the other. He squeezes my muscles, ducking down so our eyes are level.

"You can tell me anything."

"What other sins have you committed?" I ask quietly. "Besides fucking my Dad, obviously."

Gabriel's face hardens. "That's between God and me, child."

"You said I can trust you, but I won't. Not until you tell me everything."

He releases me, steps back. His eyes narrow as he studies me. Then he takes in the room again, turning as he crosses his arms over his chest. "I don't know why I thought things would be different," he says, so quietly I step forward on instinct to hear him better.

"What things? Are you talking about you and my dad?"

"I thought I could...explain."

"He cheated with you on my mom and you expect me to *trust* you?"

Gabriel runs his hand over the dusty metal desk, and my gaze follows the trails he leaves behind right to the marks my butt made when Apollo set me down on the edge.

Gabriel outlines that heart-shaped smudge in the dust as if he can see into the past.

An invisible hand grips my throat, and not nearly as kindly as Zach or Reuben ever did.

"Dear child..." he murmurs. "There's so much you still don't know. So much I have to tell you."

And then he opens one of the drawers.

The screech it makes drags ragged nails down my back.

Tell me? What the hell does that mean? Is this...is it about the Brotherhood?

No. He'd never tell me if he was guilty. No one in their right minds would.

"So tell me," I say.

I step closer.

Gabriel reaches inside the drawer and comes out holding an envelope. He glances at me from the corner of his eye, his back still turned, and frowns. "Is this what you came here to show me?"

He holds up the envelope.

T RIN

. . .

Th<sup></sup>ere's a heart over the I.

Tears blur my vision.

Suddenly I don't want Gabriel to see anything. I want him to keep talking. But when I lean forward to take the envelope, he moves it out of reach.

His brown eyes dart over my face, hunting.

"What is it?" he asks.

I have no way of knowing, but the second he asks that question, it's as if I can see right through the fucking envelope.

"A photo." I lick my lips. "It's a photo of you."

He tilts his head a little. There's even a hint of a smile on his mouth. "Of me?" That smile stretches. "I hope they got my good side."

I laugh, but it sounds like I'm seconds away from losing my mind.

Or maybe I have already.

Gabriel lifts the envelope a little. "May I?"

My head nods, but it's as if someone else is doing it for me. My eyes move, but not because I ordered them to.

I watch, frozen in place, as Gabriel opens the envelope.

Takes out the photo.

The coy smile he'd been wearing melts away. For a second, his face could have belonged to a corpse.

Then his gaze flashes up to mine. "So young," he murmurs.

He tips up his chin, staring down at the photo a second longer. When his eyes lock with mine again, my body goes ice-cold.

"Who left this here?" he asks.

I can't move, let alone speak.

Gabriel comes closer, glancing between me and the photo, eyes slowly narrowing.

I stifle a gasp when he grabs my jaw, tilting my head back so he can stare at me at just the right angle.

His eyes widen a little.

"So much of your mother in you, isn't there?"

My stomach drops.

"And to think," Gabriel says, his mouth breaking into a fond smile, "She swore to Keith and me that she'd never have children."

He turns the photo to me, drawing my eyes.

Middle row, two from the left. A young Gabriel Blake, hands behind his back, stern expression on his face.

"But then she fell pregnant. A boy, did you know that?"

Middle row, four from the left. A young Keith Malone. Solemn, bleak. But so were all the kids in that photo.

My eyes fly back to Gabriel.

"She didn't keep that baby though. Or the next. But she kept you, Trinity."

Gabriel's eyes move back to the photo, and my gaze follows.

"She kept you, because you were special."

Middle row.

Three from the left.

Inches shorter than the boy to her left and the boy on her right.

A young, pretty Monica Stevens.

My mother.

So petite looking there between Gabriel and Keith.

"Do you know why you were special, Trinity?"

A tear breaks free when my eyes shift so I can look at Gabriel.

Again, premonition fills me with a cold, frigid dread.

Don't say it.

Don't say it.

DON'T SAY IT!

But he does.

"Because you're mine," he whispers. His grip on my jaw tightens. "And I wouldn't let her."

## To Be Continued...

Trinity and the Brotherhood's story continues in Deliver us From Evil...grab the next book in the series, or binge read the rest of collection today (PLUS a bonus, exclusive novella) by downloading the entire trilogy boxset.
https://authorloganfox.com/sosa-boxset

Can I send you my secret dark romance novella that's never been published...?
Join my VIP newsletter and you'll receive your own exclusive copy of My Darling, and I'll keep you up to date with my new releases and promos!
https://authorloganfox.com/my-darling-signup

# MORE BY LOGAN FOX

For more books by this author, reading order, playlists, trigger warnings, socials, and more…please visit:

https://authorloganfox.com